FINDING NATHAN

By

Dana Bowen and Chloe Brogan

In loving memory of Dustin Graham Brogan, the grief on these pages is for you.

To everyone who's loved and lost, who have seen tragedy and still have the desire to survive. We see you, we understand, and we hope that you find the truth in this book.

Love is friendship that has caught fire. It is quiet understanding, mutual confidence, sharing and forgiving. It is loyalty through good and bad times. It settles for less than perfection and makes allowances for human weaknesses.

--Ann Landers

Trigger Warnings:

Emotional Abuse, Addiction, and Death of a Parent,

TABLE OF CONTENTS

Prologue

Nathan

I pull my keys from my pocket and open the front door to the little apartment I share with my fiancé. The smell of kitchen cleaning supplies and whatever Carolina is making for dinner wafts toward me. I look at the photo we have framed from our first Christmas together at my family's house. She and I are standing off to the side, all of us children standing around my parents. We look like babies, but it's still one of my favorite family photos. It gives me hope for the family I want someday, and the life I have to look forward to.

"Carolina! I have exciting news!" I close and lock the door behind me, walking into our small kitchen where she is loading the dishwasher. The gentle waves of her black hair flopping to the right hide her face as she bends over to load a cheap white ceramic plate dirtied with yolk from this morning's breakfast. I pull my phone out of my pocket and scroll through messages.

"What?" Her tone is sharp. Carolina flips her hair out of her face to unveil her irritation.

"Sofia had her baby this morning! His name is Armondo! Look, *Mami* sent me pictures!"

"We are supposed to leave tomorrow. Remember?" She frowns hard and my stomach tightens.

"I know, but we can probably reschedule. I figured we could call and look into changing our reservations. Normally, under family emergencies, they'll make accommodations." The excitement that was just bubbling through me now mixes with unease. I was hoping for a better reaction than this.

"This is a family *emergency*?" Carolina raises her eyebrow and folds her arms, clearly guarded.

"Sofia is going to need help. Carlos still isn't back yet, and she has no one to help with housework or getting the rest of the baby stuff set up. *Mami* is over there now, but she needs help as well. And for the next few days everyone is going to pitch in to make sure they're comfortable when they get home." I close my phone and shove it back into my pocket. All the excitement is overshadowed by irritation at this point. I fight to not roll my eyes at her. How does she not understand this? She knew the baby was coming. I was really hoping she would be excited. I love my nephews and niece. Someday, I hope Carolina and I can start a family of our own.

"Are you kidding me Nathan?" Carolina stands at exactly five feet, but her fury makes her seem three feet taller. She slams the dishwasher closed, turning to face me fully.

I was so excited to let Carolina know that Sofia had Armondo early this morning that I didn't even take my shoes or coat off at the door.

"I don't understand why this is a big issue." I don't know what she wants me to do.

"We have plans, Nathan. Hotel room. Plane tickets. ALL WITH MY MONEY because you refuse to take on a better fucking job," She hisses.

"My sister had a *baby*, Carolina. How was I supposed to know he would be three weeks early? I promised to help once the baby came. You knew this. You knew the due date and you made plans for Cancun, anyway. You never really know when babies are going to come. The only reason I agreed to the plans is because Sofia went past her due date with Oscar and Catarina."

"She has her own fucking husband to help her!" Carolina crosses her arms like a child being told 'No' to ice cream. Her voice keeps getting louder and louder with everything she says, and it makes my blood boil.

"No, she doesn't. He's gone driving a truck and he won't be back 'til Wednesday. She needs help, which I promised, and YOU said that it was fine." I clench my jaw and grit my teeth, trying to keep more hurtful words from spilling out. I take a deep breath, deciding to plead with her on a different level. "Sofia has been nothing but nice to you since the beginning. She's offered help to you when you need it. When I got my wisdom teeth removed right after college, she and Oscar helped us move into here when the apartment became available quicker than we expected. You went with her to church. She has invited you on girls' weekends. She truly treats you like you are family."

"I've never asked for any of that. What am I supposed to do? Snub her? My family has never been like that. It's weird. I don't get why your family can't just be normal? And of course I said 'Yes.' What am I supposed to say in front of a psychotic pregnant woman? No? For no reason? This trip was a surprise!" Her long, curly black hair bounces as she yells at me.

"'Psychotic' is a bit harsh, don't you think? Why do you always have to attack my family? And when Sofia asked for help, you hadn't even booked this trip yet. It's not like you consulted me when you made reservations." I feel ridiculous right now. I can't help but stomp my foot for emphasis. I hate that she can pull this anger out of me. A sick feeling settles in my gut. My family and I have always taken care of each other. Sofia has always been there for me and my sisters, and I can't imagine not doing the same. All we've ever had is each other, and I finally thought Carolina understood; I thought she wanted to be part of it. What kind of person would I be if I backed out of promises I've already made to them? I wish Carolina understood that.

"WELL, I'M SORRY THAT I WANTED TO DO SOMETHING NICE FOR US AND ONCE AGAIN YOU CHOOSE YOUR FAMILY FIRST!" Carolina turns away from me, facing the fridge that holds a strip of pictures of us from one of those little photo booths at the county fair. "What am I to you? I'm your future wife and they always come before me. Your *Mami* and *Papi*. Sunday dinners being squished at the table between Mariposa and Amaya instead of heading to the city to go to the museum, or even just going out to brunch as a couple. We always make our plans around what they want, especially Sofia. Sometimes I don't even know where I rank in your life. Don't you love me? Don't you appreciate all I do?"

"You know it's not about that." I glare at her. "You know they'll be there for us when we have kids." I try to lighten the mood and gently put my hand on her petite shoulder.

"Are you sure you're going to even fucking be there? You sure you won't be helping Sofia with her children? Or maybe helping your mom and dad remodel their bathroom *again*? Or taking Amaya to the park? It seems like your family comes first and our children would be pushed to the side," Carolina says it softly, but it feels like a slap to my face.

I drop my hand from her shoulder and take a step back. "You can't be serious right now. You're overreacting. I get that you're disappointed, but this is my family. They will drop everything to come to help us when we need it. They'll cancel plans, so why shouldn't we do the same?"

"I thought when we got engaged, *I* would become your family. I thought you'd finally prioritize *me* above *them*, but you're right. This isn't about that. This is about us, and how you constantly choose THEM over ME!" She turns and faces me again.

"I'm not fucking doing that! SHIT, Carolina!" I turn toward the counter and brace my hands against the cool granite. I can't even look at her for a moment. "You're being so fucking selfish!" The words are out before I can stop them, and then we stand there in silence. I can feel myself shaking, grateful for the granite helping to steady my weight. I hate fighting, but I feel stuck. If it's not this moment, it would be something else; it's always something with her.

I take a deep breath and pull it together. I straighten up and face her again, studying the tension in her face. "I'm sorry for yelling, I can't be choosing my family over you. You are my family, but marrying me makes them your family, too…"

She throws up a hand. "I agreed to marry you, not them. Yeah, they will be family just like mine is to you. But I could never imagine choosing my family over you. Yet you always choose yours over me." She seems calmer, but I know Carolina. This is just the calm before the storm.

"Choose your family over me? You're an only child. Your parents live in a full-service retirement community. They are completely catered to. The only thing they ever need help with is deciding where to vacation every year. It's a little different than with my family because we can't buy the solutions to our problems. My parents will never have the option to move away and retire somewhere that takes care of them. They'll always be here. We'll always have to support each other. There will never be an option to buy our way out of things." Carolina spent most of her life being cared for by nannies. She does not understand what it's like to be the oldest of six, the only male trailed by five sisters. All she's ever had to think about is herself. I think a piece of her resents the relationship I have with my family.

"At least my parents didn't breed like fucking rabbits when they couldn't afford to. It's not about that in the first place, it's about how you always choose your family's poor choices over our happiness!" Carolina's face twists in a mocking grin like somehow that was any form of witty.

It hits me like a splash of ice water. There's no way she can mean it. I try to put an end to the argument and walk to the shoe rack to slip off my sneakers.

"You're welcome to go to Cancun without me. I am not going on a trip when my sister needs me."

CRASH

I turn around back to our small kitchen. The little bright pink ceramic change bowl that my youngest sister Amaya made me in daycare is shattered across the floor, stray pennies and nickels everywhere. Carolina's face is blank, void of feeling, staring at the fireworks of pink ceramic across the floor. My jaw drops in utter shock. I feel a hollow spot open in my chest and my throat burns looking down at the shattered ceramic that Carolina knows is important to me.

Red—

Red is all I see as rage fills my very being.

"ARE YOU FUCKING KIDDING ME!" I scream, no longer worried about trying to make peace with Carolina. Right now I'm just trying to keep myself from punching a hole in the wall. Our eyes meet the flecks of seething embers shooting between our gazes. "WHY? WHY, OF ALL THINGS, DID YOU BREAK THIS? SHATTER MY MUGS, AGAIN! BREAK THE TV, AGAIN…. But not this…"

Carolina startles and covers her ears as she starts to sob.

"Why are you crying?" I take a challenging step forward.

She cowers from me and sobs harder.

I take a deep steadying breath, willing myself to calm down and reach for her. "I'm sorry…"

She steps out of reach when I try to take her hands from her face, turning her back to me. Her refusal to let me comfort her reignites my anger. Nothing about this is fair. Not the way she is forcing me to choose between my family and her. Not the way she is insulting them. Not even the way she is suddenly crying.

"Why does it have to be all or nothing with you?" I plead with her, in agony over the sound of her cries but also furious over how something that should have been a happy day has been ruined. I also feel defeated. There doesn't seem to be any way I can win this. "Why can't I love you and still love them? I do everything for you! I have done everything for you since the day we met. Nothing is ever enough."

I sink to the ground against the wall opposite of the galley-style kitchen and place my head in my hands. Pieces of ceramic litter the floor around me but I don't have the energy to clean it up right now. I don't know what to do anymore. I feel lost and broken, torn into a million pieces. Every time I find one and fit it back into place, another falls.

Carolina places her hand on my shoulder, and I look up. Her makeup is streaked down her face, and she looks about as miserable as I feel. I shift as she maneuvers her way into my lap and wraps her arms around my shoulders.

"I'm sorry," she whispers quietly into my ear.

I say nothing, and my arms stay limply at my sides. I feel her warm breath on my neck and ear as she shifts closer to me.

"I hate fighting with you," she says against my ear. Her lips brush against me.

I want to pull away, but I don't have the energy to do it. "I hate fighting too."

She kisses me, placing her hands on my cheeks.

I grab her wrists. "Carolina."

She pulls away to study my face. Either she doesn't like what she sees, or she ignores it. She leans in to kiss me again, but I turn my face away. That doesn't stop her, though, and her mouth connects with my neck.

"Carolina," I say again with more force, removing her hands from me. I look at her face, and tears have fallen again, twisting my gut into a sick feeling.

"Please," she begs.

I hate it. I can't do this anymore; this endless cycle of fighting, fucking, and forgetting. She presses her mouth against mine, her soft lips singing her siren song. Leading me back into the rocky waters to perish.

ONE

Nathan

"I understand, *Mami*. I just think *Papi* would prefer to be home." I am exasperated. We have had the same conversation every few days for the last month.

My office feels too quiet today. While the clock in the corner ticks the time, it seems like the entire library is holding its breath. I study the old wood under my fingers, and the stack of papers piled in front of me. I have had little energy recently, and while it seems like a library should be relatively easy to run, paperwork stacks up quickly. I have stacks of requests from professors and students looking to book rooms for events over the coming school year. And I haven't even planned the fall and winter calendar. Thankfully at the beginning of the school year, there isn't too much to do, but I can feel the creep of time slipping by. If I don't get a start on some of this soon, I'll be completely overwhelmed.

I know it should matter, but somehow it doesn't. It's just a weight on me that adds to everything else.

I rub a hand over my face and brush my too-long hair back from my eyes.

Damn, I need to get it cut.

"*Mijo*, of course. He should be home, but I need help. They come for a few hours, but I have to work. I can't care for *Papi* and pay the mortgage." My mom sounds utterly defeated. We were hoping for a transplant, but Papi doesn't qualify since up until he was bed bound less than a month ago, he still wouldn't quit sneaking drinks. Mami's anxiety has slowly gotten worse over the last few weeks. I can hear it in her voice. Every time I see her, this void of hollowness seems to be swallowing her whole.

"What about his pension and retirement? He worked for years with the police department. Can't that cover the difference?"

"Nathan, it's not enough. We have to look into a hospice center." Her tone is clear and stern.

"Let me pay for the nurses' extra hours. I moved out so he could be home. I can afford this. Please, *Mami*." I can't watch him deteriorate faster than he already is. Anger and frustration always seem to be boiling under my skin whenever I have to talk about my dad. I fight now to keep it from my voice. I can't add more to Mami's plate.

"Nathan, I can't ask that of you…" Her voice is quiet. My parents have never asked for financial help, but I can hear it in her voice. I can hear the silent plea behind her words.

"Fine, don't ask. I'm telling–I will call the hospice and get it set up. Okay?"

"*Mijo…Gracias.*" The thanks come out in a sob that shatters my already battered heart.

"I have to go. I'm at work te amo, Mami."

"*Te amo.*" Her tears seem to creep through the phone and run down my cheeks.

Click

"FUCK! WHY IS THIS SO HARD?" I yell to myself and slam my phone on my desk.

This isn't how it should be. I shouldn't be preparing for Papi to die. He is only in his fifties. Things took a turn for the worst right as the snow started to melt, and we've spent the last six months watching him die. My mom noticed one weekend that his skin started to take on a yellow-y hue. I don't think she thought much of it, but that same weekend I got called in the middle of the night because Papi had collapsed at the bar, and Cici had called an ambulance.

The next few weeks felt like a blur. Cirrhosis, stage four. When he collapsed in the bar, he had suffered a stroke that left him with limited mobility. I moved out so that we could turn my old room into a sterile hospital environment and Papi could receive care from home.

He's deteriorated rapidly over the past three weeks. It seems like every day I go to see him, he is awake less and he's lost more and more weight. Someone has to be with him most of the time because he is going through severe withdrawals on top of his deteriorating body. Most of the time it is just shaking and sweating, but once, in the first week after not drinking, he had a seizure that sent us back to the hospital. Mami has remained upright and by her husband's side the whole time, but now that we are nearing the end, her resolve is falling short. Our whole family is battered and tired, and part of me just wants it to be over–but the other part of me knows that once it is over, that will mean Papi is gone.

In reality, he is gone. He rarely has lucid moments anymore.

I sit up and stare at the dark computer screen in front of me. The reflection of the man on the black screen seems like a stranger. That Nathan has long greasy swept back hair. I keep mine short. He has a beard when I shave mine. His face is hard and the lines on his face defined. My face is soft, and I have always been more rounded. Whoever this man is, he is going through some shit. That Nathan is not me. It can't be me…

There's a knock on my oak door, pulling me, startled and disoriented, from my thoughts.

"Hey." Amber's head pops through the crack she made in the door frame. My friend of five years gives me a look that says she sees through the wall I hastily throw up to guard my emotions. She's got her red thin-framed reading glasses pushed up on her head, holding her light blond hair away from her face. Concern pulls her eyebrows down in the center, and the expression looks out of place on her normally calm-when-not-exuberantly-happy face. "Are you okay? I heard some frustrated mumbling from outside, I thought I'd see how you're doing?"

I drop my face into my hands, trying to ground myself as she steps into the room and closes the door behind her. Through cracks in my fingers, I focus on my shoes. Planted, rooted on the ground where the weight of my legs presses downward onto the beige carpet.

"Shouldn't you be working?" The knee-jerk reaction doesn't seem to phase her, and she crosses her arms, waiting for a real response. I take a steadying breath. "My dad is getting worse. I need to get hospice care in place." The words sound muffled through my palms, but I know Amber hears me–she comes over and perches on my desk in front of me. She's wearing yellow Keds that would normally seem childish on anyone else, but they make her look like she's walking on sunshine. I don't understand her personality, all glowing edges and rainbows, like budding springtime after April showers.

But when she needs to be, or rather when her friends need her, she's hard as diamond, unbreaking and steady. I appreciate her so much over the last few years. A genuine friend in a world full of fakes.

"I'm so sorry, Nathan." She puts one of her small hands on my shoulder. Her touch is warm, and the smallest bit of tension leaves my body.

"Can I do anything for you?" she asks quietly. When I don't answer right away, she leans down, wrapping her arms against my shoulders in a tight hug, her cheek pressed against my forehead. "I know it's hard. But you know if you need me, I'm here."

We sit like that for a few moments, and I allow myself to draw comfort from her embrace. Amber has been my rock through the summer, taking every single one of my emotions and air-headed forgetful moments in stride. When Catherine moved in with her this spring, I tried for a while to keep things separate. I didn't want to add more to her already burdensome friendship with me. However, even in the midst of my sort-of-breakup with the person I am convinced I will share my life with, she has remained constant. She's picked up pieces at work when I've needed it and has offered friendship through it all without making me feel bad once. She may be a small spitfire blonde, but she's tough as nails and fiercely loyal.

"I just feel helpless, ya know?" I sigh. "I mean, I never expected things to get better. That was apparent from the beginning. Now that we are here, I don't know what to do. My mom seems like a shell, and everyone's tiptoeing around the fact that my dad could be dead by the end of the month."

Amber presses a soft sisterly kiss to my forehead and draws back---turning my shoulders so that I'm facing her in the process. "Nathan, I don't think you're supposed to have all the answers right now. You are doing everything that you can, and it's good enough. Give yourself a break. I mean, have you even let yourself mourn yet? Are you sure you've let yourself deal with the emotions that you have about what's going on? Not just absorbing everyone's stress and grief and trying to claim them as your own?"

I feel a second of anger and frustration, but then I look into her big blue puppy dog eyes and remember she's not the bad guy here. I exhale a deep breath, fixing my eyes back on my desk. If I'm being truthful, the answer is 'No.' I haven't even brushed the surface of what's rolling around in my mind and body. I feel trapped–a slave to my own control and willpower. And part of me really doesn't want to know what might happen if I slip.

"Thank you, I appreciate all you do. Those are all great questions that I'm just not ready for. If you don't mind holding down the fort, I'm going to bail and set some stuff up for my mom."

Amber gives me a sad look, as if hoping I'll divulge more, but I just can't right now.

"Yes sir! I've got you covered, captain! Me and Mr. Broody-Pants will take care of things here." She's clearly trying to lighten the mood.

I can't help but chuckle a little at Amber's nickname for the college guy we hired in Catherine's place. He is an annoying, quiet man who obviously didn't want to have this job any more than we really wanted him here. But we had to fill the position and he was available the times we asked for.

Catherine… I do my best not to think of her, but it's nearly impossible. Every time Saul—Mr. Broody-Pants, as Amber has taken to calling him around me—shows up for work or comes to my office to ask another stupid question, I miss Catherine. I miss hearing her and Amber giggle when I go downstairs to have a meeting or talk to someone. I miss cinnamon vanilla lattes and morning chats in my office.

Fuck. I can't even sit in my office without thinking of the way she looked sitting in my desk chair, eyes searching, lust-addled and reaching for me…

Catherine showed up out of nowhere this past winter. She was running from her abusive ex and I was lucky enough to be the person she stumbled into. Everything happened so fast, we just clicked. She needed time to heal, and I respected her decision to take time to be herself. Catherine's the love of my life and I'll wait forever for her.

Fuck. That was stupid and cheesy.

"Thank you." I grab my leather satchel and pile in the paperwork I need to finish. "I'll finish the rest of this at home." My tone is sterile. If I don't hold this in, I will cry, or lose my resolve and all the carefully constructed walls I have in place to keep me steady. I push my black leather computer chair and stand. At 6'2", I tower above Amber's petite frame, drowning in a Bethton Grove University pullover that looks eight sizes too big.

"Please take care of yourself." She looks at me, her eyes full of concern.

But I can handle this. I have to.

I roll my eyes. "Yes, Mother." I pat her on the head.

She responds by tackling me in a hug. I give her a gentle squeeze back and she releases me. I walk to the oak door, hold the silver handle, and take a big breath.

Opening the door, I step away from the security of work and dive headfirst into the unknown purgatory that my life has become.

***

I lock my apartment door and head down the stairs to the galley kitchen of The Grove Coffee Shop. It's way past close, but Larry is standing in the kitchen slaving away over a giant stand mixer. There is a glorious smell coming from the oven, and even though I've been living above the coffee shop for months, it never gets old.

Larry overheard Amber and me discussing places for me to live while we were waiting in line for coffee one morning. It was right after Dad had the seizure and I was trying to find somewhere to go. Larry had offered to let me rent the space above the coffee shop. I had questioned it at first, but after he told me I could rent it for close to nothing, and it was already furnished, I couldn't say 'No.' It's a small studio apartment, just big enough for a bed, a basic bathroom, a refrigerator, and a small stretch of counter with a breakfast nook in the corner. There's a small closet space, and I didn't need to do anything but move in my clothes and a few other personal items. It's right across the street from campus and work, and only a ten-minute walk from home.

So here I am, leaving through the coffee shop at almost midnight on a Thursday night.

"Where ya headed off to so late?" Larry wipes his face down with a towel he has thrown over his shoulder. There's a few smudges of flour across his nose and brow that he misses and I think about pointing it out but decide it doesn't matter.

"The gym. I can't sleep. I thought you worked at the bar tonight?"

"Naw, I was going to, but Kitty picked up my shift. Tips are good this time of year with football starting, and she asked if she could have it. I told her no big deal, I needed to bake tonight anyway."

He gives me one long look before turning back to his stand mixer, dumping what looks like ten chickens' worth of eggs into the giant cauldron-like bowl.

My heart pounds unexpectedly at the mention of Catherine. I tried my best most days to not think about her because it always sucked me into a whirlwind of emotions. I promised her I'd give her all of the space and time that she needed, but I didn't realize at the time the amount of turmoil that would put me in.

At first, I tried to completely avoid her. I didn't want her thinking I was following her around or anything, but after a while I started to care less about that. I honestly hoped most days that I'd see her by accident. Maybe on mornings when I was leaving The Grove before the morning rush to get to work. Maybe I'd run into her while getting takeout from soups, and maybe I had walked past the bar more often than I'd like to admit going to the gym. I sometimes drop work at Amber's, but usually Catherine's already left for work before I make it to their apartment.

It's a delicate balance between completely avoiding her; turning down Amber when she invites me to take my lunch break with her, most likely trying to force Catherine and me together without our consent; and seeming like I'm stalking her by trying too hard to run into her.

Apparently, I love torturing myself.

But we rarely cross paths. Now and then I catch a glimpse of her leaving The Grove in the morning with Amber or passing through campus on her way to who knows where. It stings every time, like seeing the ghost of someone.

I miss her, and it is getting to the point where I am going to break my own promise to myself and to her. I want to see her so badly, and at the same time I don't want to, but I feel more and more like I need her. I feel like if I just talk to her, she would be able to make sense of all the things swirling around in my head. Just having a conversation and seeing her smile would lift my spirits a little.

"Well, I'm off, Larry." I head towards the storefront. This way takes longer to get to the gym, but it will give me a nice warm up.

It also takes me past her aunt's bar where she works.

Maybe I'll run into her.

"I thought you said the gym?" Larry shouts over the mixer. "Isn't it quicker to just go out the back?"

Well, fuck. I didn't think he was paying that much attention. "Oh, I take this way sometimes as a warmup."

Please don't ask me any more questions, Larry. Please...

"Alrighty then…" he pauses. "Tell Kitty I say hi!"

"GOODNIGHT, LARRY!" I slam the shop door behind me, and I swear I can hear him laughing.

Am I really that obvious? I don't bother to turn and lock the door. Larry will lock up whenever he leaves.

It's quiet out on campus for a Thursday night. My guess is most students are at the computer lab or the library getting ready for midterms in a few weeks. I walk slowly, the chill of the September night refreshing on my skin. It's still pretty warm during the days, but in the evenings, I can feel the fall air creeping in.

I tune into some classic rock on my phone and put in my wireless earbuds. This was one of those random splurges I made a few months ago because Amber said I just had to have them. At the time I thought they seemed ridiculous because I didn't listen to music a lot, but now that I had been working out regularly, I am grateful that she made me purchase them.

I see the overly bright neon glow of the sign above Cici's Pub. It's the only neon sign that never seems to have a piece that isn't working. Last call is in a few minutes. I know Cici doesn't like to keep the place open super late on weekdays to discourage college kids from being there all night.

Just as I'm about to speed up, the door opens and there she is, a broom in hand, pushing dirt and debris out of the front door. She turns toward me, and I slow to a walk, unsure of what to do. Her brow quirks up at me almost like she's amused to see me passing by. A small smile tugs playfully at the corner of her mouth the closer I get.

It's as if I'm dragged by an invisible current—unable to slow my walk toward her even if I wanted to.

"Hello, stranger."

Two

Catherine

Steam fills the small bathroom as I step out of the shower, small wisps floating off my shoulder. I dry my feet on the light blue bathmat before walking on the cool tile to the steamed mirror. I reach out with my right hand and wipe away the fog.

My dark brown hair reaches below my shoulder now. It's crazy to think it was only about six months ago that it was to my waist and a seriously unflattering auburn color. I also can't believe eight months ago I was engaged to that piece-of-shit Marcus. I can't believe he had such a hold on me that I even let him dictate everything from friends to my own damn body. When I got rid of him, my old high school friend Meg helped me get rid of the awful hair color and cut. I should proba-bly reach out to Meg to set up an appointment at her salon.

My cheeks are rosy from the heat of my shower. I have a gross little zit brewing on the tip of my button nose, but I'm thankful, that's all. I'm working on being okay with how I look. Amber calls it 'body neutrality.' Recent stress has made me a little more teen-revival pizza-faced, but I don't hate any of it anymore. I don't hate the way my stretch marks pull across my stomach, or the way my chin wrinkles in pictures when I laugh. I feel whole, like my body matches the person I am on the inside. When I decided to chase myself for once, I never would have expected to end up where I am now. I never thought I could feel so stable again.

The time to myself has been good for me that way.

The past few months have been hard to become fully independent financially. Marcus broke our lease, killing my credit. He was on my credit cards and he closed them, so I lost all that credit history. He was serious when he'd threatened to call in favors and close my accounts. I lost every penny of my savings. Cici had to loan me the money for the deposit on the apartment with Amber. Both of them want me to take Marcus to court, but I don't want to see that little weasel's face no matter how much money he took from me. It's not enough to cost me my peace.

"Catherine, are you done yet?" Amber knocks lightly on the door.

"I still need to blow dry, then I'll be out!" I shout back to her.

"I really gotta pee!" Amber squeals.

"Then just come in. It's unlocked!"

Amber throws open the bathroom door and runs to the toilet. I plug in the dryer and whip the warm wind through my hair. I hear a tiny sigh of relief come from behind me and I can't help but giggle at Amber. I love having independence, but I don't love having to share the world's smallest bathroom with a girl who has the world's smallest bladder.

I pull the mascara tube off the stained sink counter and start brushing it on my lashes.

Amber pulls her jeans up. "So, I was thinking we could go get coffee and go shopping. I need some clothes."

"I didn't get tipped well, so I can't buy anything today, but I don't mind tagging along. I was actually considering going in for a few hours tonight to try and make up for it." I let out a sigh, tucked in my towel toga as I head down the hallway toward my bedroom.

"But the weekends are for the girls!" Amber groans behind me. "What if I hold you hostage with information?"

"I don't know what information you'd have that's more important than money." I laugh and rummage through my canvas boxes in my white dresser. It's cheaper than buying an actual dresser since I spend most of the few dollars I have on clothing myself. Even though he canceled all my credit cards and closed my bank accounts, Marcus still sent my clothes to Cici's address.

But I won't wear anything from him or our past. I told Cici to keep them and happily added them to her dragon's hoard of clothing.

I pull on a black v-neck with a graphic of Kurt Cobain that Cici bought me and slide on my black jeans. I stare at myself for a minute in the mirror I have hooked on the wall. I've lost a little bit of weight in the last few months. Cici says it was all the stress weight I gained while I was with Marcus. My stomach doesn't seem to protrude from my body as much, and I like the new shape my face has taken recently. The deep bags that used to live under my eyes are much lighter, and even though I have a bit more acne than I'd like, overall I feel more like myself than I have in years. I have gained a bit of confidence over the last few months and really feel like I've found my voice. You have to speak up when you work at Cici's bar.

Amber leans into the doorway as I flop onto my twin bed. Amber gave it to me after she upgraded to a full.

Her eyes sparkle mischievously. "I talked to Nathan"

My ears perk up immediately. "And?"

"And…" She takes her time coming into my room.

I try to act like I don't care, but my heart is pounding in my chest.

"He's been talking about you a lot lately."

"He has?" My heart pounds even harder.

She crosses her arms and leans on the doorframe. "Well, not in so many words exactly. But he misses you. I think it's about damn time you two sit down and talk instead of avoiding each other."

I roll my eyes and continue to get ready. "I did tell Cici I would come in and close tonight because Larry said he had something else he needed to do and Cici made a cryptic comment about needing to go do 'something' with Charles."

In my years of experience, Cici's 'something' usually entails the two of them alone at someone's house. For long periods of time. Making a lot of noise. It's funny to think for most of my life I just assumed they truly were just platonic best friends. Until I started working at the bar and I walked into them having a 'meeting.' I was shocked, then relentlessly teased that I was too oblivious to catch on to the benefit aspect of their relationship.

I shudder internally and push the thought from my mind.

Amber is still staring at me.

"What?" I know I sound bratty and annoying, but Cici and Amber have both kept me up to date on all of Nathan's family stuff. "I really don't want to get in the middle of things and end up causing more stress where I'm not wanted in the first place. I kind of left on a weird note." I really care for Nathan, but I needed time to heal. It was hard to turn in my two weeks and end our relationship at the same time. He respected my decision, but I haven't heard from him either. I really don't know how he really felt about that moment. If he was angry, or if now he has moved on. That's not true, Amber would've told me if there was someone else at least. If he was waiting on me, though, he'd call.

Right?

She huffs. "His dad isn't doing great. Nathan's struggling and he doesn't want to talk about it with anyone…but I think he would listen to you. He needs you."

"I don't think he needs me," I say flatly.

"Fine. Maybe 'need' isn't the right word. But he misses you, Catherine. I've known Nathan for a long time, and I've known his family as a whole even longer. I also know, he's different around you, and he's been absolutely miserable without you. You asked for space, and he's given it to you. It's time you get yourself together, swallow your pride, and reach out. Because he won't do it first."

"I know… It's just been so long. And so much has changed. What if he doesn't like the changes? Or what if I'm really not what he needs right now, and I make things worse for him?"

"How are you going to make it worse?" Her question is genuine.

I spray myself with a little perfume and grab my socks from another little basket in my room. Sitting on the bed, I turn to look at her. "I don't know. I just don't want to be selfish and end up making him feel like he has to choose between time with me, or time with his dying father."

Amber nods slowly, "I get that, but you also could be the reason he can make it through dealing with his family."

"Can we talk about this more later? I don't mean to cut you off, but I really do need to work a few hours tonight." I'm arguing with Amber in spite of myself. Honestly, I've wanted to reach out for a while now. I wasn't there the night that Oscar had a heart attack in the bar, but Cici called me as soon as it happened. If I had been less of a coward, I would have found Nathan that night. My heart broke into pieces knowing that he was going through turmoil, and knowing that Oscar was the cause.

Amber sticks her lip out in an exaggerated pout. She's still mad that I'm going into work tonight.

"I know, I know. I promise you will have me all day tomorrow and Sunday, though."

"Fiiiiiine." She rolls off my bed and into a standing position.

"Do you really think he wants to see me?" I whisper only loud enough for her to barely hear.

"Absolutely."

I nod and she disappears from the doorway. I tuck her words away to deal with later as I pull on my shoes. It's Friday night, so with any luck, the bar will be packed, and I'll be walking out with good tips.

It hasn't been the same without Oscar. When drunks would get handsy, the cop and the father in him would come out and he'd put those guys in their place. *'Ey! That's mijo's chica!* Leave her the fuck alone' was a nightly comment. He made me feel a little safer. Oscar also kept me updated on Nathan even though we aren't seeing each other right now. He would insistently tell me to hurry my ass up and get back together with Nathan.

I grab my purse and my keys. My car's a trash heap, but it's *my* trash heap. It's a gold Camry. Cici ended up spotting me a little extra because she didn't like the first car that I could afford. If we are being honest, this one isn't much better, but it gets me around town and that's all I need.

I grab the door handle and pause for a moment.

Nathan.

All I want to do is call him, ask him to meet me at the bar. I want to hold him and comfort him as he did for me when I was fighting to find my place here away from Marcus. That's not fair to him though, to just show up after months. Is it? What would I even say? *Hey, Nathan, I wanna start back where we left off while your dad is dying before your eyes!*

The ball's in my court, and even though I wish he'd reach out first, he's respecting my boundaries… I think I'll call him tomorrow.

That's it. I'll call him tomorrow.

The bar is packed full when I get there, but my aunt is nowhere to be found. Charles is running around like crazy, though, trying to divide his time between the front and the back. He looks up gratefully as I come around the bar and clock in.

"I'm gonna be working in the back tonight. Larry is doing something at the coffee shop and can't come in tonight and Cici has been on a call in her office for the last fifteen minutes."

"Got it, old man." I blow him a kiss as he heads toward the back again and I start filling the orders in the front. The night goes quickly, and around 9:00 when he stops serving food, Charles preps me for the evening and then says he's going to take off. It's not unusual for someone to do the last three hours or so alone, but tonight is uncharacteristically busy, and I can barely tell my right from my left as I fill drink order after drink order.

Before I know it, the little alarm we have behind the bar starts flashing, letting me know there are ten minutes before the last call.

"ALRIGHT, TEN MINUTES! GET YOUR DRINKS WHILE YOU CAN! CLOSE OUT YOUR TABS AND REMEMBER TO TIP THE BARTENDER!" I shout to the noisy bar-goers, hoping I can snag a few more bucks before heading home.

One of the usuals comes to close out his tab.

"Hey, Catherine, have you heard about ol' Oscar recently?" He slurs. His name is Brinks. I vaguely remember Amber telling me it's her ex-boyfriend's dad, but I don't remember for sure. He probably was handsome when he was younger, dark skin and an easy smile, but now he looks like he's following in Oscar's footsteps. He spends more time here at the bar than at home.

"No, I haven't. I know Cici called Nelly to check on him a week or so ago." At that last check, Oscar was still doing okay and talked Cici's ear off.

"Visited the old bastard two days ago. He's looking pretty rough. The wife took Nelly out to dinner tonight. You should consider reaching out to Oscar's son. He'll need a shoulder here soon." He grimaces. He's never really spoken to me outside of the normal jokes that he shares–*shared*–with Oscar at my expense, along with other random ramblings of a drunk man. But he seems kind. He even covered Oscar's tab a few times.

"Tab is sixty-five tonight." I hold my hand out for the cash. "I was just thinking about that. It's hard though, he's going through a lot, I don't want to cause issues."

Brinks smirks. "Nobody has an issue with getting their wick dipped when they're sad. Keep the change." The older black man laughs from his beer belly and slaps a hundred-dollar bill into my palm.

"Oh, you get out of here, old man." I smile in thanks, seeing that he tipped more than usual.

I watch as a group of older men funnel out the door behind Brinks and slowly everyone else follows. He's the second person who's said something about Nathan tonight. I think the cosmos is asking me to do something.

Or maybe everyone is just making this small-town business.

Walking around the bar, I head to the door to flip the closing sign. I grab the broom on my way to sweep up the leaves out front. In the fall, the leaves seem to all land right outside the front door. I step out and the bell chimes. look up and see a man jogging my way.

The universe isn't asking, *it's telling*.

"Hello, stranger." I smile. My heart is pounding so hard I can barely hear his response as he slows to a walk a few yards away from me.

THREE

Nathan

"Hey." My voice sounds like I swallowed marbles.

Catherine.

I clear my throat and will myself to stop walking a few feet away from her. I can feel my body being pulled on her current, but some small part of me feels like this is a fever dream, and if I try and touch her, I will wake up.

"What are you doing?" She leans slightly on the broom handle, and I can't stop my eyes from roaming over her. She looks good. The light from the neon above the door casts a warm pinkish glow over her skin. Catherine's dark hair is longer, well past her collarbones now, and falls in soft waves around her face. She looks slimmer, less hunched, and she holds her head high as if she's not afraid of being looked at. Now she exudes confidence, and it radiates off her.

I look down at my gym shorts and t-shirt. This is the first time I have ever had trouble forming sentences. "I was heading to the gym. I thought I'd jog the long way to warm up."

She nods and her eyes roam over me the way mine just roamed over her. The glint in her eyes makes my stomach flip-flop a little. I know I've changed a lot in the last few months, but she's looking at me like I'm a different person. I guess in some ways I am. A lot has happened in very little time. I have a lot more time to myself since I moved out, and I've spent it at the gym. I know I've changed physically, slimmed down and toned in places I wasn't so much before. Mentally though… I'm afraid that the shell I've become shows through in every inch of my body.

"It's good to see you, too," Catherine smirks.

Her lips… I remember how they tasted, sweet and soft.

"Sorry, uh, I feel like I'm doing this whole talking thing really poorly. Can I start over?" I give her a sheepish smile and run my fingers through my hair. *Get yourself together Nathan, you're acting ridiculous.*

"How about you come inside and let me finish closing up. Then we can go to the diner and try talking again?" She opens the door and heads back into the bar. I watch the way her hips sway when she walks, and my mouth goes dry.

I swallow hard past the pile of rocks lodged in my throat. I follow her like a lost puppy, drinking in the scent of her perfume–and the way she looks over her shoulder at me as she walks back behind the bar.

I can't seem to get myself together tonight, and I want to cringe at my awkwardness. I've never been one to be stuck in my head, or at least I've always done a great job of hiding it. I'm caught between falling to my knees, begging her to take me back, begging her to give me even a shred of attention–and trying to play it cool and respect the space she asked for what seems like a lifetime ago.

****

I pour myself another cup of coffee as I stand in my office. My brain feels shrouded in fog. I couldn't barely pull myself from my bed this morning, and had no desire to come into work. Last night was shitty. I thought about going back or texting Catherine so many times last night, but I didn't see how I could.

I laid a boundary, even though I hated it, and I can't go back.

There's a knock at the door, and I glance at my phone. It's about time for Amber to be coming in. I assume she is here to tell me that Catherine won't be coming in today. Not that I'm surprised. After last night, she probably needs the day off. Some part of me is also afraid of the confrontation I'm sure she will want to have sometime soon.

I walk across my office in four strides, opening the door absently. "Good morning." I look up and her hazel eyes stare back. I don't know what my face is doing, but my stomach hits the floor. "Oh, I thought you were Amber." I motion her quickly into my office, closing the door behind her. "I honestly wasn't sure if you'd be in today." As I walk around my desk, I want to buy time. For some reason, I feel like we need the space between us for whatever she's about to say. There's a buzz that starts in the back of my brain when her eyes meet mine, and a sinking feeling that has my chest tightening.

I'm not sure how long we sit in silence. Catherine stares at me with a look I don't quite understand and do not like at all. Finally, I cave and break the silence when I no longer can stand the look on her face.

"Are you okay this morning? Can I get you coffee?" I feel like I need something to do with my body or I'll explode, so I walk back over to the coffeepot and pour a little more coffee on top of my already full cup. I feel stupid, but she seems too preoccupied to notice.

She declines coffee, so I sit back down at my desk. I fold my hands across the hard surface and I hope my face portrays all the things I don't feel. Calm, open, and ready to talk.

"You didn't answer my first question," I say, focusing on her face.

"I'm okay." Her brief response seems sincere. But when she says nothing else, I start to feel concerned. I don't know where this conversation is going. I do my best to remain quiet, though. When I told her I would be what she needed, I meant it. This morning she needs someone to listen, and if I'm the person she wants, I'll sit here and wait.

"So," she starts, "I actually came here to talk to you about something."

I steal myself for whatever she's about to say. Her leg is bouncing, and I don't think she notices. It rockets my anxiety skyward, but I do my best to remain still.

"I need to quit." Catherine's gaze is unwavering.

I study my hands, schooling my expression and tone of voice into one of passive resolve. "I see." I flinch internally. Once the words leave my mouth, they sound flat and hollow, bouncing around my office with all the finality I don't want to feel right now.

"This isn't because of you, or us. I mean it, kind of–I don't think I can work every day with you and keep my hands to myself. But, this is because I think I'm lost right now. Last night you said you wanted all the parts of me, and the more I think about it, the more I realize I can't offer you that right now because I don't even have all the parts of myself figured out." Catherine takes a deep breath, like she hasn't breathed since she started talking.

Even though I don't want them to, her words hit me like a punch to the gut, knocking the wind out of me. All I can manage is, "I understand." It feels like a lie. I want to understand, and rationally I do, but part of me is also screaming for her to take it back.

"I think I'm going to move in with Amber for a while. Maybe work at Cici's bar or get a job with Larry at the Diner." She attempts a smile that is full of so much emotion it just makes her look sad.

So many thoughts whirl around in my head. I want to argue with her. When I told her I wanted all of her, this wasn't what I meant. I want everything even she doesn't know about. I want to ask if this is forever and I feel ridiculous for caring so much. In a matter of weeks, she has wiggled her way into my life in a way I never thought someone would be able to.

When she challenged me that first night on the street, I went home and thought about it all night. I couldn't shake the feeling that I needed more of this stranger. And when I ran into her at the library, on the second day, it felt like fate. And then the universe threw me another scrap when she walked into my office asking for a job.

However, I cannot overlook the strength I see in her today. Her eyes are clear, bright, and determined. It's the most sure I have seen her since we met. I have to admire the strength it takes, because I don't think I could have done this. Even though I needed space from Carolina, I didn't sever things; even when our relationship became too toxic to handle. When I needed to, I couldn't walk away. I can't do that again. I can't risk pushing for a relationship that may end in resentment. Part of me is relieved that I don't have to be the one to do it. As much as I'd love to turn a blind eye and fight for what Catherine and I have, I can't.

"I think I like you even more than I did before." The words are out before I can stop them. I don't know how much truth they hold right now, but I can admire and respect the space she's asking for. And all I can do is hope against hope it won't be forever.

"What? Why?" Catherine meets my eyes, bewilderment clear in her expression.

"You are one of the strongest, smartest people I know. You deserve to find yourself. I hope someday soon you see yourself the way I see you. And then I hope, when you get there, you'll let me take you to dinner again, so that I can hear all about it." My voice cracks on the last word, but I try to smile through it.

Catherine stands and stumbles around my desk and into my arms. I cling to her tightly through the waves of emotion crashing into me. She smells like vanilla and something like citrus. I don't know how long we sit there in silence, Catherine clinging to me, and I to her.

"I don't want this to be forever." Her words are laced with tears. I hold her tighter, trying to piece together my own feelings through the shattered bits. It feels surreal to care this much for someone, to want what's best and still have to fight myself to let go. I can't be selfish. This isn't about that. We haven't known each other long enough, but it doesn't matter. Sometimes you meet a person, and you just know. Catherine is that for me. I will wait as long as it takes for her to come back to me.

"I'll be here when you get back." The admission feels heavy and vulnerable, but I don't care. I mean every word. *"I want to be what you need me to be."* I press a kiss to her forehead, drawing comfort from the feel of her.

She sits with me for another few minutes. I can feel her taking deep breaths, still holding onto me like she will fall off the edge of the earth if she doesn't. *"I should probably go…" she says finally. She wipes tears from her cheeks and my heart cracks again.*

I stand with her, taking her hand to lead her toward to door. Something in me says I need to touch her as long as I can because I will not get this chance again for a while. I press a soft kiss to her back of her hand, studying every part of her face as I do. I commit her to memory like I may go blind as soon as she leaves.

Once she is outside and my door is closed, I lean my back against the hard oak, closing my eyes and taking a few breaths. My throat feels like it's full of rocks and the first few breaths are choked and slow. Finally, I open my eyes, my office is quiet, and I go back to sit behind my desk.

This isn't forever.

***

"I don't normally see you walking by to go to the gym." Catherine's words break the silent tension and I'm again reminded of how much I love her voice.

"Oh yeah, because I wanted to take a jog instead of running on the treadmill." *Because I wanted to see you.* All I've wanted is to see Catherine, to hold her. I have spent so long convincing myself I don't need this, that I am big enough and strong enough not to invade her time when she needs space. It is all being smashed to pieces before me with every look she gives me from behind the bar.

"I see. So how are you doing? How's work? Amber told me a little about my replacement. He's an interesting guy." She gives me a knowing look.

"Saul is the exact opposite of interesting. I'm sure Amber keeps you updated on all of it, though. He's certainly not as easy on the eyes, either." I give her a little smirk.

"Amber tells me the same thing almost every day. Except the easy on the eyes part." She sends me a little wink.

My heart stutters a little at her sense of humor. I have missed her sarcasm and easy joking so much.

She gives me another knowing look and returns my smile. She's counting money now, So I just sit and watch her, saying nothing else. Catherine thumbs through it quickly, then gets a bank bag from the drawer under the register, pockets one stack of money, and shoves the rest into the bag that she drops in an office that I'd assume is Cici's.

"Well, that's it for the night. But now you're all dressed up with nowhere to go. Do you still want to go somewhere?"

"Yes!" My response is quicker than I mean, and I clear my throat awkwardly, trying desperately not to sound so ridiculously… *desperate*. "I mean, yeah, let's go. Is the diner still good?"

"Sure, it's a classic." She strides easily to the door and holds it open for me. "Just let me lock up." She turns the key in the lock and shoves it back into her purse. "Shall we?"

***

The bell on the door jingles as we enter the old retro diner. I'm not sure if it's considered retro if the business just never upgraded. The place is practically empty, which makes sense since it's almost one in the morning by now. Catherine brushes against my hand as she comes through the door, sending electricity up my fingertips.

We settle into a booth, sitting across from each other, and I'm reminded of our first unofficial date when we came here in the spring just over six months ago. Sadly, I know Larry is preoccupied at the coffee shop, so some pimply faced kid takes our order. His voice cracks when he confirms our drink orders and I wonder if he's actually even old enough to work the night shift.

"So," Catherine breaks the silence. "Fill me in. How have things been? Truly."

Her face is full of the concern neither of us are acknowledging, and I kind of hate it. Everyone's been tiptoeing around me for months now, and it's impossible to feel even a little bit 'normal' or 'okay' when everyone keeps looking at me like I'm going to break.

She looks at me for a moment, waiting for me to answer. When I don't, she continues. "I live with Amber, so I'm not clueless. I work at the bar, and everyone lets me know about your dad's condition, and even how your mom seems to handle everything. No one says how *you're* feeling, though, and that's who I care about."

Who I care about… I can tell she means it. But my mind feels too garbled to make sense of my own thoughts.

"Have you been training with Cici on how to interrogate people? You really don't waste time jumping right into the rough shit. You pulled a full Cici right there." I laugh, but it's strained at best, and even though I mean to joke, I can tell she isn't impressed.

"Well, she had many talks with me about my shit. Now stop redirecting from yours." She doesn't skip a beat, but she smiles softly at the mention of her aunt.

"I honestly don't know where to start. Dad is nearing the end, and things feel like everything is crumbling before me. I feel like I resented him so much and missed precious time. I constantly have to make sure my mom doesn't have a mental breakdown. I also have missed you more than you could imagine." The words tumble out before I can catch them, and I am surprised how easy it is to just tell her everything. I want to tell her everything. I have imagined so many nights looking for her, confessing that I'm falling apart, that I miss her, that I need her… And every single one of those nights I hate the weakness I feel, and how little control I have over my life and thoughts these days. My heart races as I wait for her reaction.

"You should've called me then, dumbass. I would've been there." She grins at me a little to show she's teasing.

"I wanted to respect your space. I didn't want to burden you so soon after you found your freedom."

She nods, and something like sadness crosses over her face. "I appreciate your diligent respect, but I also hate a little that you thought I would ignore you or turn you away."

She reaches her hand across the table toward me. "I never intended for my request for space to mean that we couldn't be friends, or that I wouldn't come running if you needed help or support. I do care for you deeply, that hasn't changed. And if you would have called, I would have been there in a heartbeat. I'm so sorry that I let my own fear and hesitation get in the way of reaching out to you."

My heart hammers violently against my ribs, and old tired butterflies float around in my stomach.

I pull out my phone and hit call.

Catherine's phone vibrates the booth. She answers. "Hello?" The sound echoes on the call.

"I miss you," I whisper into my phone mic.

"I miss you too." She is smiling from ear to ear.

"Are you ready yet?" I send her a smile back. My throat stings a bit as I see the emotion shining brightly in her eyes. She takes a moment to answer me, and I feel like a teenager, waiting for the girl he likes to check 'yes' or 'no' on a folded piece of paper. But unlike a teenage crush, the paper is my sorrow-creased heart, and if Catherine checks 'no,' I don't know what I'll do.

"Yes," she whispers back into her phone. I grab the hand that is still out-stretched on the table and squeeze it tight and hang up the phone as relief floods me. Her hands are small and soft, her nail polish is black and chipped, probably from washing bar glasses.

The waiter comes back and drops our drinks at the table. Catherine takes one big drink of the black coffee and grimaces but tries to cover it with a smile.

"The coffee here has never actually gotten better, has it?"

"I have better stuff back at my apartment." I realize what I'm saying, and she stares at me through the steam of her cup as if she doesn't know if I'm being seri-ous or not.

"I didn't know you moved," she says finally.

"I moved when Dad got worse a few months ago. Sold the car, too."

"You sold your car?" She sets her cup of coffee down and looks at me seriously again.

"Yeah, I moved into the studio above The Grove. Got a really good deal on the space. Mom needed my room for Dad, and the car bought the hospital bed. That way mom only had to worry about the home care nurse. It made sense. The coffee shop is just across the street from the library, and I don't go anywhere farther than a mile most of the time as it is. So, the car would have just been sitting. Honestly, it probably would have been towed if I left it in the wrong spot for a week."

She gives me a sympathetic smile that makes my skin crawl a little. I know people look at me like I'm a martyr, but I don't see it that way. I spent so long feeling like the worst son in the world, it made sense to help my mom the best I could.

"Well, I have my car parked out in front of the bar."

"You got a car?"

"Yeah, Cici thought I'd need one since Amber and I live a few miles away from the bar. She matched what I could afford to help me get one."

"That's amazing." I can't believe how much Catherine has grown, and I'm so proud of all the things she's done for herself so far. Not that I ever doubted she could. I'm glad things are looking up for her.

"So, let's go then?" She stands and throws a ten down on the table.

We hurry down the street to where her car is parked behind the bar and get inside. It's a little 2010 Camry in gold. The inside is slightly cluttered with papers and random grocery bags. Catherine makes some mumbled apology and then we start the slow drive to my apartment. It's barely two blocks down to the coffee shop, and we drive most of the way in silence.

"You know…" Catherine starts slowly. "I was going to call you tomorrow. Amber had mentioned something to me today when I was getting ready."

"Mentioned what?"

"Nothing in particular. Just that she noticed it was about time we talked."

"That's funny because she's been bothering me for weeks about calling you." I can't help but laugh a little because Amber would be the one to finally convince us to talk again.

"I'm sorry it took so long," she says quietly.

"Don't apologize. I know you needed time. I agreed to that time."

"I know, but I should have reached out sooner… It's just that…" she shrugs vaguely at nothing in particular. "It's just, at first it was hard. I was so afraid that I hurt you. I didn't want to come back prematurely. Then months passed, and I knew about your dad from the guys at the bar. I didn't want to complicate things for you."

"I appreciate the sentiment."

"But then Amber would not stop nagging me." She chuckles and rolls her eyes, and I love the way her face looks as we pass beneath the streetlights and they douse her in light every ten seconds, making her glow.

"It's alright. I could have said something way sooner, and I didn't either. Things were looking up for you. I didn't want to drag you down in my shit when you were just getting some reprieve from your own."

The silence in the car isn't uncomfortable, and Catherine remains steadily looking out the windshield. But I'm rocked by her thoughtfulness, and also her vulnerability, another thing that seems to have changed in the last few months. She talks with more confidence, even if it's something vulnerable.

"Next time, I think we need to be more selfish." She smiles at me again as she pulls into one space out front.

"Yeah, fuck your feelings. Next time I'm not keeping my distance."

She turns the car off and laughs, and it's the most beautiful sound I've heard in a long time.

I'm thankful that Larry is gone when I let us in through the front door of the coffee shop and head upstairs through the stairwell in the kitchen.

Catherine looks around the shop with a sense of wonder on her face that makes me smile.

"It's honestly super cool that you live above The Grove. Very romance novel-y of you." She cracks a smile as I unlock the door and let her into my apartment.

Four

Catherine

"Well, welcome to my humble abode." Nathan swings the door open to a small studio apartment.

His unmade bed is in front of the large flat screen tv. A single picture of his family hangs on the wall. I can only assume Nelly attempted to de-bachelor this place a little, with the few knickknacks placed about. Her attempts obviously didn't work. His kitchen is solely one counter with a microwave, and one of those mini fridges that you see in college dorms sometimes. There's a crockpot–again probably because of Nelly–and a coffee maker shoved in the corner. I guess when you live above a commercial kitchen and bakery, the need for a fridge and oven isn't there.

"It's not much, but it's home right now." Nathan rubs the back of his neck, clearly embarrassed. He makes his way around me and fills the coffee carafe with water.

There's a little breakfast nook shoved into the corner, with a wrap-around bench and a window overlooking the street corner below. Stacked along the back edge of the bench, right along the windowsill, are books. I can't see the titles from here, and I consider making my way across the room to see, but I feel awkward in the new space and decide to look for coffee mugs in the cabinets above the counter. I open the one above the sink and realize there is no way I can reach them. Nathan has them stacked on the second shelf above what appears to be plastic jars of protein powder and drink mixes.

His hard body presses against my back as he reaches for the coffee cups and I freeze, my heart pounding. I'm reminded of the night we spent together in Cici's kitchen before I started working at the library, back when he was just a big brooding man who helped my drunk ass home late one night.

***

I feel him brush against my back as he opens the cabinet above the sink. My heart fully stops. For a moment, I cannot do anything, and I feel my body threatening to sway again, dizziness surging through me with his front lightly grazing my back. His hand snakes to my hip as he lightly presses me back upright. I hadn't even realized my body had tilted.

"Woah, there," his voice has a husky undernote that sends shivers through my body. "One fall was enough for tonight."

Even after I'm steady, his hand stays in place for another three long beats of my heart. Time seems to both be frozen and also racing. I turn in his arm, and before I can react, his other hand grasps my hip and he lifts me onto the counter next to the sink. My eyes are heavy watching him check my palms. My left hand appears to be relatively fine, but my right hand must have caught some ice or gravel. There is a patch of raw, bleeding skin that traces a short distance from my thumb down my wrist.

He works quietly and carefully, rubbing disinfectant into the cuts. I hiss under my breath from the sting of his touch, and his eyes flick up to meet mine.

"Are you okay? Does your wrist hurt, too? It doesn't hurt when I move it, does it?"

"No, it's okay. It just stings a little." I know my voice betrays all the muddled feelings I have. It comes out shaky and low. My heart jumps into my throat when Nathan brings the palm of my hand close to his mouth and blows gently on the cut. The coolness of his breath sends shivers up my arm and down my spine, and lessens the sting of the antiseptic.

***

Nathan's breath brushes across my shoulder, but he doesn't step away from me as he sets the cups on the counter. I turn slowly to face him, his hands braced on the counter to either side of me. But I don't feel boxed in. I know if I were to place my hand on his chest, or make a move to get away, he would let me pass.

"Hi," I say breathlessly, allowing myself to look into his dark eyes. That familiar scent of his cologne hits me in the gut, and suddenly I can't breathe. I can't move. I can't speak or step away. I have ached for him so many times. And now I feel like I'm caught in a dream. If I move, I'll wake up, and a voice in the back of my mind is screaming for him to touch me, kiss me, do something because I feel like the distance between us is going to kill me. Another moment without him feels like too much to handle.

"Hi." He gives me a small smile, but his eyes are trained on my mouth. And then he's kissing me. His lips are just as soft and warm as I remember. It's not like other kisses we'd shared in the past–this kiss is soft, and not very long, but my heart jumps as if remembering exactly what it's been missing.

Nathan's rough working hands graze my chin and hold my jaw gently. I think I melt into the floor then, almost sagging in relief at the feel of his touch. The beard is new and tickles my lips. I slide my hand in his long black hair, and my other hand places itself on his chest. He's leaner and stronger than before. It's new but familiar. Almost like when you leave home for college and your parents buy a new couch. It's different, but still feels like home.

I giggle as his short, dark beard tickles my nose.

"What?" Nathan startles and pulls back, his cheeks flush from embarrassment.

"The beard needs getting used to." I smile to reassure him. He seems to relax a bit, and I'm surprised to see that he seems genuinely self-conscious. I never would have expected that from him. But I guess a lot has changed recently.

"Yeah, I mostly forget I have it. I prefer being shaved." He hands me the mug with the BGU logo printed in the school's classic deep green.

"Why don't you shave then?" I ask, wanting him to let me in. There's a wall surrounding him like a dark cloud. From the moment we made eye contact tonight, it's been looming over him like the darkness that precedes a storm. I can't quite put my finger on what the issue is.

Nathan steps back and shrugs. "I don't have as much energy. Work, gym, and help out Mom." He walks over to his coffee maker and takes the carafe, pouring my cup first and then his. "I made decaf. I hope that's okay." His body tenses, reinforcing the wall around him.

"Yes, that's fine. Does your mom need a lot of help?" I lean on the counter and take a drink of the scalding liquid. I assumed moving out would mean he had more free time.

"Yeah, she is working two jobs right now, so I usually have Amaya. I also help clean because when she's home, the nurse takes off, so honestly it's like she's working three jobs right now." Nathan stands awkwardly, facing the counter, his head turned away from me. He is holding his cup in both hands. It catches me as a little funny how small the coffee cup looks in his hands compared to mine, even though they are the same sized cup.

"That sounds really stressful, I can't imagine."

"My mom's a trooper." Nathan sighs.

"No, I mean for you." I close the distance between us and place my hand on his shoulder and he relaxes. I feel like I can physically see the cracks forming in the dark wall around him.

Nathan turns around to face me. He smiles, but sorrow is in his eyes. "It is stressful, but I'm managing."

"Says the guy who looks like he's been stranded in the woods for months fighting bears." I tease the long messy hair away from his face, stepping into his personal space to push the soft locks out of his eyes.

"You kind of have an 'unshaven jungle man' look to you." I mean it as a joke, but Nathan's face falls a little and my heart hurts for him. I take a moment to really study his face as he stares down into his cup. His normally bright eyes are duller than usual, and dark bags surround them, making his sockets appear sunken depending on the light. His posture reminds me of a cornered animal, tired and strung out, ready to fight at any moment. Nathan is rigid and stiff like he doesn't fit his skin anymore.

"Maybe I am moonlighting as a jungle man. You don't know." His smile falls.

"Is it really that obvious? I thought since the mentally unstable look was chic now, I could get away with looking like I'm brooding and full of angst." Nathan pulls a strand of black hair into his vision. He gives me a halfhearted smirk. "I guess, I am probably a few months overdue for a haircut."

"So you're stressed and you're supposedly managing even though that's definitely debatable." I prod him a little more. "How are you feeling? Like really feeling?"

He wanders into his living room that is also his bedroom. He looks a bit lost, staring around absently before settling his eyes on his massive bed. "If you're going to make me talk about my feelings, I'm sitting somewhere more comfortable."

I follow behind him and he sits on the side of his bed, staring down at his feet. He places his cup down on the little bedside table that is barely wider than a shoebox.

I sit on the floor criss-cross applesauce, cradling my cup, letting its warmth seep into my chilled fingers. There is a lack of sitting space, and I feel like there is something really intimate about sitting on his bed with him. I don't want to just assume I can sit there when he hasn't specifically invited me.

Nathan sighs. "Come up here, goofball. We can both be comfortable."

"Sorry, I didn't want to get in bed with you without your consent." I laugh a little, standing up to join him on the bed. I set my mug down next to his, careful not to knock over the spindly little excuse for furniture.

He scoots to the top of the bed and stretches his legs, crossing them at the ankles.

"Catherine, you always have my consent to get in bed with me." Nathan's tone is light but his eyes smolder, and those familiar butterflies start making their way into my chest.

"Is this how girl sleepovers are? Sitting on the bed and gossiping?" Nathan's laugh is genuine as I make a face at him and sit at the foot of his bed, crossing my legs. "In the movies, they always put in curlers and practice kissing." He smirks and puckers his lips dramatically.

"Is this gossiping, or a therapy session? Maybe I should be charging you," I tease.

"I'm pretty sure paying you to be in bed with me is illegal." Nathan winks. I can feel my face heat, even as we both laugh.

"I've missed our banter." I really have. He's always been so easy to talk to. I know that he will never use anything I say against me.

"I've missed you. Shit's hard out here for a sad, lonely librarian whose dad is dying of liver failure." His sarcastic tone shows he's messing around, but I think there is some truth to that.

"So that's how you're feeling? Sad and lonely?" I keep my tone equally playful, but I scoot a little closer.

"You were serious about the 'feelings' talk then?" He rubs a hand over his face, and when he looks at me again, all the playfulness is gone, and I have a clear glimpse of the heartbreak bubbling under his sturdy exterior. "Well in a way, 'sad and lonely' is pretty accurate. I have missed you. I know you needed the space, but I thought about you every day." My heart stutters a little in my chest. "On the whole 'dad dying thing,' I'm angry."

"You're angry at your dad for dying?"

"No, not for dying. For leaving us. I'm angry at Dad for playing a role in his own death. I guess maybe it's like prolonged suicide in a way. But I'm not angry about him dying. Everyone dies eventually. They go to meet their maker." He slumps down a little farther in the bed, staring over my shoulder at the dark TV screen.

"It's amazing finding out how much he drank. Even when I thought he was sober, he wasn't. I've been mostly raising Amaya if she isn't with Mom. Amaya and Sofia butt heads so much. Although, Sofia butts heads with pretty much everybody." Nathan looks so defeated.

I recognize the soul shattering pain of discovering your family isn't who you thought they would be.

I crawl up the bed and move to sit beside him. I place my hand on top of his, rubbing the back of his palm with my thumb. "That sucks. I'm really sorry." I give his hand a little squeeze, and when he looks at me, I smile softly.

"You look tired," I say after a moment.

He leans his head close to mine and we both settle deeper into the pillows of the bed.

"I am exhausted." He closes his eyes as he adjusts his head to a more comfortable position.

"I can leave if you want me to? So you can sleep." *I'd rather stay.*

"No, please, don't go yet." He looks up with those deep brown eyes. "I've missed you and I feel better around you."

"Alright, then." I shift around, rolling to face him.

"Tell me about everything," he says, rolling and draping an arm easily across my hip. "Fill me in on everything you've been doing recently."

I take a moment to answer, savoring the comfort that I feel around him even though it's been so long. Nathan's warmth and the sound of his voice remind me again how much he feels like home.

"Hasn't Amber kept you updated?" I raise my eyebrows knowingly.

"Of course she has, but I'd still like to hear from you. Your voice is much more relaxing than Amber's coffee rambling." His eyes are shut, but his words are still clear.

"Well, I live with Amber, I work at Cici's bar, and I still haven't talked to anyone from Georgia." It's true, I've been able to live calmly and simply on my terms the last few months.

"I heard Marcus gave you a hard time with your finances." Nathan peeks open one eye to see my reaction, then closes it again. "Sorry for bringing it up. Amber said you might take legal action then I didn't hear anything about it."

"I decided I'd rather start over than ever see him again. I think since he couldn't see me, he'd tried to force me to see him through court hearings. It's just not worth it." I can't imagine ever having to look at that pathetic man again. "Cici and Amber were upset about it, but they still supported me to get a little more financially secure. I wouldn't have survived without them. My credit's fucked, though."

"I get that. I don't want to see that creep ever again, either. I might be driven to violence." He snorts, followed by a small smile. Nathan's voice gets quieter as he speaks.

I slide down and move my head even closer to his. I stroke his cheek. A tiny smile pulls at the corners of his mouth, and his face softens. I kiss his forehead gently, still a little tacky from his run. I tuck a small lock of hair behind his ear. "I should go."

"No. Stay, please," Nathan mumbles quietly.

"Okay." I crawl under the covers, throwing the other corner over Nathan, and close my eyes. His warmth envelopes me and his arms pull me in. I curl up and his arms tighten reflexively around me. We are both still fully clothed, but by the look on Nathan's face, sleep is mere moments away. I briefly wonder if this is weird, if we are going to wake up in the morning and realize we made a mistake. I decide that is tomorrow's problem, and for now I just allow myself the peace this moment brings.

This is what I've been missing these last few months. I never could quite place where the empty hole in my life came from, and I didn't let myself believe it was him. I can hear his breathing slowing, and my own eyes are feeling heavy. Somewhere in the back of my mind, I think I should text Amber and tell her where I am. I can't bring myself to disentangle from Nathan's embrace. I never texted Cici, either, to tell her I locked up for the night.

The last thing I remember before sleep overtakes me is the deep rhythmic breathing of the man next to me lulling me to sleep.

FIVE

Nathan

I wake to a face full of hair, and it takes me a moment to orient myself to what's going on. My body feels heavy with sleep, but I can hear my phone ringing where I left it in the kitchen. The ringtone rattles my brain as I pull my arm from under Catherine's sleeping form and roll to my feet. The ringer stops and I pause, standing in the middle of my apartment.

Maybe it was an accident. I glance over my shoulder to the woman lying in my bed. She's facing me, curled up into a ball. Her features are soft, and her breathing is slow and even. Even like that, she is undeniably beautiful. A stray piece of hair lays across her forehead and I take a step back toward the bed to smooth it away.

But my phone rings again and I jump, crossing the small space in five long strides.

A picture of my mom and Amaya lights up my screen and I answer it quickly.

"Hi, *Mami. ¿Qué pasa?*"

"*Es Papi.*" Mom's voice is shaky on the other end. "He's really not doing well tonight. *El ve a Dios.*"

He sees God…

I rub my hand over my face. The clock on the counter reads just before four in the morning.

"He's not going to make it much longer, *Mijo*. You need to come home." Mami's voice is heavy with fear and pain.

"Okay, just breathe, I'll be there soon." About once every week for the last three weeks my mom has called me like this, and every time I go over, sit for a while, and Papi always wakes back up.

"I have a bad feeling this time, Nathan."

You have a bad feeling every time, Mami.

"I'll be there in a few minutes. Let me get my shoes on." I can hear Sofia in the background ranting loudly in Spanish, and my mom shushes her but doesn't say anything else to me.

"I'm going to hang up now. I'll text you as soon as I walk out the door."

"Okay." I hear her shuffling around and a deep inhale on Mom's end meaning she's stepped outside for a cigarette. "Just hurry, *por favor*."

"I will."

I end the call and sigh. The exhaustion weighs heavily on me tonight, and all I want to do is crawl into my bed, wrap myself around Catherine, and go back to sleep.

I walk to the bed and look down at her. That stray piece of hair is laying across her forehead again, and I sit on the bed gingerly and smooth it away. Catherine stirs, and from the dim light in the room, I can see her eyelids flicker.

"I have to go. You rest. Mom called about Dad," I whisper, gently encouraging her to stay safe and warm till my return.

"Do you want me to come?" she groans sleepily from the pillow, pushing up on an elbow, sleep coated eyes framed by concerned brows.

"No, don't worry. I'm sure it's a false alarm. Mom calls me at least once a week like this."

Catherine lets out a tired 'ha' and rolls back over to the deep slumber I woke her from.

I slide my blue tennis shoes on, giving myself a small sniff.

I can't believe I didn't shower. I smell like a jungleman.

Poor Catherine has been cuddled up to my stench all night. I'll shower when I come back if she's still sleeping. I need to come up with a code word with Sofia to determine the level of seriousness a call is. Then again, she is just as dramatic as our mother, I'm sure she'd tell me it's an emergency every time anyway. I grab a black hoodie with BGU scrolled across it in vibrant green from a hanger. I'll enjoy the walk, it's only ten minutes.

I head down the staircase to the cafe's kitchen. I can still smell the warm scent of the baked goods Larry made this evening, then I head straight out the back door towards the alley that separates the café from the school campus. It is dark and a little wet from the early morning dew. I head straight left on the path I've traveled many times for Mamis' late-night calls.

As I walk down the alley and emerge onto the street, I hang a right. I can feel a tickle of annoyance. Why tonight of all nights? Catherine is finally in my bed, and I have to leave. Mom's call frequency has upticked, but Papi's condition hasn't changed much. The street lights flicker above me, and I flip up my hood. It's frustrating that Sofia is there. He'll be fine till morning. He always is.

Except Mom said he was seeing God.

Hospice told her that towards the end he might start hallucinating. This is just the first time he has, though. I'm sure we'll have eight more scares before he actually goes.

Anger starts to swell up in me. It seems like every time Catherine comes into my life, it gets interrupted. Dad's been pushing me to make things go quicker with Catherine to demand her to make up her mind. Now I have her and he's pulling me away.

One of our first dates together was ruined by his arrogant drinking. I wouldn't even have to be leaving her if it wasn't for his God damned drinking. I remember so many times picking him up from the bar, destroying my social life. If it wasn't for him, imagine how many events I wouldn't have missed.

How many opportunities have been lost?

His damned drinking is why I'm having to be a dad to my own damn sisters. Amaya has never had a normal dad. It makes me so angry that I'm the only one who goes to school plays and soccer practices. Amaya's home right now seeing this side of Dad, seeing our dad hallucinating and freaking Mom out. No child should go through that. She spends a lot of nights in my nasty bachelor pad to get away from the hospital her home has become.

Dad won't get to see Amaya graduate.

Dad refused help time and time again.

Mom should've gotten to grow old with Dad, never having to work a day in her life.

My children will never know their grandfather.

Dad won't come to my wedding.

Dad won't teach my kids to fish or tell old cop stories to scare them. My dad's days are nearing the end, and he's stealing every important memory we should have made together. Now we have to suffer and miss out because of his fucking choices.

My heart is racing as I clench my fist and grit my teeth. Why am I going at four in the morning to some jerk who's taken so much from me?

The brick campus buildings fade into the neighborhoods of Bethton Grove. Large trees, planted way back when this area was settled, line the street. To my right is a small park where Dad would take Sofia and me to swing after school while Mom cared for the younger kids. The houses are old and remind me of simpler times growing up.

***

"Papi and Nathan. Papi and Nathan." I sing as I hold my papi's large hand. It's rough but gentle.

"Ah mijo, you lucked out today. All those stinky chicas are at home and we are free!" Papi laughed. Sofia had to stay home and do schoolwork.

Papi swung me up onto his shoulders. I fan my arms out wide. "Papi, I can fly!"

"Si, Mijo. Fly high enough to touch the skies!" Papi yelled.

We make it to the park. My Papi places me on the ground, and I run straight for the swings. I love the rush of going as high as Papi can push me. I pick the blue swing in the middle. It has the best momentum. The ground underneath this particular swing has been dug out by dragging feet.

My small six-year-old legs don't touch. I watch as my papi lights a cigarette and slowly gets behind me to start pushing me. Papi and I don't get much time together, between work and all of the girls. His undivided attention is like winning the lottery.

"Don't forget to kick. How was school today?" Papi is the best. He always asks me good questions. Mami tells me that's why he's a good police officer.

"It was good! Sister Luanna says I'm her favorite," I boast.

"Oh, really now? And why's that?" Papi has the best laugh.

"Sister Luanna says it's because I'm a super reader!" I shout as I begin to swing higher and higher.

"Ah, yes, a very talented boy you are, reading so much. Curiosity is a good thing, Nathan. Never stop being curious." Papi pushes harder.

"Papi! I can touch the sky!" I shout as I become horizontal with the swing set.

"Si, Mijo! You can!" An excited…

***

Yelling, I hear yelling. I turn right at the stop sign. I pick up my pace. The yelling is coming from down the street.

"POR QUE?!" The yelling becomes clear. It's weeping.

"Shit! *No*. No!" I jog faster. My ears heat up and start ringing. All I can hear is the thump of my feet hitting the ground.

THUMP

"PAPI!" Another cry.

T*HUMP*

"NO! POR QUE DIOS!" My mom is crying.

THUMP

Why is my mom crying? My heart sinks, it knows the answer.

THUMP

I can't. Dad can't…he's not allowed to be gone.

THUMP

"PAPI!" A yell tears from my throat as I end up in front of my parents' home. My mother is sobbing and wailing. Then it hits me and…

I feel nothing.

Six
Catherine

The bed shifts under me and I roll to where Nathan sits on the edge, pulling off his shirt and shoes.

"What time is it?"

"Seven-nineteen." Nathan's voice sounds like he swallowed glass, and every muscle in his body seems to be pulled tight like thick ropes under his skin.

I didn't even realize I had fallen back asleep after he said he was leaving this morning. Part of me feels guilty for not pushing harder to go with him, but I know it's not my family, and not my place.

He lays back gingerly on his pillow, like he's making sure the bed is real, and stares at the ceiling.

"Nathan?" I don't have to say more. He turns his head slowly to look at me and the agony is painted thickly on his expression. Any shred of light in his gaze is gone, and the deep circles around his eyes seem impossibly darker than before. Every emotion seems to strain under his skin, fighting to be the one in control.

I take his hand and pull him closer, wrapping my arms around his shoulders in the process. He doesn't fight, but comes to me limply, like his body has forgotten how to work. That doesn't deter me, and I only squeeze him tighter. Nathan's entire body is rigid with grief, and I slowly start to rub his back, applying pressure to his tight muscles as I do my best to channel comforting energy from my body to his.

With every shaky breath he takes, I feel his body slowly relax. I don't dare let go, though, not until his breathing has turned deep and even and his muscles fully relax with sleep. I pull back slightly to peer down at his face. Even though he's sleeping, his brows are furrowed as if he's having a bad dream. I gently touch his scruffy face, then lean closer and place a soft kiss right between his brows.

He smells faintly of cigarettes and sweat, no doubt from his brisk walk to the house this morning, and then his walk back. I remember vaguely that his mom was a smoker. She is small and petite. I remember thinking how she looked like a twelve-year-old smoking when really she's in her fifties. Thinking of sweet Nelly, my heart hurts. Every time I had the chance to be around her, she was so vibrant and loving. Her endless love towards her children is something I wish I had from my parents growing up.

And her constant dedication to her husband....

Oscar.

My heart aches thinking of the kind man who used to sit at the end of the bar and yell at the TV. When I first started at the bar, I wasn't even sure if Oscar remembered me. We had only met on two occasions, and he was drunk for both of them. Then one night he called me over and asked me if I was the reason that his son had been 'Haciendo Pucheros.' I was honest and told him the abridged version of what had happened. He had merely nodded and went back to yelling at the TV, and a few days later he called me back over.

***

"Chica! Ven Aqui!" Oscar motions furiously for me to come to him. The bar is really busy tonight and I look around first, making sure no one needs anything, before heading to the end of the bar.

There is another older man sitting next to Oscar, but he doesn't even pull his eyes away from the TV as I approach. I think his name is Brinks, but I'm still working on remembering the regulars' names.

"What's up, Oscar? Need another?" I can't help but notice his still mostly full beer bottle.

"No no no. Do you love my son?" His words come out slightly slurred and broken, but they still feel like a slap in the face. However, Oscar takes my silence as an invitation to keep talking.

"I think he loves you. One time, when I was barely out of the police academy, Nelly and I got into a fight and split up. I was an ass. It was my fault. But anyway, I loved her, and all of my friends made fun of me for pining over the little Latina instead of moving on. I knew I loved her because there was a hole," he pats his chest hard, right over his heart, "in my heart and soul."

He downs most of his beer in four big gulps and sighs deeply.

"I don't know how I feel."

"Ah, but cariño mío, I think you do know because you didn't say, 'No.'"

I scowl and sigh, popping open another beer and sliding it across the bar to him.

*"I think you're drunk. I also think right now I don't deserve your wonderful son."
I tell the odd older man.*

*"Yes, probably. I am old and drunk, which I think, if you ask me, old means wise.
I don't deserve the family Nelly gave me. Just because you think you don't deserve
love doesn't mean someone else shouldn't give it to you. Someone will find you
deserving, and if that someone is my son, then you are a lucky chica indeed. My son
loves well, like his Mami, and is a fighter like his Papi," Oscar says as I start to walk
away and help people who have gathered along the bar to get drinks and refills.*

*The conversation jars me, ripping open wounds that I have just begun to stitch
up. The weight of what he said stings. I want to be deserving of Nathan. I don't want
to take him for granted.*

***

I don't remember drifting back to sleep, but I wake when Nathan's body goes
rigid beside me. His face is tucked into the hollow of my neck, and his arm is
draped over my side. He sucks in a deep ragged breath, and when he exhales, some
of the tension goes with it. I can't help but let out my own breathy sigh, followed
by a giggle when the scruff of his beard tickles my shoulder. It's involuntary, and
I catch myself and try to pull away, but Nathan's arm tightens around me, and he
nuzzles his face deeper into the crook of my neck, winning him another giggle.

"I like the sound of your laugh," he murmurs against my skin. Then, his lips
press against my collar bone, and my body forgets how to breathe, giggles giving
way to something between a sigh and a moan.

"What time is it?" My voice is breathy even in my own ears, so I know what I
must sound like to him.

"I don't care," is what I think he says against my skin, but I can barely hear him over the pounding of my own heartbeat in my ears.

Nathan trails soft kisses across my collar bone and up my neck before settling them on my own lips. I press into him, savoring the fact that we've made it back to this point. His hand starts to lazily explore my body under the covers, and I'm reminded that I went to bed last night in jeans and a t-shirt, but right now I don't care. His body is all hard, lean muscle under my hands, and pressed against me.

I wrap my arm around the back of his neck, deepening the kiss. Every single nerve ending in my body vibrates with desire when his fingers find the hem of my cotton shirt and caress their way under. He trails featherlight touches up my hip and then dips down to my lower back. It sends tingles up my spine, and the memories of our kiss in the library. The heat floods as I flash back to the gentle kisses on my center that taught me I could feel ecstasy without expectation of the same in return.

The tender kiss is over too soon when Nathan pulls away and rests his warm forehead against mine.

"I'm so sorry," he says softly. "As much as I would love to just stay here all day and forget about everything else…"

"I know." I run my fingers through his slick black hair, and he closes his eyes, inhaling deeply.

"Can I see you again tonight?"

"Of course. You can't get rid of me now. I spent the night in your bed." I sit up dramatically. "What would Cici think?!"

Nathan rolls to his back and laughs. I almost forget what I am going to say next as I get a very clear view of his defined abs and strong scruffy chest. Veins run in thick ropes up his forearms as he places his hands behind his head. I think he catches me staring because his mouth quirks up in the whisper of a smile that has my cheeks heating. I hate the way he makes me blush. It makes me feel like an open book, easily read and on display.

"I must defend my honor," I joke.

"I thought that was the man's job," Nathan muses.

"Except you, my dear, tricked me into sleeping with you!"

"I did no such thing!" he gasps loudly, faking offense.

We both laugh and he rolls to grab his phone.

"Shit…" he mumbles, pushing his hair out of his face. The glimmer in his eye fades as he sees the time and whatever else is on his phone. My heart starts to fall into my stomach. I wish joking in bed could save him from the pain that I know he's feeling.

"What's wrong?"

"I have to shower and work on heading back to my mom's soon. People are coming at noon to start making arrangements, and we still need to call some of our distant family." He sits up and rubs his eyes with the palm of his hand. "I need a hot shower."

"I'll make coffee," I offer.

He looks at me gratefully and nods, standing and walking to the bathroom. His strong back muscles flex with every step and my mouth goes a little dry.

I get out of bed, smoothing my bed head down. I haven't looked at myself since I left my house yesterday. After feeling the tangles in the back of my hair, I fish the elastic from my jeans pocket and pull the front of my hair back into a low bun.

I clumsily rummage around in the cabinets. Both of our coffee cups from the night before are sitting on the bedside table, almost completely untouched. I wash out both cups while the coffee brews. Just as I am filling my own cup, I hear the door to the bathroom open slowly.

I turn and the hot coffee becomes a solid mass in my throat. Nathan stands there, looking like a deer in headlights, in only a small gray towel. He clutches it tightly around his hips and gives me a sort of sheepish smile. I can feel my face turning ten different shades of red as my eyes move of their own volition up and down his built body.

"I, uh, forgot to grab clothes." Nathan's cheeks look a little pink as well, but it could just be from the heat of the shower. His body is glistening, only defining his muscles more.

I finally manage to swallow and pull my eyes back up to his face. If I thought Nathan-in-a-t-shirt-and-basketball-shorts looked good, Nathan-in-a-towel is synonymous with an Aztec warrior, or at least an actor they'd have play one in the movies. The 'V' of his abs disappears under the towel like an arrow with a dusting of dark hair from his belly button to…

Every single part of him is chiseled to perfection, with his long ebony hair slicked back away from his face, and his honied skin…

"Catherine?"

"What?" My face feels on fire because I realize at that moment that he's said something else to me.

A husky chuckle rumbles from his chest. "I need to get dressed…"

"And?"

"And…" Nathan makes a vague motion with his free hand like maybe he wants me to turn around.

I lean my hip on the counter and manage to choke down another sip of scalding coffee.

He shifts, his leg muscles rippling with the motion.

"And, what?" I say again, teasing. "You can either get dressed right here or grab your clothes and change in the bathroom."

Nathan smirks at me, and I see him consider for a moment. I fully expect him to grab clothes and walk into the bathroom. He walks over to the dresser that his TV is perched on and rummages around in the top drawer.

Then he throws a look at me and drops his gray cotton towel.

My entire body goes rigid, and I nearly shatter the coffee mug between my hands from how hard I grip the ceramic.

Is it hot in here, or is it just him?

Holy shit… I don't even bother to hide my open-mouthed stare. Nathan steps into a pair of scarlet boxers, slowly, making it very obvious that he's ignoring me as he gets dressed. Every movement of his body is a show for me, and I know it.

Well, he is well-endowed…

Once everything is safely secured inside of his boxers, he pulls out a black undershirt, and he steps to the far side of his bed where he has a clothing rack for his button-down shirts and nice pants. He still hasn't looked at me once, even though a smirk is still pulling the edges of his mouth.

I can't look away.

Nathan goes to his closet. He flips through a few hanging dress shirts. He settles on a plain, dark green button-up shirt and pulls it from the hanger. Each movement he makes seems to cause ripples in muscles that I didn't even know existed.

Nathan slides his arms into the sleeves and slowly buttons the shirt, hiding away his heavenly body. This is the point where he finally turns and looks at me for the first time since he dropped the towel.

"So, tonight," he says casually.

It takes everything in me to focus on his words and not wonder whether or not his shirt is even going to fit him. The fabric across his chest and shoulders doesn't even come close to hiding the sheer mass of him.

"Tonight?" I take another drink of my coffee, trying to clear my throat of all the hormones coursing through my body.

"I'll text you," Nathan says, smiling. "I don't know how long I'll be today, but I want to have dinner with you again." He randomly selects a pair of khaki-colored dress pants and tucks his shirt in before doing the button and grabbing a belt.

"Okay." *Man, I'm killing it with these one-liners today.* "Do you want some coffee before you leave?"

Nathan stalks toward me as if I'm prey, skirting the bed easily, and closes the distance between us. My heart stutters, and heat pools low in my stomach. He doesn't stop until my back is pressed firmly against the counter and the only thing that separates us is the small BGU coffee cup still clutched in my hands. But that's gone a second later when he pries it from my fingers and sets it down somewhere off to the side.

I shiver as his fingers land feather-light on my hips.

"I really don't want to go today," Nathan whispers. There's so much pain in his voice, and his eyes drop out of focus.

I pull him close, standing on my tiptoes to wrap my arms around him, but he still has to bend over a little to wrap his arms around my waist. He smells like clean laundry and some sort of spicy soap. I bury my face in his neck and inhale deeply, trying to memorize how he feels.

"Do you want me to come with you?" I ask into his shirt collar. His cologne stirs something in me.

"I do," he says, but then pulls away to cup my face in his rough hands. "But, I don't think it would be helpful to anyone else right now. My family is fragile, and now is not the time."

I nod, swallowing the bit of emotion that bubbles up in my throat. "That's understandable. How about I at least drop you off at your mom's, though? I have to go back to the apartment. I'm sure Amber is going to be pissed. I never came home or texted her where I was." I pause. "Come to think of it, I haven't checked my phone at all yet."

"Okay," he says after a minute. "That would be nice."

I pick up my phone. The wallpaper is of Cici, Amber, and me on the couch with white sheet masks on our faces. I changed it a few weeks ago, from the one that Cici had taken a few weeks after I moved back. It was a ridiculous photo. Cici was annoyed that my background was still a picture of Marcus and me. One morning she took my phone, made a ridiculous face, and made that my background. I left it for months. Last month, however, Cici, Amber, and I had the most glorious girls day. We started out shopping, went to dinner, and then retired back to Cici's to smoke and watch HGTV. When we got there, Charles had made fry-pies with fruit he picked up at the farmer's market. He handed them to us and then ushered us into the living room before he went upstairs for the night. Sitting on the couch, I marveled at the life I had been given. It felt like a second chance at happiness, and yet, even in my wildest dreams, I never expected to be given this. I snapped the picture randomly. Every time I see it on my phone though, my heart swells with so much love and happiness.

Odd. Amber hasn't called or texted. We text each other even when we are next to each other on the couch watching bad reality TV. She's normally an early riser, so I hope everything's okay.

"What?" Nathan notices my furrowed brows.

"Amber hasn't texted yet, maybe she finally put the tracker on me. Didn't text her I had overtime ONCE and she thought I must've died in a horrible car wreck or something," I joke. Amber is near and dear to both our hearts. "She called me four times and left panicked voicemails that were each two minutes long."

Nathan chuckles. "Yikes. I was late to work once after a late night picking up Dad. She called my mother when I didn't answer." We laugh at Amber's expense. Then his face gets sullen. "Fuck, this is gonna be weird. I just need to get over it." His face becomes dark. "The new man of the Alvarez Family needs to be making sure things are in order."

I grab his rough hand and squeeze. He squeezes back.

Nathan grabs his tan leather shoes and a navy peacoat with gold buttons and throws them all on. I slide my black tennis shoes from work back on. He opens the door and we make it down the stairs into the kitchen to lanky Larry standing with a tray of muffins. Nathan leads ahead and I'm behind him.

"Good morning, Nathan." Larry pauses and stares open-mouthed at me. "Oh, my… Good morning, Catherine." The ginger-haired old man grins.

"Stop it. Nothing happened." I defend myself. My voice pitches slightly at the end and I sound guilty. My face is turning red again, betraying me. I have to fight down the urge to over explain.

"Of course, sure," Larry teases again.

I know how it looks, me and Nathan coming down the stairs from his apartment first thing in the morning, and after what I saw under Nathan's towel, I wish something had happened.

"If you say anything to Cici, I will kill you," I threaten.

"Mum's the word." Larry laughs loudly and balances the muffin tray on his one arm to carry it out into the cafe.

"He's going to tell everyone and their cousin." Nathan laughs as we head out the back door.

"I know." I groan. Larry is everywhere and knows everything. He will most certainly spill this incident over text with Cici.

I follow behind Nathan out the back and around the building to the front to get to my car.

"Sorry, Larry doesn't like me going through the cafe during open hours." Nathan rubs his neck, apologizing for the detour.

"No worries. Let's get going." We slide into my old car, him in the passenger and me in the driver's seat.

I reverse out of the parking spot and go to pull into the street. Then I hit the brakes. "Wait, why don't you borrow my car?"

"What, why?" Nathan looks at me confused.

"Well, I mean, you're gonna have to drive a lot for arrangements today and tomorrow. I don't work until Monday. Anywhere else I might need to go is a walk away." I haven't been to a funeral for a long time. I never met my mom's parents and my grandparents on my dad's side died when I was younger. I remember there was a lot of driving for all the arrangements when they did.

"Are you sure?" Nathan's defeated look says he wants to say 'Yes' but doesn't want to impose.

"I won't accept 'No' for an answer." I smile at him.

"I don't know, Catherine." Nathan's voice wavers.

"CHINESE FIREDRILL!" I swing open my door and run to his door. Nathan does the same and runs to my door. We slide back in and laugh as a car passes us. The old lady in the driver's seat looks mortified.

"You are ridiculous. It's one of my favorite things about you." Nathan smiles and sighs. "I'll drop you at your place." He reaches across and holds my hand warmly in his as we pull out of the cafe parking lot.

SEVEN
Catherine

Nathan insists on walking me up to my door, even though it's twenty feet from the parking spot he pulled into. The apartment that Amber and I share is on the first level. The building is a crisp white color, with gray roofing and trim. Our apartment is the corner one, which means we get a living room that is two feet bigger than everyone else's. It was a main selling point for Amber.

"Are you sure you want to walk me to the apartment? You're kind of already going to be late." I don't want to be any more inconvenience than I already am.

"I mean," he starts, "you did just spend the night at my place, regardless of what we did, it's bad manners not to walk a girl to her door."

Nathan's smile is warm and so comforting as he holds his hand out to me. We walk slowly and carefully. I don't feel like rushing inside to a gushing Amber, and I know Nathan doesn't want to rush anywhere, either. It feels like we are both hanging onto the last moments of peace, the calm before the storm.

"I really enjoyed my evening with you," he says as we reach the doorstep.

"I'm sorry about your dad," I say stupidly. The words come tumbling out before I can stop them. What a stupid thing to say? Why couldn't I just say *I had a good time, too'* like a normal person?

The crease between Nathan's dark bold eyebrows deepens and I reach up without thinking, pressing my thumb against his warm skin to smooth it away. As I go to step back, Nathan catches my hand and gently kisses each fingertip. His lips send electricity ricocheting down my arm, and I shiver from the contact. Then he pulls me closer, wrapping my arms around his waist as he reaches for my face. Nathan's strong hands hold me firmly as he kisses me.

I melt against his sturdy body, holding him tightly for support as his lips tease mine. His hands move expertly, one tangling in my hair while the other trails lightly to my lower back. A soft sigh escapes me, but it's lost somewhere between us.

"What. The. Fuck?"

I jump. I did not hear the door open behind me.

And that voice is *not* Amber's.

Nathan peers over my shoulder, a puzzled look on his face as he lets me retreat from his body back into my own space.

"What are you doing *here*, Mar?" Nathan is the first to speak. "Shouldn't you be at Mom's?"

My face burns as I stare holes into the concrete at my feet, trying to regain my composure. I turn to see who's standing there.

The woman bears an uncanny resemblance to Nathan. Her eyes dart between Nathan and me, her expression a mix of confusion and anger. Her eyes are red-rimmed and puffy like she's been crying.

She scowls at me while she answers Nathan's question. "I'm staying with Amber. Sofia wasn't cool with Yuri staying at the house, so Amber said we could crash."

Nathan's sister.

I remember vaguely Amber telling me about how she had been really close with one of Nathan's sisters in college. I'm pretty sure that she lives in New York now with her girlfriend, whom I'm assuming is Yuri. I wonder how much Amber or Nathan have told her about me? Well, you only get one shot at a first impression.

I clear my throat. "I'm Catherine. It's nice to meet you."

Mariposa turns her sour expression on me, and I try not to shrivel under her strong glare. She's not nearly as tall as Nathan, but she's tall for a woman. She has perfect curves that not even her oversized lavender sweater and black leggings can hide. Her perfect dark black wavy hair hangs down almost past her breast, and her soft mocha eyes glitter with emotion. The angles of her face are the same as Nathan, the plump curve of her lips identical to his. I realize that all of the older siblings that I've seen so far bear an uncanny resemblance to Nelly from the few times I've met her. Sofia and Mariposa could be twins.

"What the fuck are you two doing making out on the doorstep? Your timing is fucking horrible." The tone of her voice grates against me uncomfortably. This is my apartment after all.

Before I can speak, Nathan takes a step toward his sister. "I'm heading to Mom's. Do you want to come with me?"

Deflection. Good strategy.

Mariposa doesn't look away from me when she speaks to him. "I'll head over soon. I need to shower. I smell like gas from the car, and I want to make sure Yuri is settled."

"When did you guys get in?" Nathan asks.

"Three hours ago. Sofia had a meltdown as soon as Yuri and I stepped through the door, and Mom did literally nothing. Sofia wanted Yuri to stay in a hotel or some shit while we were here. That homophobic bitch said it was disrespectful to the family." Mariposa's voice has steadily grown louder as she's spoken, and the angrier she gets the less she looks like Nathan.

"Okay," Nathan says quietly, obviously used to this level of passion from his sister.

"You know, I expected to see you at Mom's this morning. I desperately wished you were there. It would have been really fucking nice to have someone on my side. It's not like Dad…" She trails off and sniffles before rubbing her eyes vigorously with her hands. "But, no, apparently you were preoccupied!"

Mariposa grabs the front door, and for a second, I think she's going to slam it in our face. Then she seems to remember that this is also partly my apartment. Mariposa gives me a quick fury-filled look, then she turns lightning-fast on her heel and storms away.

My blood boils at her dismissal of her brother and me.

She left the door wide open. I turn to Nathan. His wall of stoicism has slammed back up around him, his expression stony. He turns slowly to me, and the strained look in his eyes makes me feel like a stranger. Then it's gone, and his eyes are warm again, making me wonder if I imagined it.

"I'll text you later?" he asks. There are so many questions behind that one.

I don't know how to answer. I don't even know how to process what just happened.

I plaster on what I hope is a very real smile. "Of course. Let me know if you need anything."

"Thank you for letting me borrow the car today. I owe you one." Nathan winks and smiles, but it seems like he's trying to hide his sadness.

Stepping into the living room of my apartment, I'm greeted by the smell of strong coffee and one of the prettiest people I think I've ever seen. She has short black sleek hair, cut into a bob right at her chin. Her dark, almond-shaped eyes pull up slightly at the edges and she has some of the most amazing cheekbones I've ever seen. Her lips are full and perfectly shaped, and even in her baggy travel clothes she appears sleek and put together, like maybe she's going to be on the cover of *Vogue* modeling the latest styles for cross country travel. She's not very tall, maybe an inch or so taller than me. She stands with her shoulders back and her chin high like she's ready to fight.

The look she gives me is sharp, but she stands and sticks out her hand. "Sorry to meet like this. I'm Yuri, Mariposa's girlfriend."

"Nice to meet you." I offer what I hope is a smile, but I'm pretty sure it's a grimace. "Where's Amber?"

"Her bedroom, I think. Looking for her air mattress." Yuri walks into the kitchen and grabs a coffee mug from the little decorative shelf where we keep them.

"Amber made coffee a few minutes ago. Do you need any?"

I kind of like the way she says 'need' instead of 'want.' I file that detail away. I think under different circumstances, she and I would be friends very quickly.

"Not at the moment. I'll be right back." I drop my purse on the counter and head down the hall into Amber's room.

I knock lightly on the half-closed door before pushing it open. Amber is rummaging through her closet, pulling out the air mattress she let me sleep on for a few weeks before she gave me her old bed. She pulls out a bunch of blankets as well that I didn't know she was hoarding.

Amber turns when I knock and gives me a weird smile.

"Hey." Her eyes are glazed a bit, as if she's coming in and out of focus. I've seen this look many times. She's overwhelmed and trying not to panic. Her eyebrows are threatening to become one with her hairline as her face is frozen in this sort of hyper aware I'm-struggling-to-accommodate-everyone-and-still-maintain-my-sanity look.

"Hey. So, what's going on? What did I miss?"

Amber sags a little and sits on the bed, looking tired. The smile is wiped from her face, replaced by mild concern and aggravation. I try to keep my temperament even, because I'm sure she's just as put off and stressed as I am right now.

"I'm sure you've run into Mariposa and Yuri." Amber's words fall haphazardly out of her mouth.

"Yeah. At the door and in the kitchen?" I tease.

"Her mom wasn't happy with her bringing Yuri, so when she called me, I told her they could stay here. I didn't think it was a big deal," she echoes what Mariposa said at the door.

"It wouldn't be. I just wish you would have texted and given me a heads up about it." I hesitate for a second before saying, "Nathan walked me to the door, and Mariposa was the one who let us in. She was *not* happy about it."

Amber's eyebrows almost disappear in her hairline again as she stares at me. "You were with Nathan? Well, that heads up would have been nice as well."

She stands and starts rummaging around her room again, opening boxes and moving things in her closet. "I mean, I get that you were probably preoccupied, but you didn't say anything to me last night. I figured you had to stay late at work, and when I checked your location, you were over that way. Then I woke up to Mariposa's call this morning and then I realized you still hadn't come home…" She trails off.

"I know, I'm sorry. But it's not like you let me know you invited strangers into our house."

Amber stops and turns, putting her hands on her hips, her tone biting. "They aren't strangers to me."

"Fair, but still they are to me. You'd be pretty upset if I had people stay the night with no warning. AND It's Nathan's sister. Even if we hadn't reconnected last night, you don't think that would have been awkward for me?" I don't mean to attack her back, even though my tone is at least as harsh as hers.

She sighs. "I can't find the pump for the air mattress." She plops back down on the bed. "I know it might have been awkward. I just didn't feel like I could put them out to find a hotel. I didn't expect that you would have spent the night with *'him',"* she whispers it like it's a dirty secret. "It literally only happened an hour or so ago. They are going through a major family crisis, and we had an opportunity to help."

I nod, I am still a little annoyed by the fact she didn't warn me, but I know she isn't wrong.

"How about you just let them take my room. I'm pretty sure the air mattress has a hole in it from when you tackled me one morning to wake me up. I can go stay at Cici's. I'm sure she will be fine with it. Just let me go grab some things."

Amber gives me another weird, uncomfortable smile. "Thanks. I owe you one."

I stand and hug her. "It's fine. This is gonna be a rough week for everyone."

"Yeah, it is. I don't know anyone who didn't know Oscar." She gives me a devious smirk. "You still owe me all the details about last night though!"

I head to my bedroom to pack a few things. I send a quick text to Cici, who responds almost immediately that she will put sheets on my old bed in the basement and it will be ready when I get there. Even though I'm giving up my own bed for the weekend, there is a small part of me that's excited to have some time with Cici. It's been almost a year since I moved to Bethton Grove. Cici's house has been a safe space since I was little, always full of laughter, food, and sarcasm. After the night I spent at Nathan's, I could use some advice from Cici.

I throw a few pairs of pants and a few shirts in a backpack, then wait for Mariposa to be done in the bathroom so I can grab my toothbrush and a few personal items. She doesn't even look at me as she heads to where Amber and Yuri are sitting in the living room. Her wet hair swishes down her back, and Amber hands her a cup of coffee as she steps into the kitchen.

I go into our small bathroom, and it looks as if a tornado of beauty supplies came through. A hair dryer on the floor is still connected to the outlet; an eyelash curler sits in the bottom of the sink; and makeup palettes of all shades lay perched on every level surface in the room, including the top of the toilet tank. The lavender sweatshirt and black leggings that Mariposa had been wearing when she opened the door now lay on the floor in a pile in front of the shower.

At least I won't be the one yelled at for leaving things everywhere for once.

I grab my toiletries and exit the contained disaster. All three women are huddled in the kitchen now.

"I'm headed out." I give a sheepish wave.

Both Amber and Yuri wave goodbye. Mariposa smacks Yuri on the arm and shoots daggers with her glare towards me. Mariposa is gonna be a tough one to win over.

I have to show Nathan's family that I am deserving of such a wonderful man. I may not be wanted here but at least I'm wanted at Cici's.

***

The walk to Cici's house isn't far, just across campus, and the weather is cool. All of the leaves are starting to change colors and fall to the ground. It's beautiful. I'm reminded of why I chose to stay here. The quiet calm of Bethton Grove brings me a peace I haven't found anywhere else.

I consider texting Nathan to check in on him as worry runs free in my mind and longing in my heart. I decide it's probably better if I leave him to be with his family today. My heart hurts for the broken man I saw last night and this morning. This is my time to step up for Nathan like he did for me. However, I don't know what that means. I don't want to be a distraction. Texting 'How's it going?' seems shitty too. His dad just died; it's not going great. I decide to wait until later. I'll check in sometime after lunch.

I walk into Cici's house without knocking. It's the one place that I've always felt was home. The air smells sweet like cinnamon rolls. Charles has to be here as well.

There's a clattering sound in the kitchen, so I slip off my shoes and head that way. I'm greeted by Cici's back and Charles' hands firmly planted on her ass. One hand has pulled her skirt up, and I see more than I have ever wanted.

They are clearly in the middle of something.

"What the hell, guys!" I spin so that my back is to them and clamp my hands over my eyes, trying to forget the image of my aunt in such a compromising position.

"Shit," Charles says. A few seconds of clattering and the kitchen goes quiet.

"Is it safe now?" I ask, not brave enough to turn around without being completely sure.

"Yes, it's safe." Cici practically clobbers me in a bear hug as I turn. "I have missed you so much!" She squeezes me almost to the point of pain and I fake a wheezing sound.

"I literally saw you last night!" I hug her back, glancing at Charles over her shoulder.

He has his back to me, taking stuff out of the oven, and when he turns, his face is a bit flushed. I don't know if it's the heat of the oven, embarrassment, or what remains of his little make-out session with my aunt.

"What are you guys making?" I peer over his shoulder to see what he pulled out of the oven. The sweet warm smell of fresh bread and cinnamon lifts my mood a touch.

"I made cinnamon rolls" He smiles at me. The deep rich tenor of his voice and British accent feel like home. He throws an arm over my shoulder, pulling me against his side into a hug.

"Oh, that sounds amazing, I'm going to go put my stuff downstairs and I'll be back."

My old room with the green shag carpet and flowers painted on the walls looks exactly like I left it when I moved in with Amber almost seven months ago. Cici even put the same comforter on the bed that I used at the beginning of this year.

I put my backpack on the bed, planning to come back down later and unpack my things.

I head back upstairs and Cici is whispering conspiratorially to Charles, who is staring out the kitchen window. When I walk into the kitchen, they both turn and smile at me almost like it was rehearsed. Cici reaches for her sunflower-painted box from the cabinet and pulls a joint from it.

"So, what's up that you need to come stay here?"

I sigh. I hate being the bearer of bad news.

"Oscar passed this morning…"

Cici's eyes glisten, holding back tears. Charles wraps his arm around her to comfort her. She inhales deeply and exhales slowly. She wipes the corner of her eye and looks at Charles's crestfallen face.

Oscar was more than a patron to them. They all grew up together, the first of death among their friends a sign of growing older.

Charles kisses her forehead. His voice is low, not quite a whisper. "Nelly called us yesterday to let us know he didn't have much longer. We were planning to go this morning to say goodbye."

Cici takes a long drag of her joint, lets out the fog, seemingly to reset herself.

"Well, that fucking sucks. How the fuck do you know before I do? I'm always the first to know." Cici's teasing, clearly avoiding her feelings. Cici has always used humor to cope. You would've thought her parents' funeral was a comedy set. She swipes at her eyes roughly, and her glasses go crooked on her nose. Charles absently pushes them back into place before she huffs and turns around, staring back out of the small kitchen window.

"Well, that leads to why I need a place to crash. Nathan's sister Mariposa and her girlfriend, Yuri, needed a place to stay, so Amber offered to let them stay at the apartment. It was really awkward, and we couldn't find the pump for the air mattress, so I offered my room."

"That's nice of you and all, but I don't understand why it's awkward." Cici gives me a pointed look over her shoulder through the lenses of her coke bottle glasses. She turns and offers me the joint, and I am grateful for the moment to gather my thoughts.

"Well." I stare between the two of them and the words die in my throat. Nathan. Saying something like 'Oh, we reconnected last night' seems weird. Or explaining how Mariposa reacted when she opened the door and caught us kissing feels really dramatic.

"For fuck's sake, Kitty. What's going on?"

"It's not like that. It's just that… Last night, when I was closing up the bar myself, Nathan was walking to the gym or something." I study Cici's face, waiting to see what her reaction is, but her expression is pretty unreadable, so I continue.

"We sort of reconnected. And went to the diner for some coffee."

"Okay?" Cici and I both know that isn't the whole story, but before she can dig in, there is a knock on the door. Cici and Charles both look at each other, and then at me before Charles turns to start washing dishes and Cici sprints toward the stairs. "I have to get ready for work. Kitty dear, would you get the door please?" Cici shouts from the stairwell.

She's already gone before I can answer her. I give Charles a look, to which he replies with a shrug and a blank look on his face. The way he side-eyes me makes my heart do a weird flutter in my chest.

He knows something I don't.

I walk toward the front hallway, ready to sign for a package, or yell at the Mormons to go away. The textured glass on the door makes it impossible to see through, but I can clearly see someone standing in front of the door. Then there's another knock right as I reach the entranceway.

I slowly pull the door open. All I see is the back of a man's head. He's talking quietly to someone just behind him.

My heart starts to thunder overwhelmingly in my ears.

The man turns slowly as the woman behind him fixes her eyes on mine. There's a placid smile pasted on his face, and it falls as our eyes meet.

"Dad?"

Eight

Nathan

I've been sitting in Catherine's car in my mother's driveway for ten minutes, working up the courage to go in. The pain from the morning washes over me, reminding me of why I'm here. There are already cars lining the street in front of the house, and I can see people moving about through the big front windows.

My mom steps onto the porch, a pack of gold Newport cigarettes and a lighter in hand. She's in a knit black sweater and light blue jeans. Her hair has a striking silver piece in the front. Mom gives me an odd look as she settles into one of the rocking chairs on the porch and lights her cigarette. I can't sit in the car anymore. I've been spotted. I get out and shut the car door. Well, it's more of a slam since the Camry's door sticks.

"*Gordito,* whose car did you steal?" My mom's skin looks ashen, and the deep bags under her eyes are a garish shade of purple and blue. Scarlet rims her eyes, and they appear swollen in the bright light of the late morning. My mom has always been petite, but right now she seems small and defeated. I squint up at the sky, angry that it seems like such a beautiful day when everything is shit.

"Just a friend's, *Mami.*"

She huffs and nods, taking another deep puff of her cigarette. "Your dad's sisters got here about fifteen minutes ago. They brought food if you're hungry."

Even though my stomach is empty, I can't imagine trying to eat right now. "I'm okay."

"They came and collected his body a few hours ago." My mom stares blankly off into the distance, she seems like a shell of a person, just going through the motions of moving and breathing. Her eyes aren't fixed on any one spot, shining with tears that haven't fallen yet. "Soon, someone will need to go down there and make arrangements."

"That's why I have a car today," I say as I take the steps to the front porch.

"You can take Sofia with you. She needs to leave the house for a bit."

I nod, remembering the frantic phone calls my sister made to our siblings the moment after I arrived at the house when Dad passed. She probably needs a lot more than just to get out for a while.

"Are you okay **Mami**?" My mother has always been a bit on the dramatic end. To see her so stoic is eerie. There's no more wailing and crying like early this morning. She looks as if she's aged ten years in the span of five hours. It rips something open inside of my chest and the emotion threatens to swallow me whole.

"No, *mijo*, but I will be." She looks at me, eyes red and devastated.

I squeeze her frail shoulder as I pass by to enter the lion's den. I tug open the broken screen door and swing in the yellow front door behind it. The chatter and bustle of all my tias in the kitchen makes my ears ring. Sofia stands in the front room, scolding her children as they run through the house. Her husband Carlos sits in one of the recliner seats on the sectional watching football with their four-month-old asleep on his chest, unphased by the noise.

Carlos is a quiet man with a hidden sense of humor that only comes out if you're around him enough to listen. He seems like the perfect match for my sister, in the 'opposites attract' kind of way. I remember when she brought him home over a decade ago. That was the first time I had met him. I pitied him a little because I thought my spitfire sister would eat him alive. Carlos has this way with her, diffusing her expertly. He looks tired and a bit disheveled, like he didn't sleep last night, either. His short black hair sticks up in the back a little like he was pulled from bed, and he hasn't shaved.

I shut the door behind me, and silence follows as everyone turns to me.

"*Tio!*" my niece and nephews shout in unison. They come charging at me like a herd of bulls.

Sofia's oldest son, Oscar, reaches me first. I half squat to catch him as he collides with me. He is a husky kid, knocking the wind out of me, broad shouldered like his father and in general tall for eight years old.

"I'm glad you're here. Mom and *Abuela* are losing it." Sofia gives her son Oscar a glare that only a mother could give. His eyes sparkle as if to say to me 'See what I mean?' Then the kid flips up his gray hoodie and mouths 'S. O. S.' and joins his dad and baby brother, Angel, in the living room, sitting on the couch next to his dad's reclining form.

Sofia's only daughter Catarina-five-grabs my right leg, wrapping herself around my calf. She is extremely petite for her age, barely reaching my hip when she stands up straight. Her dark hair falls down her back in an unruly mess, and she's still in pjs. You would think her little copycat, Armando--who latches onto my left leg–is her twin instead of her three-year-old brother. They're practically the same size, the girls taking after their petite framed mother and all the boys taking after their dad.

"OH NO! SOFIA, MY BOOTS ARE SO HEAVY!" I pick up my feet, taking slow monstrous steps through the living room, and a chorus of giggles follow.

"ENOUGH!" Sofia snaps, rubbing her hand over her face in exasperation. "Enough goofing around, we have grown-up business to do kids. So, please, let your *tio* go."

I nudge the two on my legs to coax them into going. They both give me big pouty faces and I wink at them. "I heard your *tias abuelas* have yummy snacks in the kitchen. *Vamanos* before your mom gets mad."

The two young kids run into the kitchen, giggling again. They are both so unphased by the chaos and grief around them. I feel the smallest sense of relief that not everyone is going to be forever devastated by the next few days' events.

My sister stands expectantly, arms crossed and a stern look on her face. Sofia's barely five feet tall, and her dark hair is thrown on top of her head in a giant dark messy bun. She's still wearing the same leggings and long oversized cream sweater she was in this morning. Her posture sends out the same aura as a pit bull.

"Why weren't you here when they took *Papi* away?" Sofia hisses at me.

"I needed to get changed and showered. *Mami* said she didn't need me here for it." I sigh and turn towards my sister. I don't think I could be here as they took him, the thought makes my stomach turn. "I borrowed a car so I will be able to deal with anything else for today."

Sofia looks exhausted. She's been crying too. Her face and neck are covered in red blotches, and if she doesn't look angry, she just looks empty.

"You better be. I've been here dealing with everything when it's your job, Nathan. Lucia took Amaya with her to pick up Andria. I guess Andria's van broke down at a mechanic in Ohio. She has a friend driving her halfway. I thought it'd be better for Amaya to be out of the house instead of here dealing with this. They should be home this evening." Sofia starts walking towards the kitchen. "Carlos bought Nadia a plane ticket home. She was able to email her professors at MIT and get the week off. Now come on and make your appearance to our *tias*." She gestures into the doorway that heads to the kitchen.

"Do I have to?" I drone. She grabs my green sweatshirt sleeve and leads us into the kitchen. The smell of fresh tamales and roast permeate the kitchen.

The kitchen walls are painted a burnt orange. My niece and nephew sit at a small, blue children's fold-out table, devouring whatever food my tias threw at them. I turn to see three small plump abuelas speed-cooking in the kitchen. All three are in brightly colored, floral dresses.

"*Hola, Tia Marta. Hola, Tia Ann. Hola, Tia Sofia.*" I wave to my father's three older sisters.

"*Gordito!* So good to see you! I am sorry it's this way." The oldest, Tia Sofia, runs over and gives me a hug. She barely comes to my chest. Her curly hair is more gray now than brown, and it's piled on her head, barely contained by a big black claw clip. "You are so thin! Don't worry, we will plump you right up. I'll be staying with *tu madre* so you come here to eat, understand?" The chunky older white-haired woman pokes and prods at my belly.

"Oh, Sofia, leave the poor kid alone. He's fine." The youngest, and slimmest sister, Marta, pats Tia Sofia on the back. The sisters giggle as my quiet Tia Ann, with her salt and pepper hair tied back, continues to cook.

"Ann, dear, you think Nathan is fine, right?" Tia Marta has dark eyes that sparkle, rimmed with dark lashes. She always seems the most mischievous, with her brows groomed and polished to perfection as if she's always smirking.

Tia Ann and my dad could have been twins. They both have the same round brown eyes that crinkle at the edges with smile lines. She is also the tallest of the three of them, coming to my shoulder rather than right in the middle of my chest. Unlike her sisters, Ann still looks like she's in her forties not sixties. "Of course! Our *Gordito* needs to be thin, that's what's in now. We need him to find a wife."

The other two sisters nod in agreement.

"It's shocking to see such a fine young man still single. You know, my daughter has a friend. She's a bit of a spinster, but you're the bookish type. You'd get along well," Tia Sofia offers.

I blanch a little at the thought of anyone other than Catherine.

"No, no, he needs someone better than that. My niece on your Uncle Ralph's side is single and young. She has wonderful birthing hips, but her eyes are *muy juntas*." Tia Marta makes a squinting face. My other tias look like they're seriously considering if birthing hips are worth eyes that are too close together.

My stomach rolls uncomfortably.

"And on that note, Sofia and I are off to go to the funeral home." I try to keep my eye roll to myself, remembering why I love my aunts, but I don't always love to see my aunts.

Sofia stands with her arms crossed, trying to hurry me along. I'm not sure which I'd rather do less, endure a deafeningly silent car ride with Sofia, or stand in the kitchen while my tias arrange me a marriage.

My tias give me a hug, say adios and head back to work, preparing months' worth of meals for my mother. I walk past Sofia, nudging her towards the front door. She walks to her husband and her two sons as I watch and wait by the front door. She gives Carlos a short summary of what we're doing. He nods, she gives him and her sons each a kiss on the head. I swing open the door for her and we step out.

Mom is still sitting in her chair on the front porch.

"We're off, *Mami*." Sofia leans over and kisses our mother softly on the head.

"*Adios.* Be good you two." Mami's voice cracks behind the cigarette she's smoking.

We step down off the porch and get into Catherine's old Camry. I open the driver side and climb in. Sofia walks slowly, inspecting the old Camry before she pulls the door open.

"Whose car did you jack?" She scowls at me as she slides into the passenger's seat.

I wait a really long moment, almost deciding to tell her to mind her own business, but then I settle for the truth. Probably should just get it out of the way as quickly as possible.

"Catherine's." *Here comes the fight.*

"Seriously? Are you fornicating around with her again?" Sofia hisses.

"What the hell, Sofia? *Fornicating?* Who says that?" I can't help but roll my eyes at her. I start the engine and back out of the driveway. "I thought you liked her."

"Yeah, then she dropped you." She crosses her arms, pouting like a child.

"She did not *drop* me. Catherine had shit to work out," I pause, giving Sofia a look from the corner of my eye. "And now, she's worked them out." I have explained this time and time again.

"When you're in a relationship, you work it out together. Carlos can't just bail to work things out for a while. If she has issues later, is she just gonna leave? You let Carolina walk all over you and bail on you constantly. I don't want that for you." Sofia refuses to listen. She crosses her arms and turns her entire body in the passenger seat to glare at me.

The venom on her voice burns as she reminds me of my mistakes with Carolina. Eventually they leave. I already hate the scrutiny that I am under, and the lack of support from my family unsettles me further. I don't want who I choose to date or marry to cause problems in my family. I know what I want; I want Catherine. I have always wanted Catherine. How can I manage a household though when my family doesn't respect my choices?

"We aren't married, Sof, and it's not like it was even a serious relationship. We'd only known each other a few weeks. Who am I to force something on her when she wasn't ready for it? We weren't obligated to each other."

Sofia's traditionalist ways have worked for her, so she thinks they work for everyone.

"You should date for marriage, not for whatever you two are doing," she scolds.

"Well Sofia, as always, that's my business, and when it goes wrong, you are more than welcome to say I told you so." The annoyance in my tone slithers out into a hiss.

"I can't wait." The only way to end a fight with Sofia is to let her know she's probably right.

"Do you remember when I first got my license?" I ask after a few moments of quiet. "*Papi* gave me that old Honda Civic?"

"I remember watching you learn how to change a tire."

"I remember being shit at it."

Sofia snorts, and I can see the side of her mouth twitch like she might smile. There was a time when Sofia and I were close, and sometimes I miss it. We will always be family, but I miss when we could spend time together without something turning into an argument.

"Remember, you decided to show me up, *Papi* was so irritated that I kept forgetting to tighten the bolts correctly. You said you could do it, and *Papi* let you."

"He made me go everywhere with you for a month." She shakes her head and gives me the faintest smile.

"Even on that one date with Carolina. I had to buy you a ticket to that art gallery, and you hated it."

"I still think you made me go there just so I'd go home and complain so you wouldn't have to take me places anymore. All you guys did was oogle each other and hold hands and kiss. It was terrible!"

"Do you remember what *Papi* said to you that night?"

Her face goes stony, and I realize too late that I might have pushed her in a direction she didn't want to go. "He told me that one day I'd be thankful that he made us spend time together, because one day when he was old and gone, we'd be all we had." Her eyes have gone icy again as she looks at me. "If only we knew then what we know now."

I'm not completely sure what she means by that, if she's referring to the fact that we wouldn't have nearly as long as we thought, or if she's referring to spending time with me. It doesn't really matter either way, I don't feel like she's all I have. I don't even really feel like I have her on my side at all. And Papi is still gone.

The ride is quiet and uncomfortable with too much time for thinking. Sofia and I are close, but she has always been the mother hen. Even as a child, she would scold me even though I'm older. She had the Bible memorized by six while I was having my knuckles cracked by sisters in school. Being less than a year apart, and with Sofia being so intelligent that she was in my grade, we essentially grew up as twins.

I remember at eight she decided she wanted to become a nun.

***

"That seems like a pretty boring job, Sof." I tell my little sister.

"You're a pretty boring job. Nuns help a lot of people. That's not boring. They aren't just mean old ladies who yell at you in school, Nathan," Sofia says as she pulls a chunk of grass from in front of her crossed legs. We are sitting in the front yard

after school. It's springtime and warm enough in the afternoons to be out for a while with just a sweatshirt on.

"Yeah, whatever. You have to dress really weird and never get married, though," I refute. I just don't understand Sofia. It's like she was born an old lady.

"I look great in black, and it symbolizes more than just weird clothes. Boys are dumb anyways. At least you are." She pulls another chunk of grass out of the front lawn and throws it at me from where she is sitting.

I blow a raspberry at her. "What if you find someone you love, and he asks you to marry him?"

"I'll do what God tells me, not a stinky boy." She pulls another clump.

Our dad shouts from the front porch. "Ay! Don't ruin my lawn, Sofia Alvarez! It's not becoming of a good girl!"

"Hey, Papi! Sofia wants to become a nun!" I shout.

Our dad stands up out of the rocker, putting out his cigarette on the black iron railing.

"That true, Sofia?" he asks with a tone of curiosity.

"Si, Papi." she says confidently.

"I couldn't possibly be prouder. You have a Godly heart, Sofia. You will do well." He smiles brightly and descends the steps to join us.

***

Then she met Carlos in high school, a quiet but popular teenage boy who was our Catholic school's best linebacker. They got married two months after graduation. They moved into Abuela's house right behind Mom and Dad's. Sofia cared for our Abuela for three years while Carlos apprenticed with an electrician and built up a nice nest egg. They had their first son and named him after dad shortly after Abuela passed. Raising her family in the home passed to her from Abuela.

The silence between us continues as we make arrangements at the funeral home, Sofia only speaking to confirm my choices. Neither of us were raised to encourage deep conversation or emotions although I catch her swiping a tear or two from her eyes. The car ride back is much of the same silence…with the elephant in the backseat–that dad is gone.

***

I pull into our mom's uneven driveway where another new car is pulled in. A small baby blue Fiat with a racing stripe down the middle. Mariposa is here. Sofia's scowl tells all as she gets out and slams the car door behind her. Mariposa and Sofia have never gotten along. Sofia the rule follower, and Mariposa the rebel. Sofia, always up and ready for Mass, while Mar refused on more than one occasion. Most of the arguing in the house growing up was between them. I let out a loud groan, leaning my head back on the headrest.

Deep breaths, in, out, in, out.

The shit is about to hit the fan. The exact thing I don't need right now. Fuck, I am not ready for whatever is about to happen. The three oldest Alvarez children haven't been in the same room together in a year or more. The last time… Dad was here. Even in the midst of his alcoholism, he was always able to diffuse the tension between the three of us. As children, we always used to butt heads, then as we got older and developed our own unique personalities, the tension grew worse.

I pull open the Camry door and drag myself up the porch into the front door, carrying the weight of the whole Alvarez family on my shoulders. I inhale deeply as I grasp the front door handle, propping open the screen door with my foot, then I exhale as I swing the door open.

"Look, it's the new man of the house?" Mariposa sarcastically throws at me. She looks better than she did this morning, but I have to resist the urge to flinch at the venom in her tone.

"*Papi* passed this morning, Mariposa. Are you kidding me?" Sofia looks horrified at Mariposa's statement.

"Sorry, I was just trying to lighten the mood. *Sheesh,*" Mariposa spits back at her.

"The mood is fine. Where's mom?" Sofia sneers.

"In her room napping. She needs sleep." Mariposa changes her tone to a somber note.

"Okay, and you're here, why?" Sofia scoffs.

"I don't know. Maybe because our dad died, and I am a part of this family too?"

I can feel the fight brewing.

"Really? I thought you moved to New York so you could pretend you weren't." Sofia takes a deep jab. Her anger is barely contained inside of her small body as she widens her stance like she's gearing up for a fist fight instead of exchanging insults.

"Hey, I tried to stay here and be a part of the family. You decided Yuri and I weren't welcome." She puffs out her chest, defending herself like a cornered animal. Mariposa is an inch or two taller than Sofia, but everyone knows Sofia's bite is bigger than her bark.

"I'm sorry, but I think parading your *lifestyle* around a deeply Catholic family that is mourning is stressful on everyone." There Sofia goes. The line has been crossed, the pin pulled from the grenade.

Mariposa stands there in shock. Sofia has never directly said anything to keep the peace, but the tension has always been there. She thinks Mariposa loving Yuri– or any woman–is wrong.

I stand uncomfortably as my sisters shoot each other with daggered looks. My palms sweat, and Mariposa's eyes beg for me to step in. If Papi was here, he'd tell the girls to stop and that would be the end of it. I don't have that kind of power. I scan the room for any source of redirection and nothing can be found.

The family is starting to trickle in, standing in doorways, watching quietly like this is an interesting scene from a telenovela.

Mariposa rolls her eyes at me and turns back to Sofia. "Are you fucking kidding me? All these years, all the changes happening in our world, and you still think MY love is wrong?" Mariposa yells, clenching her fists.

"Watch your language and volume! My children are here." Sofia's face shows she knows she riled up Mariposa giving her the upper hand.

"What, the, FUCK! Nathan are you gonna fucking say anything to this homophobic bitch?" Mariposa's eyes beg for back up.

I can't take sides. I have to keep the peace, like Papi did.

"Mariposa, let's calm down…" Maybe I can get them both on a calm level to discuss this. I try to keep the exhaustion from my voice, but the words end up coming out sounding as if I'm just as annoyed as Sofia. "Both of you, just, can you stop? This is not the day for any of this."

"Calm down? Oh, right, because if she's mad at me and my *lifestyle*, she can't be mad about you sleeping around and fucking Amber's roommate last night."

"What the fuck, Mariposa?" I take a step toward my sisters, trying to regain my composure. I'm about five seconds from seeing red.

"Nathan! Language!" Sofia turns her rage on me, and even though I am both older and bigger, it's hard not to cower under her glare. "Is that why you weren't here when *Papi* passed?" Sofia's rage is mingled with pain and her voice starts to quiver even while it increases in volume. She looks like she might collapse at any moment, or maybe haul off and hit me. Both of those options scare me. I feel helpless, wishing Mami was awake, wishing Dad was here to tell Sofia to get her head out of her ass, wishing someone along the edges of my vision would step in. Unfortunately, though, I am alone.

I'm the new 'man of the family' as Mariposa pointed out.

"They were at Amber's this morning. I saw it myself." Mariposa beams, redirecting Sofia's wrath at me.

I hold up both of my hands in what I hope is a placating gesture, but in reality, I feel the need to protect myself. "Number one, my business is my damn business. Number two, I was asleep when you called. How am I supposed to magically know, out of all the times you and *Mami* have called me for false alarms, that this wasn't one." I take a breath, my head starting to spin from the tension in the room. It feels like there isn't enough oxygen for all of us. Guilt starts to weigh on my shoulders, maybe if I hadn't missed the first call or two, I would've been able to be there for Dad.

Tia Sofia comes out of the kitchen wielding a wooden spoon. She marches between my sisters to me, then winds up her weapon and thwacks me on the arm. "*BASTA*! Enough! You three are family. I will not listen to any more bickering in *tu padre's* home. His soul is still here watching you all bicker. You should be ashamed!"

"Hey! They started it!" I rub my right arm. That's definitely going to bruise.

The tiny latina abuela shoves the wooden spoon in my face. "You, sir, are the man here, you are supposed to bring our *familia* together, not participate in tearing it apart."

She shakes her spoon at all of us. "Now apologize. All three of you. This is not how Alvarezes behave."

We all chorus a disgruntled, "*Lo siento.*" The room returns to its buzzing, and my phone rings.

"I'm sorry it's work. I have to step out," I say. I look up to the three women glaring at me. Their displeased looks show me they don't think I should go. If I don't leave, I'm positive our fight will continue.

"*Lo siento*, I will be back as soon as I can," I say sheepishly.

"You better be," the three women say in unison.

Cringing, I give a little wave and run out the door to escape the mess that's here.

"Hello, Saul. I'm a little busy." I pinch the bridge of my nose, holding back my build-up of stress.

"I think I broke it," Saul says in a monotone voice.

"Broke what?" I can't help but be short. Saul is not the most competent employee.

"Everything." His flat tone makes this feel like a joke.

"What?" I am dumbfounded by this poor kid.

"I don't know how to do anything, I messed up a lot. Amber usually does this all for me."

Why have I not fired this kid?

"What doesn't Amber do for you? Whatever, nevermind, I'll call Amber and send her your way."

"Thank You."

Click.

Well, that was weird and abrupt. Amber doesn't allow Saul to do much, but he's not a total idiot. He was the only person to apply after Catherine left, so I didn't have many options. Usually, weekends aren't busy, so how did he break something?

I check my phone and I have a text from Catherine.

NINE

Catherine

"Kitty, hi." My dad looks just as startled as I am. His salt and pepper hair perfectly combed over to the side makes him look like the straight lace cop he is. He clears his throat once, twice, and then looks over my shoulder like he's not sure if I'm going to let him in.

The floor feels like it's falling out from under me, and my head starts to spin as panic sets in.

Why the fuck is my dad here?

Where the fuck are Cici and Charles? Did they know my dad was coming? Did they set this up? Why would my dad even be here? I hear Cici's phone's ringtone of "Cherry Pie" go off in the stairwell. I stare at the stairwell hoping for rescue. Cici exits the stairwell, phone on one ear and her free hand on the other to block out anything else going on. I try to send a look her way but her face is serious and she doesn't bother to look in my direction.

"Hi, Nelly. Yes, Catherine just told us. Is there–" her voice trails off as she disappears again into the kitchen.

I turn back to the door, and my dad and I stare at each other for a long moment.

He looks uneasy, like I might slam the door in his face, and I'm not completely convinced I wouldn't.

"Well, come in, I guess." Sighing loudly, I stiffen up and pull the door wide open. I haven't seen my dad in almost a year.

"KITTY CAT!" My sister runs into me knocking the air out of my lungs. The petite blonde girl squeezes me with all her might, and I lift her off the ground as she adds another layer to her hug by wrapping her legs around my middle. She smells like Lip Smacker lip gloss and chocolate.

My heart sinks and I feel awful as I hold her. She's so much bigger than she was a year ago, and she clings to me with something similar to desperation. I feel her deep exhale into my hair, and she doesn't make a move to let go. So I just stand there with my not-so-little sister clinging to me like a koala.

I kiss her cheek affectionately. "Hey, Bailey Mae. It's good to see you. How have you been?" I use my little sister to focus so I don't have to deal with Dad or Lisa.

She pulls back, beaming at me. Her brown eyes have flecks of gold in them, and she has the same light spattering of freckles that Dad and I both have.

Bailey Mae sticks her tongue through the hole where her bottom left tooth should be. "Good! I lost a tooth! Then I got a dollar, AND then Daddy said we had to drive up here cause his friend is gonna die forever. Mommy said it's forever, it's not like sleeping, but it's okay cause he loved Jesus so Daddy will see him again." She continues rambling, but I don't catch much of the six-year-old's rant. I try to keep my eyes locked on hers though, nodding and smiling like I'm taking in every word she's saying. It keeps me from having to look at my dad, or Lisa who is standing sort of awkwardly behind my father.

"Bailey Mae, enough. Hi, Catherine." Lisa is, I guess, my stepmother. She has the same sun-kissed blonde hair as my little sister and the same gold flecked brown eyes. She and Dad started dating when I was a junior. Then graduation came and we moved to Georgia for her job.

They got married, then Bailey Mae came. Lisa has always been kind to me, but we're just not close. I was too old for her to step in as my mom, and I kept my distance as well. She has texted me a few times since I left, unlike my dad. She gives me a small, slightly awkward smile and straightens, stepping around my dad. I look at the petite woman in front of me long enough to realize she's either smuggling a beach ball or is very pregnant.

"Well, look at you." I turn my attention back to my little sister, faking excitement even though the sight of Lisa pregnant is making my heart sink. I was a hard teen to deal with, my dad's and my relationship was on thin ice when he started dating Lisa. Then it broke when Lisa announced she was pregnant at the housewarming party when we moved to Georgia. I was blindsided in front of a crowd of people. "I see you have a new playmate coming soon!" I set Bailey Mae down and look Lisa in the eyes. "Bailey Mae said you're here for a funeral? I didn't think you kept in contact with anyone here. I certainly don't remember you being a social person while we were here. It's also quite a long drive for a pregnant woman and a child."

My dad shuts the door. He looks tired. They must've driven. He's still wearing pajama bottoms and a blue Georgia Panthers hoodie. Michael Martin still maintains a well-built figure, gray hair and crows' feet the only things betraying his age. You'd guess he was graying early, not that he was passing fifty.

"Ah, well, my buddy Oscar from the force isn't doing well," my father answers me curtly. There's a clipped tone in his voice that makes it seem like it's an inconvenience that I'm asking.

He doesn't have a right to be short with me. All it does is stoke the flame of resentment in my heart.

Lisa rolls her eyes at him. "We also thought it would be a great opportunity to see Cici and you."

"I didn't know you knew him. Oscar died early this morning," I respond in the same short tone he gave me. I feel a twinge of guilt at my brusk tone as my dad's eyes jump to mine and then to Lisa before his shoulders sag.

Lisa shoots me a warning look as she walks over to my dad and wraps an arm around his waist.

I would never admit it out loud, but I like the way she looks at my dad. I remember the fighting and the arguments that he and my mom had all the time. I can honestly say that Lisa is probably one of the mildest, most affectionate people I have ever met, and she really seems to care about my dad.

She looks protectively pissed, standing there comforting my dad while he regains his composure. Her eyes never leave my face, and I can feel the 'I can't believe you just did that' rolling off her. She might not come off as a fighter, but I have a feeling she would do her best in a fight to defend him if needed.

When I was in high school, I always imagined my mom would come crawling back, and that she would apologize, and there was a part of me that was so angry when Dad started seeing Lisa because I thought she would get in the way. Not long after that I realized with certainty that mom was never going to come back and be the person Dad and I needed. Cici filled that void for me, and even though I resented it, I know Lisa is who my dad needed.

"I did know him. He was a good man. I wanted to say goodbye and it seemed like a great opportunity to see Cici. I honestly didn't think you'd want to see me, so I'm surprised to see you." My dad's voice is calm. He studies my face, like I'm an old acquaintance and he's trying to remember my name. Or like he might know my face but can't remember where he met me last.

"Why wouldn't I want to see dear old Dad?" I try to lighten the situation, but my resentment slithers out in my tone.

Lisa nudges Bailey Mae who's still standing close to me, peering confused between me and Dad. I'm thankful Lisa is redirecting because I can feel my grip on my own control slipping.

"We should probably go to Auntie Cici." Lisa takes Bailey Mae's hand and tugs her toward the kitchen. Even Bailey Mae realizes something is wrong, following her mom with no fuss.

Another thing I am grateful for is that Lisa has never seemed put off by my aunt. Where my mom always discouraged me from seeing her too much, lest I fall victim to her 'shenanigans,' Lisa has just taken everything in stride. Bailey Mae gets to have her family just as they are. No comments. No awkward interactions. No strain in adult relationships that makes her feel like she has to choose.

Except for me. I'm the asshole in this situation.

My dad sighs, hangs his light blue jacket on a coat hook, and sits down on the bench by the door to take off his shoes. I stand, waiting for a response. He doesn't look at me.

"Hello?" I prod my father. Seething anger bubbles just beneath the surface of my skin. I think I always assumed when I finally saw Dad again, it would feel better than this. I imagined that he would come up here to Bethton Grove to save me. I assumed it would be a relief. But really, seeing Mike Martin again just opens every wound I have taken so much time to heal. All I want is a safe place where I don't feel exposed or unwanted. But seeing my dad in Cici's house, my escape plan no longer an escape, has sparked every fight or flight instinct I have, setting me on edge.

"I am tired, Catherine. I really don't have time to have this discussion right now." His tone becomes short and angry.

He hasn't seen me in a year, and he doesn't have *time*? The heat inside me starts to boil over, but then it's like someone turned down the flame and I switch to self-blame. I was going through hell. I guess he didn't see it. *I didn't let him know. Maybe I should've called him back.*

No. I will not pull it back on me, not like when I was with Marcus. That's what I just spent the last few months figuring out. It takes two. This is just as much on him as it is on me.

"Discussion? You don't have time to even have small talk with me? Is that all you have to say?" I hiss at him. He's the one being short instead of speaking to his daughter. "It's been almost a year. We could have at least suffered through pleas-antries. But if you want to cut straight to the chase, then by all means–" I cross my arms expectantly.

"What do you want me to say?" He looks up at me and all of the light has left his face, leaving him looking tired and older than when I last saw him.

"Honestly, anything. Literally *anything*. You show up out of fucking nowhere.

I have been gone for months and you have said nothing." I feel the venom in my tone. "I get that you didn't come here for me, but still, you walked into this house and I'm here."

"Cici knew we were coming. It was not my intention to ambush you." He groans as he pulls himself up. His eyes look pained, but his voice is so calm and monotone it just makes me angrier.

"You have my number, right?" I ask, trying to keep my cool.

"I do, and you have mine." Our eyes meet and his eyebrows draw together, challenging me. His dark eyes are like looking in a mirror. I see all my own emotions thrown back at me.

"So then why the fuck didn't you text me you were coming up? Or, I don't know, like ever?" I practically spit the words at him and internally excitement bubbles through me. The old Catherine never would have been so bold.

"Can you stop cursing at me!" His voice switches from dismissive to stern, and it only makes me angrier.

"Now my language is a problem, too?"

"Bailey Mae is in the next room, Catherine. Lisa is not a fan of profanity around her, and you're already being vocal enough! I did call you. When you first left you chose not to call me back. I called your aunt to make sure you weren't murdered and were safe. You're an adult. I can't harass you into calling me." Dad's tone is cold. "I waited for an explanation, for a call telling me what the hell was happening. I had your ex-fiancé practically knocking down my door looking for you. I called Cici trying to get answers, but she just kept telling me that you would talk when you were ready. But when I would call you, I got nothing back. So, what am I supposed to do? I have a stressful job, a pregnant wife, and a six-year-old. I can't be chasing down a twenty-five-year-old. YOU made it clear that you didn't want me involved."

"Yes, how could I forget that when I became an adult you decided to do the family thing right and I didn't fit into that." I hit him where it hurts. I know it's a low blow, but even when I lived in Georgia, "I wasn't a part of this new family. We could've had weekly dinner, we could have been a family. You never came to visit me. It was *me* going to *you. Bailey Mae is too little to drive an hour. Bailey Mae gets car sick; we can't drive that long. Lisa has a big court hearing tomorrow so we can't come.* Finally, I stopped asking. I resigned myself to holidays and birthdays if I was lucky." I go to continue his lists of crimes against our relationship, but he cuts me off.

"Now, you listen here, young lady." His tone drops and he puffs his chest, taking a step toward me. The cop in him comes out and he looks at me like I am a person resisting arrest.

"No, you listen, do you see how fucked up that is. My life fell apart. You weren't there, MY DAD WOULD'VE BROKEN DOWN WALLS FOR ME! My dad would have come running across the country to make sure I was okay." I gesture toward the kitchen where Lisa took Bailey Mae. "Her dad doesn't give shit about me." My shout fades into a whisper, my anger to heartbreak as I say what I feel out loud. "You decided I wasn't a part of your family, not me. I tried reaching out, I wanted help, but you were always busy, you were always tired, there was always something else! So, you're right. I didn't want to tell you. I didn't want to answer your calls because they weren't enough. IT WASN'T ENOUGH."

My dad is stunned. The same range of emotions flash in his face. He stays silent and stares at his feet. Reigniting the spark to the flame of anger and hurt. He looks over my shoulder, but I don't turn around. I don't care who might hear. I wouldn't care if all of Bethton Grove was watching at this point.

"Well, I fucking guess *their* dad, like YOU'RE KIDDING, right? How the fuck did you think I'd take this? You show up out of nowhere and she's that fucking far along? Did you really think you could get away with coming up here and just not seeing me? Did you guys think you could slip in and out of town and just never run into me? Like, what the fuck? you're just going to keep my siblings a secret, never let them know they have an older sister?" My face is getting hot again. Tears prick the corners of my eyes. I swallow hard, trying desperately to breathe, but my lungs are barely cooperating. Every breath feels like fire in my chest.

"Language! What gives you the right to speak to me that way?! You are an ADULT, Catherine. You didn't call me about Marcus. You didn't tell me that you two split. I didn't know for months. You were going to get *married*. It was my time to back off. You had someone else to protect you." He clenches his jaw as he speaks.

"He didn't protect me! You knew he was a creep! I ran away to your house more than once!" I yell back.

"You went back to him every time. WHAT WAS I SUPPOSED TO DO? I CAN'T TIE YOU UP IN THE BASEMENT! How was I to know that this was the straw that broke the camel's back? You didn't tell me, you disappeared. You are the one who went off the grid. THAT'S NOT ON ME! What do you want from me?" Dad's angry side is coming out.

So is mine.

"I WANT A DAD! Cici was there. Cici has a busy stressful life. SHE still made time for me. I'm not even her goddamn kid! She calls if I don't text her even when I was in Georgia. No matter what, she keeps trying. I didn't willingly go back to him, but when I tried to leave his abusive ass, YOU let him back into my life every time. You didn't keep me safe, and I thought Marcus would kill me! YOU didn't care! Lisa reached out more than you did. Seems like everyone gives a shit but YOU!" I can't stop yelling and tears begin streaming down my face.

"You never told me he was abusing you. It was always a fight with no more details than that. I'm sorry he hurt you, but I can't protect you when I see nothing more than a young couple working out the kinks in a relationship. You can't blame me for your choices." He sternly crosses his arms.

"You're a LITERAL detective, and you fucking couldn't pick up what was going on? I absolutely can blame you for my fucking struggles. You're my dad. If you hadn't pushed me away, I would've felt safe to tell you like I did with Cici. Just like you pushed away my mom!"

His face tells me that I've gone too far, possibly to the point of no return. The fire that gleams in his eyes turns cold. His mouth snaps shut so hard I feel like I can hear his teeth rattle. I fall back a step, the weight of everything sinking in. Suddenly I'm almost too tired to stand. My vision swims and my knees turn to jelly. I hear my own angry words bouncing off the walls, and shame creeps up my spine.

"Awe, look at this family reunion!" Charles claps once uncomfortably, coming out of the kitchen.

Dad and I both shoot daggers with our glare.

Charles looks like he instantly regrets walking into the room and throws a look over his shoulder, trying to find Cici fast.

Bailey Mae shouts from behind him as Cici pulls him back into the kitchen. "UNCLE CHARLIE, THEY ARE FIGHTING."

I look back at my dad as he smirks and rolls his eyes at his daughter's commentary. He doesn't look at me again, turning so that he is facing the wall behind him. It's like a knife cutting me. Still, even in the heat of the moment, my dad still finds some twisted humor in all of this. I feel like I'm ten years old again, being reprimanded for something stupid. I can hear my own pulse beating vigorously in my ears. Bile surges up in my throat and I stare at the ground, willing myself not to throw up.

"Enough, Catherine." Cici comes around the corner. Her stern tone draws my attention.

"Why the fuck didn't you tell me?" I hiss at her. Fresh tears start falling when she walks into the small hallway, the betrayal like ice in my veins.

"Not my job to make sure you have communication with your dad. I don't share your life with him; I don't need to share his with you. I knew they were coming today but forgot when you texted me. You don't live here, and I didn't know if he told you or not. I know it's a touchy subject and you've been busy. Don't put any of this on me. He's my brother. I'm not going to turn him out because you, who doesn't live with me, don't like him." She crosses her arms, signaling the conversation is over.

"Yeah, whatever. I think I'm gonna stay somewhere else. I'll grab my stuff." I don't look at my dad and brush past Cici. I enter the kitchen where Bailey Mae is quietly poking her cinnamon bun with a downcast look on her face. While Lisa and Charles chat quietly over tea. They turn to me, and I can see panic flash across Lisa's face, but I ignore them to go down the stairs, snatch my bag off the bed, and haul back up the stairs.

Charles is standing there with a homemade Cinnamon bun in a Tupperware container. "Take it with you. I'm sorry about this morning. Call me if you need me."

I reach for the container, but instead of handing it off to me, he uses it to pull me into a tight hug.

"Thanks." I hug the older British man back tightly.

I wave and walk out of the kitchen as Lisa consoles Bailey Mae who has started crying. My heart shatters, I didn't think about how what I said would hurt Bailey Mae. It's better to just leave than stay and make things worse for her, she barely knows me anyway. Lisa's eyes flick to me briefly, but I don't know her well enough to read the expression on her face.

Cici grabs my arm as I walk past her.

"You're tired. Please try to talk to your dad in a better headspace before he goes back to Georgia." Her voice pleads with me.

My eyes scan the room and he's gone. Most likely disappeared to the bath-room.

"Yeah, I'll think about it. I just need to get outta here right now."

She gives me a little squeeze to remind me she loves me, but I don't return the sentiment. After spending so much time with Cici, you'd think I wouldn't be surprised, but my heart aches anyway. I can't stomach that she did this to me right now. Not after how much I've expressed my pain and heartache to her about my dad and Lisa.

I walk out the door and am suddenly too exhausted to go any farther. My legs threaten to give out as I step off the porch. I sit ungracefully right there on the step. Where do I go? I feel lost and alone again.

There is only one place I feel wanted right now. I pull out my phone and send Nathan a text.

Me:

Can't stay here, my dad showed up. Can I stay with you?

TEN

Catherine

Nathan pulls up about five minutes later. Outside of Cici's house as I sit on the bottom step of the porch crying, I can barely see him walk up through the tears.

"Rough day?" Nathan asks. I nod silently as I stand up, wiping the tears away. He pulls me into a warm safe hug. "Me, too. Let's go." He gives me a squeeze, grabs my right hand in his and pulls me to the car. He opens the passenger's side door and I climb in with my bag.

"Wait." I shuffle through my bag, making sure I have everything I need for his house. I realize I have no shampoo or body wash. "Can we swing by my place and get shampoo and stuff?"

"You can use mine. It's a three-in-one wash." His sweet naive smile makes me giggle.

"Absolutely not. I will not ruin my hair like that."

"Why not?" He looks so confused. For being one of the smartest men I know, he can be dumb.

"Just because it does everything doesn't mean it should. I spent too much money fixing my hair from red to ruin it again." I laugh, feeling the stress of the fight melt off my shoulders.

He pulls down a lock of his hair and inspects it. "My hair isn't ruined."

"Well, your hair is natural. Mine is colored and treated, major difference." He seems to accept my answer even though I can tell he doesn't understand. The skin between his eyebrows creases as he examines my hair for a long moment.

"Alright then, let's go to Amber's, I guess. Mariposa is at Mom's right now. I'd really appreciate us avoiding my family right now." He rubs his neck uncomfortably.

"What happened?" I prod him.

"Uh, let's talk about it when we get back to my house. It was just…A LOT." Nathan is avoiding it, but maybe he doesn't feel he can get into it now. I can't really fault him. I don't particularly want to rehash everything at the moment either.

"Fair enough. If you're hungry we can raid my place when we get there," I offer.

Nathan turns left at the stop sign.

"I am not exactly hungry with everything going on." He sighs.

"Me, either," I groan. I should eat, but I don't want to.

Nathan reaches across and holds my hand. I look at him and smile.

Safety. All I have wanted is safety, and here it sits right next to me. His hands are warm but not sweaty. Comforting, his eyes meet mine for a moment. His soft dark eyes look exhausted. Nathan flashes a smile before turning away again.

"We can always raid the back of the bakery on our way up to the apartment."

Nathan nods slowly. "That I could go for. Some coffee and cookies sound really good."

"Good old fashioned emotional eating," I say sarcastically. I sigh, turning to look out the window as we stop at the last stop sign before we reach my apartment complex. How had everything gone so badly so quickly? Less than twenty-four hours and nothing is how it was, and it will never be the same again. If there was any possibility of fixing things with my dad, I ruined it.

Nathan pulls into my apartment parking lot and finds a spot right outside the entrance. We flash each other another loving smile. He hops out and walks around to my door and opens it.

"Milady." He gestures and bows a little.

"Oh, stop it, you. Let's hurry up. Cookies are waiting," I tease.

I pull my keys out of my backpack as we get to the front door to let us in. The house is mostly quiet except for some loud clattering in the kitchen. As we walk around the corner, we are greeted by the sight of a slightly hysterical looking Amber.

She whirls on us with a forced smile that falls as soon as she recognizes who we are.

"Oh, thank God, I thought it was Mariposa. I have a bone to pick with you!"

Nathan and I both are silent, not sure which one of us she's angry with.

"Why the fuck is Saul so stupid?" It's definitely not a question as Amber points an accusatory finger at Nathan. "I show up to the library and there he is. Manically pacing the third floor looking like a lunatic! On the bright side, it's the first time I've seen him show ANY emotion aside from indifference, if that even is an emotion. But still. We trained him! How could he let the library fall into shambles in one day!"

"Shambles?" Nathan echoes, clearly as confused as I am.

"He broke the fucking check-in computer! You have to manually put in every book's information to return it instead of scanning the barcode. Then instead of staying downstairs and working on it, he was hiding upstairs with a cart full of books that didn't even go on the third floor!" Amber huffs and slams another cabinet closed, ripping open a bag of pretzels and jumping up to sit on the counter next to the sink.

It looks like Mariposa has gotten to the kitchen as well. There are half-eaten bags of chips and candy piled in the corner of the counter. Three overnight bags are thrown on the couch, each in a various state of unpacked, which just means our living room looks like Cici's closet.

"When you said Saul needed help, I thought it was something simple! But no, I just spent the last hour manually inputting every return from today into the computer. Then I had to write a sign on each cart telling him which floor to take which books to." She shovels handfuls of pretzels into her mouth, not bothering to chew and swallow before talking. "I say we burn him at the stake. Or lock him up in the library basement with the rest of the monsters! Why did he even want this job if he's an actual idiot?"

"We don't have a basement to lock him in, and killing people is not the solution." Nathan's deep voice is calm and understanding, and I can see her fizzle out in front of us.

"Well, you owe me big for that. I get that your dad…" She doesn't finish the thought. "Either way, you owe me." She says, still half glaring over her pretzel bag. "I want him fired!"

"Okay, Amber, we can't just fire him over this."

She sighs dramatically and rolls her eyes.

"Then I want an extra vacation day. Final offer."

A small smile pulls the corners of Nathan's lips. "Deal. Thank you for helping me today."

Amber nods, then turns her attention to me. "And you." She jumps down off the counter and comes over to me. Her tone is still on the harsh side, but as she steps up to me, it softens considerably.

"I am so sorry for everything that went down this morning." She wraps her arms around me, and I slump against her, relief filling my body.

"I'm sorry, too," I mumble into her hair. My throat stings a little after this shit-show of a day I had, and we stand there for over a minute. When she finally pulls away, I feel the smallest bit lighter.

"I never should have told Mariposa that she and Yuri could stay here without texting you first. This is just as much your home as mine. It was unfair for me to invite someone to stay without asking."

"It's fine." I look over my shoulder to Nathan who is still standing in the doorway looking slightly confused and uncomfortable. I give her what I hope is an apologetic smile. "I should have thought to text you last night, too. Instead of just not coming home."

"Why are you here?" Amber asks, finally starting to realize that Nathan and I walked in together. She looks between the two of us for a long minute before an excited smile spreads across her face. "Are you two…?" She doesn't say more, but something on our faces must give something away. She starts to wiggle, and an excited yelp comes out of her.

"It's not like that," I say hastily. "Nathan borrowed my car today."

"After you spent the night there!" Amber winks at Nathan, who is about twenty different shades of uncomfortable and embarrassed at this point.

I roll my eyes. "It really isn't like that."

She gives me a knowing look and I try to change the subject.

"Where is Yuri?"

"She's taking a nap in your bed. I hope that's fine. She and Mariposa drove most of the night, so she needed to sleep a little."

"That's totally fine. I just need my shampoo and some makeup."

"Doesn't Cici usually keep those things in the bathroom downstairs for you?" Amber looks confused.

My heart starts to beat uncomfortably. I don't want to talk about this right now. "I'm trying to only use the stuff that Meghan gave me. I don't want to ruin the progress on my hair with the other stuff." *Or Nathan's 3-in-1.*

Amber nods understandingly and goes back to her pretzels.

"I'm gonna grab my stuff and get going, I don't think I want to be here when Mariposa gets back."

"Me either," Nathan adds under his breath, but Amber and I both hear him.

"I'm sad you aren't going to be here for the next few days." Amber follows me to the bathroom.

"I know. Me, too." I grab my things from the shower and my drawer by the sink. "I think for the next few days, we can manage. It's best for everyone to have a safe place to go."

I glance at Nathan, who's been quiet this whole time. I know I should tell Amber about my dad and that I'm going to stay with Nathan for at least a few days, but something about it still feels forbidden. I am a little afraid that if I talk about it, it will have all been a dream or something.

"I know. You're right. Once this all blows over, maybe before Mariposa leaves, I'd like for us to have a girls' night. I know you two got off on the wrong foot," she pauses and sends a look Nathan's way. He retreats slightly, clearly so uncomfortable with everything that's happened since we walked into the apartment. "It would mean a lot to me, though, if we could all get together and have a drink. I think under better circumstances you guys would really get along."

"We can do that." I hug Amber again, thankful that she is so understanding.

"Should we get going?" Nathan looks at me.

"Love you," I call over my shoulder to Amber.

"Love you, too!" She heads back into the kitchen as Nathan and I make our escape to the front door.

Once we are safely outside, Nathan takes my hand and fixes me with a look. "How come you didn't tell Amber about your dad?"

I knew he'd ask, but I was hoping to avoid the conversation for a while. I sigh, pulling him toward the car. He opens the passenger side door and I get in without hesitation and he walks around to the driver's side. I think it's a little bit funny that we've already fallen back into this little routine without even trying.

I wait until Nathan walks around and gets into the driver's seat before I answer him.

"I just don't really feel like having the therapy session she was going to try and create. I didn't think you'd want to stay there for the amount of time it would have taken me to talk her down from wherever she would have taken the conversation."

"If you needed to talk, you could have."

"But I really don't want to." It's such a short drive to Nathan's apartment from mine that we are already almost halfway there.

We are quiet for a minute and then Nathan talks again. "I hate to be this person, but you also very adamantly denied me in front of her."

I cringe and turn slightly in my seat to face him. "I honestly didn't know what to tell her. I mean, we haven't seen each other in months, and then last night out of the blue we reconnected? And do you really want Mariposa to find out from Amber that I'm staying with you for a few days instead of at Cici's?"

He's quiet, but his grip tightens on the steering wheel as he stares straight ahead. "I guess I just forgot that it's been so long. I know we just reconnected last night, but it feels like we were only apart for a few weeks, not months." He turns and smiles at me. "It's cheesy but I really do feel that way. We just click. I also don't want to invoke my sister's wrath."

"I don't either. Everything feels fragile right now… and I might be a little selfish too. I don't really want to share this time with anyone else right now."

"I'm not upset," he says quietly. "I just wanted to make sure I wasn't missing anything."

The apprehension in his voice is sweet, and I understand the anxiety he's feeling. Smiling, I take his hand. "Come on, let's head in."

Eleven

Nathan

I swing open the cafe's door. The small bell above jingles and the smell of fresh bread hits me in the face. Catherine's hand is so small in mine it feels like mine was meant to hold hers. There is another couple probably in their early twenties sitting in the corner making googly eyes at each other. An older man sits sipping coffee at the front table while reading the news. Larry stands behind the counter waiting for us to approach.

"Well, hello, lovebirds." Larry stands up straight from leaning on the counter. There's a mischievous glint in his eyes, and I feel Catherine grip my hand a little tighter.

"Hey, can we get a bunch of cookies and baked goods? We're planning on eating our feelings." Catherine's sense of humor makes this all so much easier. She gives him this huge doe-eyed smile that I'd imagine is why Charles and Larry practically fall over themselves to take care of her. I momentarily envy the easy relationship she has with them. Between the two men and Cici, Catherine has more family than she realizes.

"I'm sure I can supply you with the goods. Come on back." Larry does a little wave with his one hand to guide us into the back kitchen and swings it open. He only has one arm and can't keep the door from smacking back into Catherine. She reels back on her feet a bit and bumps me in the process. I place my hand on the small of her back to steady her steps. She glances back at me and her cheeks look a little pinker than usual.

"I've got whatever you want in here. Go ham." Larry turns to us "On the house. You only lose a dad once."

I know he means well, but man, Larry is dark.

"Thanks, man. Means a lot." I smile, but somehow my heart is still aching. Looking at Larry, thinking of all the times he's helped Dad with house projects, or helped load Dad in my car after he'd had a night of drinking. The ginger-haired old man was strong enough to fireman-carry my father out of Cici's bar. He also has brought food over to my parents plenty of times since Dad got sick.

Larry pats me on the arm. "Now behave you two or I'll call your parents." He swings the cafe kitchen door open out to the storefront, leaving us alone with a smorgasbord of baked goods.

Catherine turns to me and our eyes meet. Her hazel green eyes sparkle, living many childhood dreams of eating as many cookies and cupcakes as she can. She lets go of me as she lets out a devious little giggle. She starts to look with delight over all the premade goodies. Then she gives me a look as if she's looking for permission from me.

"What? Larry already gave us the okay." I can't help but wonder why she needs permission from me.

"I just…I just don't want you to judge me about how much I get." She looks down, cheeks flushed at her feet.

"Why would I judge? I am going to gorge myself on all this dessert." She still looks concerned. "Plus a hot chick covered in brownies and cookies in my apartment sounds like a great time." I give a little wink and her cheeks flush to almost a magenta color.

"Well then, I need at least a baker's dozen of both to cover all of this." She laughs, gesturing to her figure.

"Do I get to eat it off of you then?"

She gives me a scolding look and punches me in the arm. We both laugh.

Her laugh is like listening to music.

"That sounds unhygienic. Do you see chocolate chip cookies? They're my favorite!" She spots some on the top shelf and reaches. Only her fingertips graze the shelf's edge. "S. O. S. I can't get the cookies!" she huffs.

I reach up and hand the chocolate chip cookies to Catherine, her face overjoyed.

"God, you are just so beautiful when you're happy." I hear myself say the words before I register what I've said.

"Thanks." She smiles a small, shy smile and blushes. She snatches a cookie and takes a bite. She grabs a tray of brownies, stacks the cookie tray on top and I grab some apple empanadas.

"I haven't stuffed my face full of sweets in forever." I swing open the door that heads to my loft. "Alright, be careful. Don't drop any cookies."

"Or what? You gonna spank me?" she coily says as she walks by, sending any evil little smile my way. She does a little taunting wiggle with her ass. Now she's making me blush.

"Yes…" My voice cracks like a thirteen-year-old boy. Shit, is it hot in here, or is it just her? Some extremely inappropriate images flash in my mind, and I have to take two deep breaths before I follow her.

Catherine cackles as she climbs the stairs knowing she's riled me up.

I catch up to her and make my way to open the door at the top of the steps so that I can hold it open for her. I slide past her, my body pressing against her. I regret the desserts. If they weren't there I could throw her against the wall and kiss her right here, right now. My hands are too full and it's hard enough to get to my key in my pocket, let alone get to her body. It's maddening to be so close yet so far. I open the door and Catherine walks through. My eyes are drawn to her voluptuous ass. The way it moves so gracefully with each step. It's firm not jiggly, she must do a ton of squats for an ass like hers. I could bury my face between those cheeks.

"Excuse me?" she says cheekily.

"Huh?" I look up, realizing she's staring at me over her shoulder.

"Are you staring at my ass?" She turns herself towards me.

"Oh shit, yeah, maybe." I smile, feeling a little embarrassed.

She starts to laugh and sets the sweets on the counter. "No offense, but when you slid past me, you smelled hardcore of cigarettes."

"Yeah, Sofia and Mom smoke like chimneys. It's truly amazing how many cigarettes they can smoke in one sitting." I sniff my sleeve and, damn, she's right, I smell awful. "Yikes, I think I'm gonna shower." I turn to head towards my shower.

Wait… Catherine is here… She could shower with me. I spin on my heels and lay on the charm.

"You could join me if you'd like." I smile and look her up and down. Imagining the water rolling down her hot, curvy, naked body.

"Nah. I'm gonna sit out here, watch your TV, and eat cookies." Catherine struts over and runs her hands down my chest and pecks me on the cheek. "Enjoy your shower."

She is toying with me. I can see it in her eyes. It takes every ounce of self-control that I didn't know I had until now to keep my hands to myself. I can smell myself now, though, and I don't want to think of Mom and Sofia when I'm… in the moment.

"I understand, but the offer is open if you change your mind." *Play it cool Nathan.* I head into the bathroom and close the door.

I turn the shower on and turn up the heat. I stare into the mirror, only seeing one thing–my dad. These small moments make me forget he is gone. With Catherine, the whole world melts away. Now I'm here seeing my dad in every feature. My jaw especially. Dad and I both have very defined square jaws. My eyes are the same shade of brown as his. If my son has my eyes, I will only be able to see Dad. Dad won't ever see me get married, or meet my children.

The weight of the day comes crashing back down in waves. The warm bathroom air is clogging my lungs, and my skin feels clammy. It's like my clothes are all of a sudden too tight, making it hard to breathe. I can feel the collar of my button-down shirt suffocating me, and the fabric turns to sandpaper on my skin. My eyes start to fill with tears. I peel off my shirt, unable to suffer the feel of the fabric against my skin any longer. I try to shake off the crushing weight of everything going on.

I step out of my pants and underwear and into the shower. The hot water rolls down my back. Everything relaxes as the heat relieves the stress. For a moment, I feel like I'm washing away the pain of today. I step back into the water, allowing it to run down my head and chest. Closing my eyes, I tilt my head until water rushes over my face, dulling the throbbing pressure that felt like it was building under my skin moments ago. The water is scalding hot, making my outside as numb as my inside. A wave of sadness hits again, nearly bringing me to my knees. All I want is to just breathe. The water that was soothing a second before now makes me feel as if I'm being waterboarded. Steam clogs my nose and throat and my chest tightens,

Breathe in, breathe out.

I just need to ground myself. I feel nauseated. I feel like I can't breathe. Another wave of emotion has me pressing my palms into the cool tile of the wall.

My vision swims.

Breathe in, breathe out, breathe in, breathe out.

The sound of knocking brings me back and I catch my breath.

"Come in!" I cough out. Air rushes back into my lungs and I have to stifle a gasp as the door creeps open.

"Sorry if it's weird, but I really have to pee."

I hear her feet shuffle past the shower.

"It's okay. Just don't flush till I get out. I will turn into an iceberg if you do." I try to say it loud enough for her to hear.

"Lisa, my dad's wife, texted me!" she shouts.

"Yeah, and?" I yell back. She still hasn't told me what happened with her dad showing up at Cici's today, but I can't imagine it was great given the way I found her.

"She wants to have breakfast tomorrow. I'm kind of pissed that it's her reaching out and not my dad." She pauses and I focus on her words, making sure I don't miss anything. "I'm gonna go anyway!" she yells.

"Why are you mad? What happened?" I know she said earlier she didn't want a therapy session with Amber, but maybe she will still talk to me.

Then I hear the glass door slide open. I look over and my jaw drops. Catherine stands there, the steam rolling around her almost like an angel in a cloud. No, a goddess. Her body is completely breathtaking. I can't help but stand there stunned by her tits. God, her tits are perfect. I must be drooling. Like *The Birth of Venus by Botticelli*, her curves and her form are perfect. I feel hot, my skin feels too tight, but not in the same way that it did a few moments ago. This is something completely different. I feel all the blood rush from my head to elsewhere. I can't help it, my heart is racing. Although I think in this situation for once we have the same idea. I just have more sense and try to keep my body to myself. She climbs in with me, her soft delicate skin pressed against mine. She starts drawing in the water on my chest, sending electricity up my spine.

I push through the mind fog she's creating and grasp onto the last part of the conversation that I can remember. "Why are you mad Lisa texted you and not your dad?"

Catherine slumps against me, resting her head on my chest and pressing her chest against my abdomen. I have to take two deep breaths before I can right my mind again. God, her skin feels so good under my fingertips as I rest my hands lightly on her lower back. I don't know how much touching is appropriate right now. I desperately want to hear what she has to say, and I want to know what's happening with her family, but my focus is torn. I keep my hands still against her, even though most of my second brain is screaming to touch her everywhere.

"I really don't want to talk about it right now. I didn't know Dad was coming up and we got into a fight because they got to Cici's right after I did."

"Okay, then we don't have to talk right now." Some part of me is relieved even though I feel like a douchebag, but I'm struggling to concentrate with Catherine standing in front of me, bringing every fantasy I've had over the last six months to life.

She relaxes into me, breathing deeply. When she inhales, I can feel her nipples glide across my bare skin, and I have to hold back the excited thrill that shudders through me. I clear my throat once, hoping to push past the brain fog.

"Here, let's trade places. That way you have some of the water." I wrap my arms around her, intending to just turn, but there isn't nearly as much room in the shower as I anticipate, and we end up shuffling around awkwardly until her back is under the hot spray.

My body feels mechanical and out of practice, like I don't know what to do with my hands. I take a half step away from her as she leans her head back into the water, closing her eyes. I lock my jaw in place, concentrating on remaining neutral as I watch the water stream down her naked form.

When she opens her eyes, there's a haziness to them that has my heart speeding up even more in my chest. She shoots me a lazy smile and then looks around the shower.

"I totally forgot all of my shampoo and stuff out in the kitchen, and I haven't washed my hair in a few days." She looks concerned.

"I mean, I can go get it." I look toward the shower door, regretting offering as I think of the cold air in my apartment just outside of the bathroom door.

"No, it's fine." She eyes my 3-in-1 shampoo warily. "Just don't tell Meghan."

"Oh, I'm definitely telling her next time I get my hair cut."

She rolls her eyes at me but reaches for the shampoo anyway. I can see the smile she's trying to hide, and she awkwardly grabs the bottle.

"Here." I take the shampoo from her small hands. "Turn around."

She follows my directions quietly, and I'm not sure she's completely comfortable, but I don't really care at this point. I need to touch her, and this seems like a safe trade. Dropping a small amount of the shampoo into my hands, I reach for her, slowly and carefully working the product through her thick dark hair.

She relaxes after a moment, tilting her head back toward me as she sighs. From here I can see her eyes flutter closed, and the top of her tits as they're pelted by the water. This seemed like the safe option a moment ago, but now I'm not so sure.

I run my fingers through her hair and get a devious thought.

"You know what's great about 3-in-1 shampoo and body wash?" I ask slyly.

"What?" she says curtly.

"That I go from washing your hair–" I run my fingers through her hair leading my hands down her curves to her tits. "–to washing your body."

She squeals a little in surprise. I keep massaging her soft tits, they fit perfectly in my palms. She wriggles under my hands, letting out a small moan that threatens to turn my knees to jelly. I want her closer. She doesn't feel close enough.

My mind is dragged backward to memories of her breathing heavily under my touch in a coat closet at the beginning of the year. My brain and body barely have time to catch up as I pull her back flat against my front, letting my fingers roam over her chest and stomach. I can barely breathe as her slippery soft skin glides under my hands.

Catherine's breath catches in her throat. I can see the change in her body language. I press my lips to her shoulder, and she sags against me slightly, my dick pressed firmly into her lower back just above her ass. I freeze, so aware of how close our bodies are and even more aware of my breathlessness. She leans her head back on my chest, eyes closed, and I kiss her neck this time, just behind her ear. I wrap my arms around her body, holding her tight against my own. I feel like I'm going to war against myself. Part of me wants nothing more than to turn her around, lift her off the ground and finish what I've started. At the same time, I haven't felt this at home in so long. The exhaustion and ache of the last twenty-four hours has me reeling still. I don't want to feel like I'm using a moment that should be special just to get some momentary relief.

Catherine must sense my warring mind because she turns slowly in my arms, wrapping her own around my middle. I don't know how long we stand like that, joined together under the hot water, but eventually it starts to grow cold, and I reach around her to turn it off.

I only have one towel, which now seems stupid, so I allow her to dry off first and then dry my own body.

Neither of us have clean clothes in the bathroom, so we head into the bedroom/kitchen and stand for a moment.

"I won't tell anyone if you don't," I say quietly. "But I think we should nix the clothes, grab the cookies, and find a comfort show on Netflix."

Catherine beams at me. "I think I could fall in love with you." She does a ridiculous mad dash to the kitchen, and I chuckle to myself as she turns to me, naked, with a plate of chocolate chip cookies in hand. The evening light is streaming through the windows at the far end of the apartment, haloing her body and making her dark hair shine as she marches back to my bed.

"You are so beautiful."

She makes a goofy face and sticks out her tongue as she settles under the covers. I can't tear my eyes away from the way her tits move as she settles back into the pillows.

"What do you want to watch?" She hands me a cookie as I turn on the TV.

"*The Office* for sure."

"Perfect."

"It's the only safe choice in an emotional crisis," she says, taking a bite of her cookie.

We settle back into the bed, shoulders touching, the plate of goodies wedged between us.

We aren't even halfway through an episode when my phone starts to ring. I groan, rolling away in bed to reach for it sitting on the charger on my nightstand.

"Hey *Mami*, are you okay?"

"I think we should find other questions to ask *Mijo*." My mom's voice is raspy with sleep.

"Okay." I don't really know how to respond.

"I sent everyone home for the night. I needed some time to myself. *La tias* are coming back in the morning, and we are having a family breakfast. Everyone expects you to be there."

"Thank you for letting me know, I will be there." I pause a moment, then ask, "Are you sure you're going to be okay in that house by yourself tonight?"

There's a long pause on the phone and then my mother sighs. "I will be okay, *mi amor*. Your *Papi* and I haven't shared a bed in months. I'll see you in the morning."

"I'll see you in the morning."

My mother ends the call without saying anything else, and it strikes me how weird the last day has been. I lay my phone back down staring at the ceiling.

"Are you okay?" Catherine's voice sounds far away, but her hand finds mine. I use the sensation to ground myself, dragging my mind back to the present, to Catherine beside me.

"I will be," I echo the words my mom said a few moments before.

TWELVE

Catherine

I lay on my side, watching Nathan as he stares blankly at the TV. It's dark
outside, and we've been lying here for a long time. The plate of cookies is no longer
between us, but empty and placed on the dinky nightstand next to the bed. His face
is mostly relaxed, except for the worry creases between his eyebrows. Nathan's body
language is still and unyielding. I just want to curl up against him, but something
stops me. I feel exposed, and raw. I know he's not doing much better.

And then there's the shower incident.

My cheeks grow hot as I think about standing in the shower with Nathan.
There's some sort of weird tension that is created when you know you're going
to see someone naked for the first time. My hands shook when I took off my own
clothes before sliding the door open to get in. I remembered the way he looked
when he came out of the bathroom the morning before, taking his time to get
dressed as I watched. It was different this time. This time there were no barriers
between us. I still can't get the image of him, steam licking his skin as water trickled
down his perfect body. His hard dick, completely on display. I almost backed up. It's
not like I haven't seen a penis before, that's not the issue.

But the way Nathan looked at me, coupled with the way his dick twitched when

I stood naked in front of him...

My heart starts to race at the memory. He's bigger than I anticipated. In the morning when he got dressed, I didn't get nearly as good of a look as I did tonight. And when he pressed up against me in the shower, the sheer size of him set my body on fire with a mix of exhilaration and trepidation.

I wanted to touch him. I wanted more, and yet I didn't want to ask. We both had terrible days, although I don't feel like mine really holds a candle to his in the grand scheme of things. But neither of us are ever in a place where it seemed like we had a good chance of getting through any type of intimate moment.

Nathan glances at me, catching me staring. He smiles softly, and the worry creases between his brows relax slightly. There's no wall built around him tonight, no dark storm cloud looming just out of reach. The space between us is empty and open. Somewhere in the back of my mind, I feel like there are still things we need to talk about, but I can't bring myself to say anything tonight.

Not when he's looking at me like that.

"You're too far away." Nathan wraps his arm around me and pulls me into him. Our skin touching feels safe, warm, and like home.

"This is nice." I close my eyes, laying my head on his chest and breathing him in deeply.

"Yeah, it is." He sighs and squeezes me tighter.

I wrap my arm around his stomach and throw my leg up over his hip. I can hear his heart beating rhythmically and my eyelids feel heavy. The emotional exhaustion from the day bleeds into more as physical exhaustion starts to pull me toward sleep. If I could freeze time right here, I would. If I could save either of us from what tomorrow brings, I would. But I can't, and as my eyelids grow heavier, Nathan kisses my forehead. He strokes my hair and I drift off to sleep.

***

I start to stir. The soft warm bed has become cold without someone else in it. The smell of fresh coffee raises me fully from my slumber and I sit up. I pull the blanket over my chest realizing I'm still naked. My nipples are rock hard from how cold the loft is. I spin my head back and forth looking for my human heater.

"Good morning sunshine!" Nathan's voice comes from behind me. I turn and see him pouring us cups of coffee. "I didn't make breakfast since we both have plans."

"Gimme a sec. My brain is still rebooting," I say groggily. Rubbing the sand out of my eyes, I look up and Nathan is sitting on the edge of the bed. He's wearing a nice black sweater and gray khaki pants.

"Here!" Nathan's got a big goofy grin on as he extends the white mug towards me.

"Fuck, you're a morning person, aren't you?" I groan.

"What? I mean, a little." He has a look of confusion on his face.

"I'm not sure this is gonna work out because I am NOT a morning person." I'm exhausted but manage out a rasping laugh.

"I noticed. I've tried to wake you up three times already." He laughs.

"Oh, God, you did?" Well, that's embarrassing. I take the mug from him, tucking the blanket into my arms not to expose myself. "Uh, can you hand me my bag of clothes? I'll just get dressed under the blanket."

"Yeah, sure." Nathan sets his mug on his nightstand, then stands up and walks towards my bag. He has a really nice butt. He stops suddenly in front of my bag. Nathan spins and gives me a devious grin.

"What?"

"I don't think I can bring it to you," he says, crossing his arms. That smile is still pulling the corners of his mouth.

"Why is that?" I try to act annoyed but can't help the giggle I feel bubbling in my chest.

"Revenge is a dish best served cold." He takes two casual steps toward me.

"You asshole." I can't hide my own smile now.

It's freezing in the loft, and I already feel goosebumps prickle my skin. And I can feel my nipples pressing uncomfortably hard against the fabric of the blanket. Hard enough to cut diamonds is not an exaggeration.

I grab his big comforter and drape it around myself, throwing it over my head and everything so that only my face and feet are visible. It takes some maneuvering, but I manage to stand up and make my way toward my bag. I stick my tongue out at Nathan as I approach, but he's just grinning. I am maybe two steps from my bag when I feel Nathan shift behind me and then I can't move anymore. I turn slightly, looking over my shoulder to see Nathan triumphantly smiling, and his foot is plant-ed firmly on the corner of the blanket that was trailing behind me. I can no longer walk and keep the blanket around me. I analyze the situation. I could admit defeat and beg to have the blanket; I know Nathan would give in quickly. I also want to catch him just as off guard as I was yesterday when he dropped his towel.

I turn my back to him, take a deep breath, trying to make my facial expression neutral, and I let go of the blanket. It pools in a puddle around my feet, and I hear Nathan suck in air sharply. I don't turn until I've reached my bag, doing everything in my power to walk naturally. I reach for my bag, bending over slowly, pick it up, and turn around to face him.

Nathan's face is blank but his eyes blaze as they work their way up from my feet to my face. His gaze lingers on my chest, unwavering for a few long seconds, and then he meets my eyes. He seems almost as frozen as my skin feels.

"Eh-em." I try to call his attention back to me. Like a deer in headlights, his gaze is wide-eyed as it meets mine. "May I have the blanket back now? It's cold as fuck."

He grabs the blanket and wraps it around me. Nathan suddenly picks me up in his arms like a groom crossing the threshold with his bride. He walks over and tosses me on the bed. I flop onto my back, my body on full display. The blanket is crumpled under my back, only one corner draped across my stomach. I think about shifting, pulling it over me to hide the amount of skin I know is visible. I'm so tired of hiding, though I like the way he looks at me. I like the way he makes me feel about myself, so instead, I shove the corner of the fabric away from myself, laying bare in front of him.

Nathan's dark eyes look at me with a deep, primal hunger, shifting from the gentle librarian into a hyper masculine being. He kneels over top of me, sliding his knees between mine. His body heat surrounds me as he crawls up my body, taking his time to look at every inch of exposed skin. Nathan pins my hands down and kisses my neck. I let out a soft moan. His kisses get deeper and rougher against my skin as he begins to press himself into me. I can feel his rock-hard cock through his khakis, rubbing between my legs. I moan louder as the friction begins to send euphoric bliss through me. He moves from my neck down my collar bones, dragging his tongue down my neck to my breasts. His hands run from mine. He sinks onto one elbow, still supporting himself over me. The other hand goes to my hip, pulling me closer, wrapping my leg around his hip. Then his mouth is on mine, teeth grazing my bottom lip. With my hands free, I cling to him, dragging his body flush against mine, pulling at his clothes. Why does he still have so many clothes on? He begins to circle my nipples with his tongue and fingers. I shudder. Then when his fingers are replaced by his hot mouth, I can't help but to exhale a moan in pleasure.

"Fuck," I whisper.

Suddenly our phones go off simultaneously.

"Noooo," we both groan as our ecstasy is interrupted again. He checks his phone.

"Can we just ignore it?" I plead.

"No, it's my mom, I have to go to breakfast." He groans. "I can't be late. I don't have a choice." Kissing me on the lips one more time, he pulls himself off me and sits on the side of the bed. "Why? Why always when it starts getting good?" He shakes his fist like he's angry with God. I roll over and grab my phone.

Lisa:

I'm here at that cute little coffee shop! See you soon!!

She uses way too many exclamation points.

Wait… SHE'S HERE!

"Fuck, I gotta go like five minutes ago!" I scramble up and out of the bed. I throw on my clothes as Nathan stares at me like a twelve-year-old who's never seen boobs. I don't care at this point. I need to go. I throw my jeans on, a bra, and a big gray hoodie out of my bag.

"Going commando?" Nathan raises an eyebrow as I slide on my canvas shoes.

"Yeah, now you have something to think about at your family breakfast." I wink and his face turns bright red. I run over and peck him on the cheek. "See you later." I run out the door and down to the cafe. I swing the door open and there stands Larry.

"Have a fun night?" Larry winks and shoots a single finger gun, gesturing with the stump of his other arm.

"Shut up. Is Lisa here?" I ask Larry and he nods timidly. Something like concern passes over his face, and I wonder if Cici or Charles filled him in on whatever happened yesterday. He at least knows Lisa from Dad's wedding. He gives me a weird smile and I don't like the energy at all. I have always felt like Larry could see into my soul, and right now it feels like he can see way too much.

I walk through the kitchen doors and my eyes meet Lisa's gaze. She's dressed in a white turtleneck and light blue skinny maternity jeans, the fabric panel peeking out from under her white sweater. She looks at me quizzically, glancing behind me to the kitchen door. Even tilting her head like a confused puppy. I'm not quite sure why.

Wait. She's probably wondering why I'm coming through the kitchen. What if she asks? What should I say?

Lisa's face spreads into a huge smile as I walk around the counter to her. She steps toward me like she might hug me, and I freeze, causing her to stop mid step and drop her arms. But her smile never fades.

"Good morning, Catherine! Thank you for meeting me for coffee this morning, I love this little shop so much. I wish we had one like it in Georgia."

"Well, sadly, Larry is only one person. I think." I look over my shoulder at the shaggy haired man behind the counter. The speed with which he makes drinks is amazing given that he only has one hand. I'm not sure how he does so many things so fast. Maybe there really is more than one of him.

"Should we order?" Lisa's smile still hasn't moved an inch on her face and I'm starting to worry for her health.

"Yeah, let's go up." Larry already has my order done when I step up to the counter, and Lisa orders a decaf coffee that is mostly cream.

"Let's go sit by the window! Then we can look out at campus. It's such a pretty day." *Shit, Lisa is a morning person, too*. We walk over to the window booth and cram into it. I take one side and she takes the other.

"So," Lisa says after the silence is apparently too much for her. "How do you like working at the bar?"

My head still feels groggy, and I take a big drink of my coffee before answering. "I like it a lot there. I get along with all of my coworkers,"-*obviously*- "and the bar is always fun even if it's a little busy."

"That's good, that's good."

Another long uncomfortable silence settles over the table.

"Catherine," Lisa starts, looking up at me. The smile has finally fallen from her mouth and now I'm slightly surprised to see exhaustion filling her eyes.

"Your dad–"

I hold up my hand. "Don't you think he should be having this conversation with me instead of you? I mean, I didn't have a fight with you."

"I know, and your father does want to talk to you. But–"

"But nothing, Lisa. This isn't all my fault." I cut her off again.

We both stare at each other, unblinking. The cafe is bustling around us, but our little booth seems to be soundproof because none of it penetrates the tension between us.

Lisa finally breaks eye contact and looks around uncomfortably, as if trying to see if people care enough to listen in on our conversation. Out of habit, I follow her gaze around the small coffee shop, and as I'm turning toward the counter, Nathan emerges from the back kitchen, my keys and phone in hand.

He sees me and gives a small uncomfortable smile as he makes his way around the counter to us. My heart starts to pound and a voice in the back of my head starts screaming for Nathan to *Stop! Stop! Stop!* It doesn't make it to my face though because he continues toward us, with that awkward smile frozen on his mouth until he is standing at the head of our table.

"Good morning." He nods his head respectfully at my pregnant stepmother.

The smile that I'm coming to hate already appears instantly back on her face. "Good morning!"

Nathan turns to me, sliding something across the table to rest next to my left hand. "Here, it's the spare key to the apartment if you finish before I'm back. That way you can just let yourself in." He pauses and stares at my keys in his hand. I know what he's going to ask before he does.

My face grows hot, and I shoot a quick look at Lisa from the corner of my eye. She's turned into a statue, only her eyes darting between the two of us. She's still sporting that sickly sweet smile, but it's starting to droop at the edges like maybe her facade is melting.

"Okay, thank you, and take the car in case you need it again today." My voice sounds squeaky as I take the key and shove it into my front pocket.

"Alright," Nathan says, finally tuning into the awkwardness of everything and the pile of tension building between Lisa and me. "I'm going to head to my mom's. The Alverezes will be pissed if I'm late."

He gives me a slight little wink before heading toward the door.

When I look back at Lisa, her face reminds me of a loading computer screen, blank except for her eyes, which are full of so many emotions. I take a deep breath, trying to mentally prepare for the shitstorm that's about to explode.

"Is that Oscar's son?"

Here we go.

"Yes."

More wheels turning in her mind. "I didn't know you were seeing anyone."

"This is what we are going to fixate on?" I can't keep the annoyance out of my voice. Taking another sip of coffee, I settle back in my seat, waiting for everything to click into place.

"How long have you guys been seeing each other?" Lisa's face brightens slightly like she's actually excited about this. "Is this where you went yesterday? Do you stay with him often? You guys aren't living together, right? I thought you still lived with Amber." She pushes her coffee out of the way. "Are you making good choices?"

Something inside of me snaps, and a whoosh of blood rushes to my face. "Stop."

"I mean, I'm just making sure you know what you're doing. His dad did just die."

"Lisa." My voice shakes a little and I have to take a deep breath to try and calm myself. Unlike earlier, the coffee shop now feels overwhelmingly loud and I can barely hear my own thoughts. "You are not my mom. I don't think you have any right to ask questions about my life."

Lisa sits back in her chair like she's been slapped. From this angle she looks as if her belly might swallow her petite figure.

"First, you come here to talk to me about my dad being an asshole, now you're going to lecture me for staying with a friend when I had literally NOWHERE ELSE TO GO?" My entire body feels like it's on fire, and my vision is going blurry around the edges. "AND the only reason I had to call Nathan is because you guys showed up, unannounced, to the last safe place I had!"

I slump against my seat and close my eyes, trying to ground myself. Lisa is silently staring at me when I open them again, her eyes misty with tears. I fight back the urge to roll my eyes because even after all of this, she is still the one who's hurt that I'm upset.

"I don't pretend to be your mother," she says quietly, each word punching me in the gut. "You made it very clear from the beginning that I had no real place in your life. So, I've left you alone. That doesn't mean that I don't want a relationship with you."

I exhale the breath I didn't know I was holding in. "But it's not about that now. How I was in high school is very different from how it is now. My mom literally abandoned me. I was a hurt kid. You and Dad gave up on me a long time ago. Whether or not you guys believe it, you did. You tried once or twice and never again. Do you know what it's like to have every adult around you leave you? Then you guys made me leave for Georgia, forcing me to leave my friends and Cici, the only one who gives a shit. Then you had another kid and I completely disappeared. We never had time for a relationship because any time I needed you, you were busy with your other kid. I was going through a crisis, and you were too busy with a toddler. I would come back to hide, and I would feel like I was in the way because I disrupted your schedule. Every time I made an effort to reach out, or ask for help, you guys never saw it as anything more than a stupid juvenile fight between a newly engaged couple."

"Catherine."

I hold up my hand, stopping her because I'm not done. Now that I've started, I can't stop. "Before you say that you guys didn't know, or that I didn't tell you how bad things were, how was I supposed to tell you when I couldn't even count on you for the small things? Even if it was a stupid fight, you were never on my side. You didn't see the signs. Do you remember that Christmas after we got engaged? We had dinner at our new apartment, and you commented continually about how thin I looked? Do you know he did that to me? Do you know how much he starved me? Do you have any idea that every time I came back to your place upset, it wasn't a stupid little fight? I had endured hours of being screamed at and having things thrown at me, only to be told by you guys that I disrupted your *schedule*?"

I drag in a deep breath, feeling like I'm surfacing water for the first time. My head is pounding. Lisa is sitting, silent tears streaming down her face.

"You know, the night that I left him, the night that I finally got away, he had nearly broken a glass over my head? It missed me by inches. And I was so relieved that for once his aim was bad. I was terrified for my life. And honestly, I thought about coming to you guys, but instead I went to the airport. I came to the only place I could think to go. Because I knew if I showed up and told you guys that I ended things, Dad would have been so upset. You would have been upset that I would have had to move back in with you. You both would have sat me down–just like you had done before–and told me to hear him out. You would have let him into your house to talk to me. I would have disrupted your precious schedule again, and you couldn't have that. You wouldn't have listened, you would have pushed me right back. So I came to Cici.

"I can't help that you guys are mad that I didn't call you. I didn't feel like I could call you. If I'm being really honest, I didn't think you guys deserved to know any-thing about my life. It wouldn't have made a difference. You would have thought I was making a bad choice, or Dad would have called Marcus like he did in the past and convinced me to go back. I couldn't risk it."

Lisa sits there absolutely dumbfounded. "I don't know what to say…"

"There is nothing for you to say. I think breakfast is over, honestly," I say, disheartened. I know she will relay what I've said to my dad. But I wanted to say it to him myself. "I have work tonight, so I'm going to go. See you later, Lisa."

I stand up and walk away from Lisa. She sits quietly. I don't bother to turn and see her reaction. I just don't care.

I swing open the kitchen doors and climb the stairs. I fumble with the keys in the door to the loft. Tears start to well up in my eyes in frustration. Frustration with Lisa, frustration with my dad, and frustration with these "FUCKING KEYS!" I yell. Finally, I get the door open.

"YOU OKAY?" Larry shouts up the steps.

I slam the door. I don't want to be bothered. *Well, Larry didn't do anything wrong.*

I creek open the door. "NOT REALLY!" and slam it again.

Thirteen

Nathan

I pull up to my mother's home and cars line the street. A space behind Sofia's SUV is left for me. I am not ready for this. The man of the family always gets the spot closest to the door. It was that way for my dad and his father before him. Just like me, my dad is the only boy amongst the four siblings. Unlike me, he's the youngest.

I know that the house is stuffed to the brim with both the Alvarez and Perez family here together to mourn. I step out of my car. The front porch is filled with smoke with all my tios and tias smoking outside. Sofia stands, her arms crossed with a cigarette hanging out of her mouth at the top of the steps as I approach.

"*¿Dónde has estado? Está super tarde!*" My sister sneers at me. I don't use Spanish in my daily life like Sofia, so it takes a moment to process. She's asking me where I was and that I'm super late.

"*Mami* told me nine and it's 8:30." I start to scale the stairs, ignoring my sister's glare and refusing to make eye contact because that'd just be an invitation for a fight.

"*¿Hablas en serio? Todo el mundo sabe que llegas dos horas antes para ayudar a prepararte para un velorio.*" *Are you serious? Everyone knows you arrive two hours early to help prepare for a wake.* **She snaps at me.**

"I'm sorry." I ignore her and walk through the smog of cigarette smoke, trying to hold my breath.

My tios stand gathered around the broken screen door discussing who should fix it and who would do a better job.

"*EY GORDITO!*" the five men shout in unison. The first to grab me is my Tio Juan Rodriguez, my Tia Sofia's husband. A plump gray-haired man, he pulls me down into a hug kissing me on the cheeks. I plaster a smile on my face, trying my best to not cringe as the older men crowd around me.

"*¿Cómo estás Gordito?*" *How are you, little fat boy?* Juan states, then steps back. "*Bueno supongo que ya no eres gordo.*" *Well, I guess you're not so fat anymore.*

"*Es un poco grosero, pero está bien.* Good to see you, Nathan. Sorry it's been so long." *That's a little rude but okay.* My Tio Rodger gives his brother-in-law a look. Rodger Denver is my Tia Marta's third but longest husband of fifteen years. His mother goes to the same Catholic Church as my parents and abuelos do. His father is whiter than a piece of paper, though. I remember the elderly man. He'd sit through services, nodding along when he didn't understand a single word of Spanish.

My other three uncles return to bickering over the screen door. Nathan Perez, whom I'm named after, is Mami's older brother and thinks he can fix it. Mami's younger brother, Francisco Perez, or 'Tio Frank' seems to be the one saying they should just buy a new one. Then Tia Ana's husband Jose stands there nodding along, pretending to be in agreement with both men at once.

"Hey guys, excuse me! Gotta get in there." The five men part and let me through.

I swing open the door and the smell of fresh conchas fill my heart and lures me in. I pass multitudes of cousins watching Sunday football. Carlos, my sister's husband, stands screaming at the Philadelphia Eagles while holding the infant, Angel. Oscar Jr., Catarina, and Armando scream at the TV along with their dad. Marta's youngest son, Nick, is sitting on the far end of the couch with his laptop out, talking to my cousin Maria who is Tia Ana's oldest daughter. They both have a few years on me, and I'm surprised to see them here. Maria lives in Philly with her husband and three kids. They're crammed on the floor in front of Catrina and Armando. I can never remember their names. Nick only lives about an hour away, but he's never around. Last I heard my dad say, he was running a smoke shop that he bought with a few of his friends.

I look to my left into the dining room. My sisters Lucia, twenty-four, and Nadia, eighteen, are setting the larger table. Lucia is in a tight black dress that looks like she could wear it on a night out. Lucia's hair is done into a tight bleached blonde ballerina bun. Her lipstick is done in an elegant red. She lives on campus but is home almost as much as I am. Whenever I can't keep an eye on Amaya she normally does.

Nadia is in black skinny jeans and a white button up blouse, her jet-black hair pulled back into a tight ponytail. Unlike Lucia, she doesn't wear much makeup. She says it's because there's no point since she can't apply it without her coke bottle glasses and she refuses contacts.

Amaya, the youngest at eight, sets the kids' table. Her hair is done much like Lucia's and is in a little black dress to match. Since they went and picked up Lucia's twin, Andria, they probably got matching outfits. With Mami working so much to make ends meet, and Sofia having her own kids to handle, Amaya spends most of her time between Lucia and me.

Nadia looks up and sees me. "Nathan!" She runs over and hugs me tight.

Lucia follows suit. My two younger sisters embrace me. They both let out sighs of relief and shed a few tears, I hold them tightly, holding back my own emotions. I know they are hugging me tightly to hold onto the memory of Dad, whose shoes I am supposed to fill. More weight added to my shoulders. I take in a deep breath to rally my strength and resist the urge to weep along with them. Amaya looks up and makes eye contact with me. She smiles and waves a little wave and goes back to what she was doing.

"How are you? Sofia is being a fucking drama queen," Lucia groans.

"You need to reign her in. Dad's not here to do it and Carlos is too whipped to tell her to chill out." Nadia nods in agreement with Lucia.

"Yeah, I noticed she's a little high-strung right now. I will talk to her when I have a chance." I will just avoid any chances to do that as long as possible. "We're all exhausted and a little over emotional."

"Well, we need to finish up. Mariposa is in the kitchen. I have no clue where Andria is at." Lucia gestures towards the kitchen.

"Don't touch anything unless you wanna get your hand smacked by Marta. She's extra fiery today." Nadia rubs her hand to let me know she found out the hard way.

I head into the kitchen as the living room cheers for a touchdown. The noise makes my ears ring, adding to my stress. I enter the burnt orange kitchen and the messy peeling linoleum seems even worse with the army of seven women squeezed in cooking huevos rancheros. My three Tias Sofia, Marta, and Ana –Dad's sisters– huddle over the stove. Mami, her two sister-in-laws–Maria, Nathan Perez's wife, and Rita, Tio Frank's wife–sit and roll tamales at the small table in the corner. Mariposa sits on the floor in a plaid black skirt suit straight out of a late nineties movie, peeling potatoes and chopping onions.

She turns to me when I walk into the kitchen and looks at me venomously. "I told them I wanted to hire catering but no. Now I'm sitting on the floor in a three-hundred-dollar skirt suit peeling potatoes. BECAUSE YOU'RE LATE!" Mariposa scowls at me.

"Like I told Sofia, Mami told me nine and I got here at eight thirty. I didn't know coming early was a thing." I defend myself.

"Yeah, cause Dad let you sleep in during his parents' funerals and he did this. So here." She extends the potato peeler to me. "Do your job."

I'm bothered by the awkward symbolism of Dad's job being passed down to me through my angry sister shoving a potato peeler in my face.

"Let me find Andria and hug *Mami* first then I will peel potatoes and chop onions." I Put my hands up like I'm being held at gunpoint.

"Fine but hurry up." Mariposa shakes the peeler at me and goes back to work.

I walk over to Mami. She's dressed in a long black dress and a black cardigan. You'd think she'd be sweating, but Mami is so short and thin. I lean over and kiss her head, wrapping my arms around her too-thin shoulders. I feel like a piece of shit for just realizing how much extra weight she has truly lost over the last few months. She seems so much smaller than I remember.

"*Hola, Mijo,* Andria is out back. Tu Grandpa and Abuela are flying in from Florida tonight please pick them up and drop them here." Mami pats my arm. "Now be a good big brother and check on Andria. She doesn't seem to be doing well."

"*Te amo.*" I kiss the top of Mami's head.

"*Te amo.*" Mami says and goes back to rolling tamales with my tias.

I head out to the back porch where Andria is sitting smoking a joint. Her hair is shaved on both sides but is long enough to flop over to one side, or part down the middle to hide the short hair she wants. She's wearing a large black zip up hoodie, black skinny jeans, and black converse. Her leg is bouncing like it always does when she's anxious. I sit on the stoop down to the backyard next to her, and she extends out the joint to me.

"No thanks. I don't smoke." I am tempted but I don't think I've ever smoked, and the wake is probably not a great place to start.

"Oh, sorry, I thought you'd be just as stressed out as me." Andria withdraws the joint. "The last time I saw Dad was months ago. I never got to say goodbye, Nate."

"I know, but maybe that's a good thing." I wrap my arm around Andria, tucking her against my side. Andria travels around a lot with a group of her friends. They started a band in high school and managed to gain enough traction that they traveled the east coast in the summer, playing events and small venues. She had a free ride for music at Bethton Grove, but she has never been the sit still type. Dad was so proud of her; I think he was immensely proud of all my sisters.

"Why do you say that?" She pulls deep and lets out a cloud of smoke. The skunky smell tickles my nose.

"Because you still called *Papi* at least once a week. You got to see him at his best. You won't have the imprint of his last few days stuck in your brain." I cringe. It seems like every time I close my eyes, I see my father's withered yellow corpse.

"That sounds like it totally fucking sucks," Andria says in a low voice.

"Yeah, it *totally* does." I mimic her to lighten the dark cloud above us.

She smirks and then turns to me with solemn eyes.

"Are you okay?" She takes another long drag and turns to exhale it away from me.

"Yeah sure, I'll figure it out." I smile to reassure her.

"Nate, pal, you suck at lying." She raises her eyebrow at me, judging me as she hits her joint again. I study her face for a moment. She's lost a little weight and you can see all of the holes from her piercings. Sofia probably told her she had to take them out.

"I know. I'm not quite there to talk about it," I confess.

Andria nods understandingly.

"Remember, *Papi* would send us to *Abuelo's* house, and he'd stand right here and shout–" she puts her hands around her mouth like our Papi would to amplify his voice, "–DON'T SEND THEM BACK THIS TIME, *ABUELA!*"

"Yep, then we'd come back, and he'd shake his head and say–"

"Darn you guys are like boomerangs! No matter how many times I throw you out, you come back," we said in unison in his same goofy tone and laugh.

"He was really a great dad." Andria wipes a tear from her eye.

"Yeah, he was." The door slams behind us.

"YOU HAD WEED AND DIDN'T TELL ME!" Mariposa yells at Andria. "Gimme, gimmie." She grabs at the air for the joint.

"And on that note, I have potatoes to peel. *Adios, chicas.*" I stand up, dust off my pants, and head back in as Mariposa takes the joint and takes a massive puff.

Fourteen

Catherine

I feel like a bitch after being short-tempered with Larry and the conversation I had with Lisa. I have wanted to say something for so long to Dad and Lisa, and it feels good to finally get it off my chest, but part of me is so overwhelmed that I don't feel like I can function. I decide to get back into the shower since I didn't have any of my own products last night and my hair feels terrible without conditioner and my detangling spray.

I make quick work of it even though I want to linger, remembering the way Nathan touched me last night and then again this morning. I dry off and rummage through my bag. Luckily, I remembered to bring the bag into the bathroom with me this time. My body aches from not sleeping in my own bed the last two nights, and barely sleeping in general.

I pick out the same jeans I threw on this morning, but change out the sweatshirt for a long sleeve floral print shirt that has a deep 'V' in the front. Since working at the bar and living in Bethton Grove for almost a year, I can tell that my confidence has gotten better. I don't hate the way I look anymore, and most days after applying some mascara and blow drying my hair, I actually like myself. I don't have most of my styling products with me and I don't have a blow dryer, so I settle on letting my hair air dry and steal some of Nathan's pomade that it looks like he's had for the last three years to tame the frizz. It will have to do for now.

I decide to make myself more coffee since I left in such a rush downstairs that I didn't bring it up with me. While the coffee brews, I sit on the floor and check my phone. I send a text to Amber, just checking in, and then send one to Cici to see what time she's going to the bar today. I figure Nathan is probably busy most of the day, and I don't want to chance running into anyone, I might as well go to work early. I haven't gotten to talk to Cici about everything yet, and I miss her so much it hurts. I hate the way we left things yesterday and I just want to fix it. Especially after my blow-up with Lisa, I just need Cici to tell me things will get better.

Once the coffee's done, I refill my cup from this morning and sit back on the floor of the kitchen. I feel numb, my body and brain aren't communicating, and I feel frozen on the floor. My chest is heavy, and it feels like there isn't quite enough oxygen in the apartment.

I hold tightly to the coffee cup, using the heat to ground me back into the present. I want the conversation with Lisa to stop replaying in my head. I needed to say what I did and that's the end of it.

I don't know why I feel so off about it though. I thought that was the conversation I wanted to have, but now I can't help but feel like maybe I've pushed Lisa and Dad too far. They caused so many tiny scratches in our relationship, and eventually all of the small hurt turned into one big painful wound. Like when you snap yourself with a rubber band, at first it just stings for a moment. After snapping it on the same spot repeatedly though, it starts to leave a mark until your skin is red and purple and the mark hurts for days.

I didn't want Lisa to be my mom. By the time Dad brought her around, I didn't need or want a mom anymore. I hoped she would see me. I hoped that she would see through my outbursts and the distance I put between us and fight through it. Now I know that was childish and selfish, but I was a child. I was already hurt, and I was so afraid of her. I think some part of me just wanted a friend in her, I wanted to be able to count on her like I never could with my mom. I didn't know how to ask, I didn't know how to make the first move, and she never really tried.

Maybe we are all to blame for the way things ended up.

My phone vibrates in my lap.

Cici:

I'm heading in at 11. After church crowd will start trickling in around 3. Need to prep for the last day of the weekend.

I text her back that I'm gonna come into the bar as well and then set an alarm on my phone. I don't bother to wait to see if she replies before I decide to climb back into Nathan's bed. I leave my mostly empty coffee cup on the counter. Exhaustion is dragging at my limbs, making me feel heavy and clumsy and I practically tumble under the covers. It's not two minutes before I am asleep.

***

When I wake again, Nathan is over me, his hands dragging lazily down my body as his head dips down to kiss my lips gently.

"I missed you today," he says quietly, dragging my shirt over my head. He makes quick work of the rest of my clothes, too, yanking my pants down my legs until I lay

completely naked under him. He hums his approval as his mouth connects with the bare skin of my chest, directly between my breasts. My breath gets stuck in my throat as his mouth finds my nipples and then works down my body until he is peering up at me from between my legs.

I shudder as the heat from his mouth sends shivers up my thighs.

And then he touches me, my back arching off the bed a little at the wave of pleasure and surprise washes over me.

"I've missed you every day since you quit the library."

Another caress. A soft moan escapes my lips. His palms press my legs further apart and my mouth goes dry.

"Every day that I walked home I thought about finding you. I thought about just ignoring the space you asked for."

A flick of his tongue has me gripping the pillowcase above my head.

***

The sound of the alarm on my phone rattles me from my sleep. I sit up so quickly I feel like I give myself whiplash.

I haven't had many sex dreams about Nathan, but this one leaves me particularly uncomfortable. My pulse still pounds in my ears as I fight through the ache for actual intimacy. I can't count the number of times I touched myself to the memories of him going down on me in his office. Now that we are so close again, it feels like my body and mind are warring with each other. Possibly it's because I'm in his bed and it smells like him, or maybe because for the first time something could actually happen. For a moment I consider sitting in bed the rest of the day. I'm sure if I told Cici that I wasn't feeling up to working she would let me off the hook. I don't know what seems worse. Sitting in Nathan's apartment where all I can think about is him while he's dealing with the death of his dad, or going into work and having the mandatory therapy session she's going to give me. I just hope more than anything that I don't run into my dad.

I almost forget to lock the door behind me when I leave, but at the last second I turn around and grab the key. I'll probably need to let myself in later. I send Nathan a quick text, just telling him that I have to work but don't close tonight, so I'll be back after the rush is over.

The steps creak under my feet as I make my way down to the kitchen. Larry is standing in the back of the kitchen by the freezer, using his one good hand to scoop mounds of dough out of a giant stand mixer. He gives me a crooked smile as I wave at him.

"Sorry I yelled at you earlier," I say timidly, not because I'm worried that I offended him, but because I hate the person that I feel like I become when some of my family is around. Although, now I feel even more like shit because I'm starting to realize that maybe a big part of what's going on is my doing.

Larry shrugs and motions to a plate of small chicken salad sandwiches sitting out on the counter. "It's alright, my dear. Take some sandwiches with you. You can't fight your battles on an empty stomach."

I take two of the small sandwiches and give him a weak smile. He wipes the dough off his hand and comes over to me, sliding his good arm around my shoulders in a sort of side hug.

"I know things aren't ideal right now. They can't stay like this forever. Things will pan out as they are supposed to."

I nod as Larry kisses my forehead endearingly and pushes me toward the door that leads to the cafe. "I'll see ya later," he calls after me.

With a handful of food, a sort of good nap, and some reassurance from Larry, I feel much more prepared to handle the rest of the day.

It's a little less than a block to Cici's Pub and I walk slowly, enjoying the cool afternoon air and the sandwiches on the way. The sign is still dark, but the door is open as I step inside, looking around for Cici.

I can see the light of her office in the back and that's where I head first. She's sitting inside behind her desk looking over delivery receipts as I step in. My aunt looks up at me and smiles. The warmth on her face makes me want to curl up in a chair and tell her everything.

"Hey," I say quietly, trying to return her smile the best that I can.

"How was breakfast with Lisa?" She looks at me over her coke-bottle glasses, raising one eyebrow at me. She has a cut up black shirt with a faded Kiss logo, and her gray hair is just as curly and unruly as ever. She looks effortlessly grunge with her smoked out black eyeliner and maroon lipstick.

I roll my eyes and plop down in a chair in the corner of her office. "It was pretty much a disaster. I think I made it twenty whole minutes. I just don't understand who she thinks she is. She actually tried to lecture me on my life choices!"

"Yikes! She texted me that it was a bust." Cici flips through some papers.

"She texted you?" I'm worried about what Lisa could have said. She's never spoken ill of me before. I wasn't exactly the kindest either.

"I texted her. She didn't say anything except that it didn't go how she hoped."

Cici doesn't flinch. She shoves aside whatever papers she's been looking at and folds her arms on her desk.

Since it's been eating at me all morning, I bring up what I said to Lisa this morning. "I sort of lost my cool this morning. Lisa was prying into where I was staying since I wasn't at the apartment, then had the audacity to ask me if I'm making good choices. Like she was my mom or something. I went off on her."

Cici sits back in her chair, appraising me in a way that always makes me want to keep talking. But I'm spent, and explaining more would be explaining where I'm staying. It's not that I want to keep it from Cici, but I also have no idea how she will react to the information even though I'm pretty sure she already has an idea and she's patiently waiting for me to tell her.

"You're how old again? Sorry, Catherine, but throwing a tantrum over Lisa trying to have a relationship with you sounds like you are in the wrong," she says plainly, sitting back in her office chair.

"Seriously?"

"Seriously." She pauses and pins me with a look. I'm reminded of the way I felt in Nathan's apartment.

I sigh very begrudgingly and play with a small hole in my jeans. "I think you may be right. I know that I reacted poorly. I just don't know what to do anymore. I don't know what to expect from them and I don't know what they expect of me. I feel like I've been fighting for so long and now it's my first reaction."

Cici nods slowly, "Have you thought about asking Lisa? Or telling her what you want?"

"I just don't know what I want. I know they're my family, but it doesn't feel like it anymore. But, when they showed up yesterday and Lisa was pregnant, and Bailey Mae was so big… I hated that I felt like an outsider."

Cici stays quiet, and after a few minutes I feel the need to fill the silence again.

"I don't want her to be my mom. I never wanted her to be my mom. Sometimes I think I'm afraid if I let her and Dad in at all, something will happen and they'll leave me again like Mom did."

We sit in silence, my revelation bouncing around the room like an echo.

We seem to be in a little bit of a stare off. I expected her to have more to say and the silence is making me uncomfortable.

Finally, she shifts, resting her elbows on the desk in front of her. "Where are you staying?" she asks, looking at me skeptically.

I take a deep breath. "Nathan's."

There's uncomfortable silence around us, as she gives me a hard look, her red-painted lips forming a thin line of contemplation.

"Did I miss something?"

"I told you we reconnected. I was going to tell you about it yesterday, but we got interrupted. Where else did you want me to go?" My tone sounds clipped and rude even to my own ears, so I clear my throat. "It's not quite what it seems like."

"Yeah, I get that. Once again Kitty needs to be *rescued*. Don't you think maybe right now should be about Nathan? You *could* stay at *your* apartment. It'd be awkward but you *could*. It's your house. You *could* stay with *me*, but you don't want to because your dad's there, so let's get that straight. You have places to go. Don't pretend you don't. You are choosing to stay with Nathan. Because you want to escape your problems and make his problems worse."

"That's not it at all. You're being unfair." I defend myself.

My aunt takes a deep breath, and I think she's fighting for control. I haven't seen Cici like this before, and it's a bit jarring. But then I remember she's grieving a friend, too, and is very protective of the people she cares about. "Then why don't you tell me about it now."

I spend the next five minutes telling her about our weird chance meeting the other night, and how I accidentally fell asleep in his apartment, and how I was there when Oscar passed.

Cici stays quiet even after I finish, and I hate that I can't tell what she's thinking. "I understand, I just want to make sure you aren't using him as a scapegoat. He's going through enough of a mess right now without having to help you too."

"What the hell." I pause, taking a deep breath trying to regulate myself.

"That came out wrong. Catherine, I get it you don't want to have a relationship with your dad. You don't want to make Mariposa uncomfortable or don't want to upset Amber. And maybe I don't understand your relationship with him. I guess I thought you had moved on from all of that already. I'm just worried you both are using each other and are going to end up hurt. And I care for both of you deeply and don't want to see that."

"You think I'm *using* him? Cici, this is me we are talking about! He reached out to me! I get that our timing is shit, but the other night was a chance. How was I supposed to know everything would go up shit creek so fast?"

"He came to you conveniently when his life is falling apart, and you're really going to take that at face value, that it's just coincidence?"

"Why can't it be a coincidence? This has nothing to do with that. I care about him, and neither of us can really help the timing."

"What is this? A romance novel? You most definitely can help the timing." Cici's stern tone feels like hail on my skin. It pelts me relentlessly, cold and hard.

"You don't understand," I say breathlessly. The rage from the last few days is building behind my eyes, but it feels as if I can't actually get it out. "Maybe we can help the timing, but I really think you're overreacting to this. I'm not using him, and he's not using me. I understand and appreciate your concern, but I really think you are being unfair. I understand that you are stressed and grieving too. I understand that I left you in a shitty position with my dad and Lisa, I really do." I soften my tone, trying to convey all of my own mixed-up emotions in the midst of this. "But I also need you to understand that this doesn't feel like a choice. This feels like a contin-uation of what we had before. I know that you aren't a fan of it, I know you aren't a fan of his family all the time, but this is still my life and my feelings, and since you aren't a mind reader, I really think it's best if you don't make assumptions because they're just going to hurt us both."

Cici is quiet for a long time, and I think for a while that maybe I've pushed someone else too far again. But I can't back down. I don't want to. I want her to understand me. I want her to see everything with an open mind even if she's not a huge fan of the situation.

"None of us like the situation we are currently in, and we are all trying to make the best of what we've been given."

"That boy is head over heels for you and has been for months. He asks me about you whenever he has the chance," she says quietly. "I don't think I like it very much, but you're right, it's not my situation to handle. I'm not trying to make Nathan's or your life harder. I just hope that everything turns out how you want and not the way I keep envisioning it."

I stand to my feet now, taking a step toward Cici's desk. "He and I have ALWAYS been on the same page. He knew I needed time. Time and space didn't mean I was moving on. I never said I was moving on. We met up before Oscar passed. We didn't know he would go that same night. Just because I distanced myself to get my shit together does not mean that I haven't been wanting him. That I haven't thought about him every day since I walked out of the library."

"I'm just trying to protect you both. This is a sensitive time–"

"You don't think it's a sensitive time for me too?" I cut her off. My hands are shaking so I ball them into fists at my side. "You blindsided me, Cici! You have your own agenda like always. You really want to say that I consistently put people in positions to help myself, but what about you? I don't believe for one second that you didn't see my needing to escape to your house as the perfect opportunity to put me and Dad in the same room again. You KNEW what you were doing."

Cici puts her hands on her face and takes a few meditative breaths. "I'm sorry,

I'm not trying to attack you. I did know your dad was coming, I was planning to say something when you came over. Talk about it and make a plan…but my brain fell to pieces once you said Oscar was gone. He is… was very important to me. I didn't tell you about your dad because you can be… explosive and self-destructive. I'm worried about you. I'm worried about Nathan. I can't trust you to not lose it again and book it. If you do, what is Nathan supposed to do? How are you supposed to fix things with your dad?"

"Maybe you should have talked to me first before making plans alone. I understand I blindsided you as well, I know everyone is struggling right now. I am not running off. This is my home now. It always has been. I don't want to leave Bethton Grove. I know I'm still coming into myself, but I am in a good enough place that I'm not going to run at the first signs of a messy situation. I don't want to be that person anymore. Lisa barely sees me as a person, and Dad doesn't see anything that makes him fucking uncomfortable. I have been trying for months to avoid this exact situation because of what happened."

"I don't believe I have to consult you, Catherine, with my plans since you don't live with me anymore. If that chain of events didn't happen the way it did, I would've been able to handle it more appropriately." She takes in a deep frustrated breath. "You have barely given your dad and Lisa a chance," Cici retorts. "You're an adult now. You are responsible to deal with your own shit before you make someone else pay for it."

"I gave them years of chances!" I say quietly, barely containing all of the emotions still bubbling under the surface. "I will tell you exactly what I told Lisa. I gave them every chance. I asked for help as much as I could from them, and they turned me down. Every. Single. Time. They let me drown. That's the whole reason I came here in the first place! Because if I would have gone to them, they would have tried to convince me to go back to Marcus!"

I take a deep, shaking breath. My body is so exhausted I'm starting to feel lightheaded.

"I really thought you understood that."

Cici shakes her head, her eyes glistening with emotion that I don't see often from her.

"I can't help the timing. I have finally found someone who makes me feel safe! For the first time in my life there is somewhere safe to go. Why am I not allowed to have that?"

Cici leans forward over her desk. "Well, that makes me feel great."

"I didn't mean…"

"I know, but your safety is built on his blind need for a distraction from the shitstorm that is his own life. You need to take a step back before both of you end up hurt again. Neither of you deserve that. Love can't be built on uncertainty. That's why you left Nathan after Marcus, because you know that's true and had to solve your own shit first." She sits back in her chair, pulling a little box from her desk. She takes out a joint and lights it, taking a deep drag before saying anything else.

"Kitty, I'm not trying to fight with you, I just want to know your choices aren't healthy for you or Nathan, and it's my job to point out when you're not making well thought-out decisions."

"I appreciate your concern for us, and I understand what you're saying. I just can't blindly listen to you this time. I'm not saying you're wrong, but this is some-thing I need to see through to the end. Because if this is the real thing, I can't lose my chance."

"But, if it's the real thing, it will still be there later," Cici says, taking another hit of the joint.

I have no response to her as she passes me the joint and I take it. I feel just as helpless here with her as I did with Lisa this morning. I take one puff, and exhale, then I hand it back and stand. "I'm going to go organize behind the bar and restock stuff."

She nods quietly, staring past me like the wall full of pictures and old memo-ries are way more interesting than what's happening in front of her.

Charles is behind the bar when I step out of Cici's office, wiping down bar stools, his face is hard, and his eyes are fixed on what he's doing. I know he over-heard everything, between me and Cici, but he's decent enough to stay quiet as I start restocking olives, cherries, and go about changing out boxes of syrup under the soda sprayer.

The day is incredibly long. There are many new faces in the bar tonight, a few of which introduce themselves as Oscar's friends or family, reuniting with each other over beers, talking about the funeral tomorrow and the kind of man Oscar was when he was on the force, or who he is to their family.

It's chaotic trying to keep up with the mix of old and new customers, college kids and regulars. Cici doesn't speak to me again the rest of the night unless it's to ask for help in the kitchen.

I want to be mad at Cici for the conversation we had in her office this morning, but I can't bring myself to hold onto the feelings. We work in mostly comfortable silence, the only thing that indicates there is tension is the lack of joking that normally permeates the bar when my aunt and I work together. I feel the loss deeper than I will ever admit out loud. I don't know what to do after our conversation. So much has happened in such a short period of time. After the first few hours I just tune out all my thoughts and focus on the work. The rest of the night goes by relatively quickly.

At some point Larry walks in and says he's going to take over for me. We meet in the back hallway as I'm grabbing my purse and he's hanging his windbreaker on one of the hooks that's on the wall for employees.

"That key Nathan gave you for the apartment will open the front door of the shop as well," he says quietly.

"Thanks," I mumble back.

He nods and then nudges my shoulder with his nub as he walks past me. There's a small reassuring smile on his face. I think Larry might be the only one on my side right now, and it gives me the smallest amount of confidence as I head back to Nathan's apartment.

Nathan and I will be fine. I'm going to make sure of it. I know that we have a lot to talk about now in light of what Cici said, but I refuse to let it get in the way of Nathan and me figuring things out. This is no longer just some little coincidence, it's our lives, and like I told Cici earlier, I need to see it flush out myself. I need to see it to the end, because the more I think about it, the more I want to fight for what we could have.

FIFTEEN

Catherine

I've been standing outside the door of the apartment for the last minute or so, trying to figure out if I'm going to knock or just use the key. I let myself into the coffee shop, and then locked the door behind me, but it feels weird letting myself into Nathan's apartment while he's here. I know that's the whole reason he gave me the key, but it still feels strange.

Just do it.

I suck in a breath, shoving the key into the lock and turning it. I swing the door open slowly, stepping into the light of the apartment.

You are choosing to stay with Nathan. Because you want to escape your problems and make his problems worse.

Cici's words still sting almost nine hours later. Nathan is standing in the kitchen, unpacking Chinese takeout. When he hears the door, he stops what he's doing, turns, and smiles at me. Butterflies come to life in my stomach.

"I didn't know if you'd eaten, so I picked up some stuff for dinner." He holds up the white and red take-out boxes. "I didn't know what you liked, so I got lo mein, orange chicken, fried dumplings, and egg drop soup."

My stomach rumbles because I haven't managed to eat since Larry gave me those sandwiches earlier.

"Shit, all of that sounds amazing." I walk into the kitchen where he's loading a plate with all of the items, then he hands me a little clear plastic container of soup and points toward the little table in the corner.

"Sit. I'll bring the rest over."

My feet are sore from running around like crazy at work, so I don't protest as I take my container of soup and sit so that I can see out the window. Nathan sets a plate down in front of me with a mountain of food and chopsticks shoved into the middle.

"I have forks, too, if you don't use chopsticks." He sits down with his own plate.

"Nope, this is perfect." I pick up my chopsticks and start eating. Everything is still warm, so he must not have gotten home only a few minutes before I did.

For five minutes there is perfect silence. I look at the window absently as we eat, counting cars as they drive by.

"I had to drive out to the airport today to pick up my grandparents, so I filled the car with gas for you."

"You didn't have to do that." When his face looks strained, I add, "I appreciate it, though."

"How was breakfast with Lisa?" Nathan asks between mouthfuls of food.

The deep timber of his voice shakes me out of the trance I was under, and I snap my head to look at him.

When I don't answer immediately, he continues.

"Things seemed pretty tense when I stopped at the table, so I'm assuming it wasn't a great time?"

I sag a bit. "Not even a little. We went from what I think was supposed to be small talk, to her questioning every single life choice I've made in the last five years. Like she even has a right to say anything to me." I'm so talked out I don't even know if I can tell the story. All of the details feel like a hazy mess inside of my head and I really don't want to start crying over dinner.

"How about you? How was breakfast?"

Nathan seems just as eager to talk about his day as I am to talk about mine. His shoulders slump, and he sets down his chopsticks.

"My sisters are not doing well. Mariposa and Sofia are pissed at me, and the twins are taking it really hard. I also have forgotten the chaos that comes with having all of the family around. I'm not sure if this many of us have been in one place since Amaya's christening."

"That must be hard."

"And it doesn't help," he pauses, rubbing one of his hands across his tired eyes, "that everyone keeps insinuating my new place in the family. Like no one knows what to do without asking me first. Because they would have asked Dad, but…" He shrugs.

"I can't imagine. That sounds so stressful."

A sad, slightly uncomfortable silence settles over us. Cici's words from earlier come back to me again and I wonder if Nathan feels like she does, that I'm asking him to pick me, or if I'm just a well-timed distraction.

"Do you think that maybe our timing is off?" I ask quietly. I watch him out of the corner of my eye, opening my soup and taking big spoonfuls to hide the shake in my hands. Part of me hopes he doesn't hear me, but the way his expression changes tells me he does.

"What do you mean?"

"I mean, you don't feel like I'm just using you to escape my own problems, or distracting you from your own family stuff?" I stand, walking into the kitchen with my empty plate and bowl of soup. I feel like I need to put some distance between myself and the situation so that I can protect myself from his response.

"What?" he echoes again, turning in his seat to face me. "Why would I feel like that?"

I shrug helplessly, already hating that I even said anything.

"I don't know. I talked to Cici today, and she made a comment about how she feels like I'm just using us reconnecting as an escape from my family. And she said it was unfair that I'm using you to get out of it. I just wanted to know what you thought. I know we have moved really fast, and I know that our timing sucks. But I don't want you to feel like that about me…" I trail off. I don't recognize the expression that has settled on Nathan's face.

"Cici said that?" He stands, bringing his plate to the kitchen and dropping it into the sink next to mine with a crash. "Do you feel that way?" he asks, turning so we are standing six inches apart. Our height difference makes it so that I have to tilt my head up to look at him. His full lips are pressed tightly together, and his eyes have a cold glint to them that makes my stomach feel really unsettled.

"I don't. That's why I'm asking. I also realize that we haven't had a real conversation about what we are doing. I didn't mean for everything to fall apart so quickly, and I for sure don't want you to think that I'm just hiding here because it's convenient. I wasn't trying to use you…" I take a step back from him.

"I offered for you to stay, and I was never afraid you were using me."

"I know, but I don't want you to feel like you have to choose between me and the situation at hand."

"Why do I have to choose? And who says I even want both?"

My heart starts to beat heavily in my chest, and every thump feels like it shakes my rib cage.

"It's not that." I sigh, turning to lean against the counter. "I mean, you were late to family things because of me. At least one of your sisters is mad at you because of me. You are sharing your space because of me." I tick each item off on my fingers.

Nathan adjusts to stand in front of me, taking my small hands in his big ones. "I was late to family things because I am exhausted and ready for all of this to be over with. My sisters are mad at me for things that have nothing to do with you, and having you in my space has been the best thing that's happened to me in years. I have been living on autopilot for so long, I have forgotten what it feels like to have someone around. I am so grateful that you're here. I don't think I could be in this apartment alone right now… and I honestly hope that you'll consider staying once everything settles again. I feel like I have missed you all of my life, then I had you and ended up having to give you back. I'm not sure I can do it again." He takes an almost predatory step closer to me so that our bodies are pressed together.

All of the air rushes from my lungs, and I have to fight through the lump of emotion that sticks in my throat.

"I don't want you to question my choices based on what's happening around us, just like I never questioned your choice to be here. I gave you the key because I trust you, and for the first time in years, I feel like I'm one hundred percent making the right choice. I have loved you from the beginning, and I don't care what anyone else thinks of what we are doing as long as we are in this together. You make things easier. You make me laugh in a way I haven't before. You make everything seem a little bit more manageable, and I don't want to lose that. Not again."

I freeze. I feel like time slows down around us as I study his face, only finding raw emotions and honesty. His dark eyes burn so much that it threatens to topple me. The trepidation I felt moments ago has been stripped away.

In the next second I am reaching for him, lunging to my tiptoes to wrap my arms around his shoulders, he meets me halfway, his mouth covering mine as he wraps his arms around my waist and holds me against him. One of his hands comes up to tangle in my hair, tilting my head to the side. He slides his tongue along my bottom lip, and I shiver against him. Our bodies become a tangle of limbs and kisses as he hooks his hands around my thighs and lifts me off the ground. I wrap my arms around his neck for support, arching into his body as he kisses my jaw and down my neck. I moan when he reaches the top of my tits and his teeth nip at the skin.

Nathan turns without setting me down and starts to make his way out of the kitchen and toward his bed. My heart is racing as we tumble into the sheets, still wrapped in each other. My hands start fumbling with the buttons down the front of his shirt and he sits up, untucking the shirt and just pulling it over his head. His plain cotton undershirt follows and then he's reaching for me again, pulling me to his lap before yanking my shirt over my head. He kisses my shoulder, running his fingers feather light down my shoulder blades to the clasp of my bra, unhooking it and yanking it from my shoulders. I adjust myself, straddling him better and rocking my hips until I can feel the hard length of his erection pressed between my legs.

My breath catches in my chest at the sensation, and I shudder in excitement. His hands come around to grip my tits, running his thumbs over my nipples. He straightens slightly, taking in the sight of my bare chest and the hunger in his eyes has me biting my lip. I arch into him as the heat of his mouth sends pleasure down my spine and heat coursing through my stomach.

Nathan wraps a strong arm around my waist and flips us on the bed, his body covering mine completely. He kisses my throat and works his way back up to my mouth. He nips my lower lip and slides his hand down the length of my body until he finds the button of my jeans. It's only then that he sits back on his knees, looking down at me as he yanks my jeans down my legs.

I lay there on the bed for a moment, completely exposed to him as his eyes roam every inch of my body. It's not an appraisal, but lust and admiration swirled together. The sound of my own heartbeat in my ears is deafening as I sit up slowly, reaching for his pants. He watches me but makes no move to stop me or help me. I unfasten the button of his pants, slipping them off his hips. I run a hand down his stomach, feeling the way his muscles ripple under his skin at my touch.

Nathan still hasn't moved, and I wonder if he's having second thoughts, or if he's just waiting for some sort of consent. My heart speeds even more as I realize he's waiting for me to decide what I want. I know if I looked at him right now and said no, he would stop, nothing would happen. He's giving me the power to decide how far we go, and something about that small gesture makes me want him even more.

We've waited long enough.

I hook my thumbs into the front of his underwear and start to pull them down. But he suddenly stands out of my grasp, dropping his underwear and his pants all the way to the floor before stepping out of them. Somehow, he seems even bigger than the night before, bare before me. His body is perfect, but he stands almost awkwardly like he doesn't know what I think.

"Come here," I say quietly. My voice doesn't feel like my own.

"You're perfect." His voice is husky and thick with lust.

I lick my lips, heat pooling between my legs. My skin feels like I'm burning up as I reach for him. He kneels on the bed, parting my legs with his knees before he settles over me. As I lay back, he takes my hands, holding them together in one of his above my head. Stretched out before him, I don't feel uncomfortable or insecure. My body aches to have him touch me, see me, kiss me, and I sigh again as he continues his exploration of my body. His lips are demanding, and I feel blinded by the anticipation of what's to come.

His hand finds its way between my legs, his thumb brushing over the sensitive bundle of nerves. I can't hold back my gasp as his thumb traces lazy circles around my clit.

Nathan moans against my mouth as his fingers trace farther down.

"God, you're already so wet." He groans against my neck, and I shudder.

He still hasn't released my hands and his fingers are sending fire up my spine, making me feel crazy with need.

"Please," I beg quietly. I wiggle my wrists from his grasp, and wrap my arms around his shoulders, holding him against me as I lift my legs around his hips. "I'm ready."

He lets out a husky groan against my neck, bringing himself closer to me. His breath is hot against my cheek as he lifts himself on his elbows and so slowly sinks into me. We both exhale simultaneously as if we've been holding our breath for days. His eyes meet mine as he settles into me, pausing so that my body can adjust to the size of his cock.

"Are you okay?" His voice waivers slightly as if he can barely contain his own need.

I nod because I don't trust myself to speak. He painstakingly withdraws and slides back in, creating a slow sort of rhythm as we get used to each other. Reaching up I kiss him softly, holding on as he picks up the pace.

His breathing becomes more ragged, and I can feel my body tightening around him as pleasure envelopes me. His kisses are gentle against my lips, and the way he cups the back of my head in one of his hands makes me feel protected and cherished. My heart swells and I cling to him tightly.

He pushes up on one arm, finding my clit with the other hand, and starts circling it again. My back lifts off the bed as I throw my head back moaning, tension building between my legs and in my stomach, threatening to burst at any second.

But then Nathan withdraws and I gasp at the empty feeling.

"I have to know," he murmurs into my neck.

"Know what?"

He's moving down my body and I think I might die. My skin is burning as he grips my thighs with both of his hands and buries his face between my legs. I don't know what to do with my hands as they fly over my face to stifle the moan that tears through me. Waves of pleasure run up and down my spine, but I'm too close and I can't slow the orgasm. I feel like I have no control over my body. I bury my fingers in Nathans's hair, but he doesn't move, and I am helpless to do anything as another overwhelming wave of pleasure hits me.

"You taste just as good as I remember." The lust-addled sound of his voice makes me shiver. I lean up wrapping my arms back around him and kiss his throat. I feel the way his breath catches as he slides back into me.

His pace is faster this time, and my breath comes in short, ragged gasps. He groans when he reaches between my legs again and my body clenches around him. His eyes close when I lean up to kiss him, locking my fingers in his hair. And just like that I feel my body prickle with heat again, another orgasm building at the base of my spine. I want to scream, I want to tell him to keep going, but I can't get my mouth to work. I can't form coherent thoughts or do anything but cling to him.

As if Nathan can tell how close I am, he picks up his pace even more, matching each stroke with his fingers. I cry out as he presses into me, my orgasm crashing into my body with unexpected force. He drops his face to my neck again, not slowing his pace as I squirm underneath him, unable to control the spasms of pleasure shooting up my spine. He groans once, the vibration shaking me to my core a few moments later, pressing his face into my shoulder as his body shivers from the force of his own orgasm.

I grip him tightly, lying with my eyes closed as we catch our breath. Neither of us seems to be able to move at the moment, and the weight of his body over me is like a balm to the rawness I feel. Relief mixes with emotions I don't have the ability to name at the moment, filling my stomach and chest as I breathe in and out.

Eventually he slides out, rolling to the side, pulling me with him. We lay facing each other, his hand draped protectively over my hip, the other resting beneath my head.

"Are you okay?" There's a hint of worry in his voice, but I just lean forward, cupping his cheek in my hand and kissing him.

"More than okay," I whisper.

A tender smile pulls at his mouth as we lay there together. My limbs feel heavy, and my eyes are starting to sting with exhaustion.

"I'm so tired all of a sudden," I say quietly, rolling into him.

He shifts, dragging me with him so I have to scoot back to stay against his chest, and he rolls us so that we are right on the bed, my head resting on a pillow.

"We should get some sleep." His voice is muffled by my hair as he wraps me into his arms. "Big day tomorrow."

I sigh against his chest. The old familiar anxiety about our situation settling back in. I'm too exhausted to pay much attention. Nathan's breathing is steady and deep, lulling me into a sort of haze between awake and asleep.

I have loved you from the beginning.

His words echo around in my head as sleep starts to sink in.

"I love you too," I say quietly, and the last thing I remember before falling asleep is Nathan's arms tightening around my body as he settles in for sleep as well.

SIXTEEN

Nathan

I wake to my face pressed against smooth, warm skin. Catherine is curled on her side facing away from me and my cheek is pressed to her back in between her shoulder blades. Images from the night before flash before my eyes when I close them and inhale deeply. She still smells like vanilla and citrus, and it's intoxicating. Her breathing is shallow and consistent.

My alarm goes off on the bedside table, and I groan as I roll to turn it off. Catherine doesn't even stir as I shift away from her, checking my phone to see if I've missed anything. There's one text from Sofia saying that I better be at Mami's at eleven so that we can drive to the church together. My heart beats harder as I set my phone back down and roll over to pull Catherine against my body.

Catherine stirs when I press myself against her, kissing her back right at the base of her neck. She rolls toward me, not opening her eyes. There's a small sigh as she settles back into my chest. I am hit once again by how beautiful she really is. Her lashes are long and dark, touching her cheeks when her eyes are closed, and her lips are full and slightly parted as she breathes deeply. Her hair is splayed out on the pillow behind her and drapes across my arm. I run my hand up her thigh and hip, savoring the way her warm skin glides under my fingers. There's a light dusting of freckles on her shoulders and her cheeks that I don't think I've ever really noticed before, like constellations on her skin.

For the first time in so long, a small amount of peace settles in my chest. I am confident in the choice I'm making to pursue this woman. Now that she is here, and she trusts me, I decide I will do whatever it takes to keep her with me.

I won't let her go again.

I press a soft kiss to her forehead and carefully slide my arm out from under her head and slip from the bed. She immediately rolls to her stomach, taking the spot that my body was just in, and sighs. I push the hair off her forehead and kiss her once more before heading to the bathroom to shower.

The water shakes me awake the rest of the way as I wash the sleep from my face. I am scrubbing my hair when the bathroom door opens a bit and some cool air rushes in.

"Want company?"

"I don't think I could say no even if I tried." I slide the door open for her as she steps into the warmth of the shower. "How did you sleep?" I ask, reaching to position the showerhead so that she can step into the hot spray.

"Better than I have in days." She smiles timidly.

"Me, too."

We are silent as she wets her hair. I watch her grab her shampoo, her back to me so I can see her ass perfectly as she bends at the hips to reach for the bottle. Blood rushes to my dick at the thought of placing my hand on her back, sliding into her from this position, and I swallow hard.

"So," she says, turning to face me as she washes her hair. Her tits sway slightly as she scrubs her scalp, and I can't keep my eyes from roaming her body. As if she senses it, a small smile quirks the corners of her lips. "Eyes up here." She tilts her head and giggles a little.

"Sorry, what?" My entire body feels hot and bothered, but I straighten.

"Today, do I need to take you straight to the church, or are you going to your parents' first?"

"Sofia texted me this morning. We are all meeting at Mom's house so that we can go to church together."

"What time is that going to be?"

"I think we are meeting at eleven. But that means I really need to be there by ten or ten-thirty."

Catherine nods, turning her back to me as she again tilts her head back to rinse her hair and then bends again to pick up another bottle of stuff. I was finished with my shower when she got in with me. I'm just enjoying the heat and marveling at the way she looks soaking wet.

"I'm going to hop out," I say after a moment, unsure of the time. Anxiety is creeping in, and I feel the pressure of getting things done on time. I also desperately need coffee.

"Okay, I'm almost done," she says over her shoulder.

Stepping into the cold air of the bathroom, I towel off quickly, then wipe the mirror down so that I can brush my hair back into a pathetic-looking bun.

I really need a haircut. I kick myself for not seeing if Meghan could squeeze me in yesterday before the funeral. I walk into my sort of bedroom, picking out black slacks and a black button-down shirt and a black blazer. The outfit isn't totally unusual for me, but I hate the idea of wearing all black today of all days. I lay the blazer on the bed and walk into the kitchen to make coffee. Opening the tiny fridge, I realize the only thing I have for breakfast is cold Chinese food or frozen waffles. Neither sound appealing today, but as I'm contemplating which is the lesser of two evils, Catherine emerges from the bathroom.

Her hair is wet, and her face is clean of makeup. She's wearing a black skirt that hits right at her knee and hugs every inch of her curves in a mouthwatering way. She has a deep purple shirt that has a skimpy piece of lace half-covering her cleavage.

I almost drop the coffee creamer as I straighten to get a better look at her. She smiles, walking toward me, and I can feel my face heat as I stare, but I can't look away.

"You made coffee? My hero." She places her hand over her head dramatically, pretending to swoon, and I laugh.

"I was just trying to decide if frozen waffles or leftover Chinese go better with it."

"Always waffles." She reaches into the cabinet above the coffee pot, takes two coffee cups down, and then takes the creamer from my hand. Pouring us each a cup, I'm overtaken again by the urge to rip all her clothes off right here. I really need to get control of myself because I can't be late today, and I also can't walk around a funeral with my dick straining against my zipper. I take two calming breaths and pull the waffles from the freezer.

"I'm going to go do my makeup," she says, walking back toward the bathroom. Her hips sway and my mouth feels dry. She throws a dazzling smile over her shoulder like she knows I am staring, and I take a long drink of my coffee to hide my embarrassment. The burning liquid does the trick and snaps my brain back out of the fog.

The waffles pop in the toaster behind me, and I butter one, sprinkling it with cinnamon sugar because I don't have syrup. I walk to the bathroom door and lean against the frame. Catherine is putting something shiny on her cheeks. I can't remember if it's highlighter or bronzer, but it makes her glow a soft pink, and when she turns her head, it sparkles slightly.

"Your waffle." I hand it to her on a napkin that came with the takeout.

"God, you are so hot." She takes a bite. She's careful not to mess up any of her makeup as she does.

I'm not really sure why her small comment stirs something in my chest. I don't think anyone has ever showered me with so many small compliments or apprecia-tions before and I don't know what to do with all the feelings raging to the surface. I chalk it up to the emotions of today and try for a joke. "So easy to please…" I say, stepping into the bathroom and wrapping my arms around her waist. Some of my control slips and I pull her back against my front and dip my head into the spot between her shoulder and neck, kissing her softly. The way her breath catches is enough to have me reaching up the front of her shirt, running my hands over her stomach.

"Stop that," she says, turning her head to look up at me. "You're going to ruin my makeup." But she's smiling and I don't think she would care if I did. I brush my lips across hers twice before letting her go and stepping back.

Catherine smiles at me through the reflection in the mirror. When she bends forward to brush something through her eyebrows, I can see straight down the front of her shirt in her reflection in the mirror. I bite the inside of my cheek.

"I'll be done in fifteen minutes," she says when she straightens.

"Okay, I'll be in the kitchen." At the last second, I pat her ass twice before stepping back out of the bathroom. I'm rewarded with a giggle as I find my coffee cup and phone. I put another couple waffles in the toaster and once they're done, I settle into the little breakfast nook, absently scrolling through social media until she's done.

When Catherine comes out of the bathroom, I have to lock my jaw to keep it from hitting the floor. "Shit…" I murmur as she refills her coffee.

"What?" She looks puzzled as she sits across from me.

"You are just so beautiful." I scoot around the half circle bench to sit next to her and throw my arm around her shoulder. "Come here often?"

She throws her head back and laughs. If I wasn't sure before, now I am positive that I will spend the rest of the foreseeable future doing everything in my power to hear it.

Then she quiets and turns into me until our knees are touching. "What do you need from me today?"

"What?"

She straightens a little. "What do you need from me today? I don't want to be in the way. Today isn't about me. So, what do you need from me? Do you want me to make friends with any particularly annoying family members and keep them away from you? Do you want me to keep my distance? I just want to know before we get there. I'm not going to be upset or offended if you need some space."

I honestly don't think anyone has ever asked me something like that before. Definitely not anyone in my family, or anyone I've dated before. Emotions surge up my throat again, making it hard to swallow.

"I don't know," I say after a long moment. I honestly don't have an answer.

"Okay, and that's fine. I can totally go with the flow. I just figured I'd ask."

I kiss her softly. "Thank you for asking." I check my phone and sigh. "We should get ready to go…"

***

A half hour later, we are sitting in my mom's driveway. I feel Catherine stare at me while I stare at the house. Sofia walks outside, lighting a cigarette. Catherine squeezes my hand, and my eyes connect with hers like a rabbit outside of a foxhole.

"I guess we should go in," I say, even though anxiety is slowly filling my lungs.

She nods and we get out of the car. Catherine waits for me to circle the car before she follows a step behind me up to the porch.

Sofia's sneer is visible as she takes a long drag from her cigarette. "*Llegas tarde.*"

I roll my eyes. "*Yo, no soy.* We are not late, Sofia. It's ten, and you said eleven."

"*¿Por qué la trajiste aquí?*" She takes another drag.

I do not have the time or the energy to justify Catherine being here with me. I ignore the question because it never should have been asked.

"We are going inside to see *Mami*. I'll talk to you later." I send her a pointed look and take Catherine's hand, pulling her alongside me as we step inside. The house is packed and loud. The family, all dressed in black, are everywhere. Some people are sitting, eating or drinking coffee, and the little kids are running around playing games. All the tias are crowded around my mom, helping her get things done.

All heads turn as the door closes behind us. It's like we hit a pause button as the silence fills the room. The sweat rolls down my neck. I have never brought anyone home besides Carolina. I don't think Catherine and I are what you would consider an 'item' yet. Catherine steps closer to me, almost like she's trying to disappear. Unfortunately, she has become the star of the show.

"CATHERINE!" Amaya breaks the silence. Thank God for Amaya. She comes barreling towards us and it breaks the tension, causing others to move slowly in our direction.

She jumps on Catherine in a big hug. Catherine embraces her warmly, and I can see some of Catherine's nerves being relieved. I can't help but smile as it fills my heart knowing Amaya accepts Catherine. She sets Amaya down and I look up to see the army of nosy family members coming to bombard us with questions. If Dad was here, he'd already have me cuffed to a kitchen chair shining a light in my face, demanding to know my intentions and telling me that I better not be fooling around.

"HOLA! ¡Cual es tu Nombre! ¿Es Novia de Nathan?" Tia Sofia essentially shouts in front of the mass of people congregating in the small entryway.

"I'm sorry. I don't speak Spanish." Catherine smiles, but her voice is sheepish as she looks into the pack of wolves.

"Oh, Los sientos, Gordito." Tia Sofia gestures, implying I should translate.

I smirk. I know this is a bit of a trap, but I have to know. I consider the situation for a second, apologizing for my family's forwardness, but I don't think this is the worst of what it will be like today.

And after last night, I really need to know where Catherine stands.

"She said, 'What's your name?' and 'Are you my girlfriend?'" I give her a reassuring look, wanting her to know that no matter what her answer is, she won't upset me.

"Oh, yes, I'm Catherine, Nathan's girlfriend," she answers confidently.

My heart leaps a little. Catherine can be hesitant. It feels good knowing that, of all things that are uncertain right now, she is certain in us and me. I translate back to my Tia Sofia she grins ear to ear, grabs Catherine's hands and pulls her in. *"Bienvenida, la Familia."*

"Well, we need to fix that whole not speaking Spanish thing," Tia Marta interjects.

"Oh! You can come here. We can have family dinner and I'll give you lessons!" My mom elbows her way through the small crowd of people. "Catherine! My dear, thank you for coming. It's so good to see you and Nathan together! It's so good to have you here today."

My mother sweeps Catherine up in a hug, and my shoulders sag a little in relief. This is going better than I anticipated.

The door slams shut behind us, and I look over my shoulder to see Sofia and Mariposa standing in the doorway. Mariposa looks surprised, while Sofia is glaring even more than she was out on the porch. Sofia looks at me and rolls her eyes.

"Mami, Veo que conociste a la puta de Nathan?" Sofia hisses.

"No seas una perra Sofia!" Anger swells inside me.

"Enough, you two! English, please." Mami tries to keep the peace, but it's futile. The only person who could keep Sofia from losing her shit was Dad.

"Fine. I said, 'I see you met Nathan's whore.' and then Nathan called me a bitch." Sofia says it with a smile while venom drips from her mouth. She scans the room looking for backing and sees none. She walks through the crowd to the kitchen, grabbing her husband's wrist on the way.

"I am so sorry for Sofia, Catherine. My Sofia is kind, but she doesn't handle stress well." Mami looks mortified.

"Grief is hard." Catherine gives her another hug.

Mami is gracious for her quick forgiveness while I am about to throw down with Sofia in the kitchen like we did when we were six.

Mami introduces Catherine to family members. I squeeze her hand and lean over.

"I think my sisters are in the kitchen. Sorry to leave you," I whisper.

"It's okay. Go." She smiles and squeezes my hand, reminding me I am free to do whatever I need today and that she's only here to meet my needs.

I walk around the crowd that swallows poor Catherine. I breathe in deep and head into the kitchen where all my sisters except Amaya are ready to ambush me.

The twins Lucia and Andria are sitting at the table with Nadia. Mariposa sits on the kitchen counter. Sofia leans on the backdoor. Carlos and the kids are most likely playing–or hiding–out back. The air in here is so thick with tension you could cut it with a knife.

"Hey, Loser." Mariposa is the first to notice my presence. She gives me this sad sort of awkward smile that I think is meant as an apology, or at least an offer of understanding.

"Did you seriously bring her? Why is she here?" Sofia immediately interjects and all my sisters watch her meltdown.

"Because she's my girlfriend. She knew *Papi* and had every right to mourn along with us." I try to stay calm, but my blood boils.

"Well, if that's all, why the fuck couldn't Yuri come?" Mariposa uses the opportunity to go after Sofia.

"Yuri can come! Who said she couldn't?" I know exactly who.

"I did! She shouldn't, just as Catherine shouldn't!" Sofia stomps her foot like a child.

"For somebody demanding for me to step up and make decisions, you sure are trying to undermine me a lot." Sofia goes to speak, but I hold up a hand to silence her and turn to Mariposa before she can. "Swing by and pick up Yuri before the funeral. She is to come to the rest of the family's events from now on."

"*QUE?!*" Sofia shouts.

"That's FINAL, Sofia. *Yo soy el hombre de esta familia y eso es definitivo.*" If she wants me to be the man of the family and take charge, I fucking will. I'm not afraid of it anymore, and I owe part of that to Catherine. "It's time to load up and head to church. Let's go."

Seventeen

Nathan

A few people are just starting to walk through the doors of the church when we pull into the parking lot. The big old limestone building looks ominous, even on this sunny day. Most of the drive over was silent. The argument with Sofia put a bit of a damper on my mood, even though Catherine seems to have been treated mostly okay at my mom's house.

We get out of the car and wait by the bumper as my family slowly pulls in and exits their cars together.

"How are you feeling?" Catherine stares up at me, worrying on the edge of her lips.

I lean forward, kissing her softly. "I'll be better once this is over."

She wraps her arms around me and squeezes. Warmth floods my body, and I lean into her a little, kissing the top of her head.

"How inappropriate for our father's funeral," Sofia scoffs as she storms past us on her way to the front doors. The youngest of her children, wrapped in a blanket, is tucked tightly into her arms while Carlos staggers behind, clutching the other two by the hands. Oscar Jr. follows close behind his dad, tugging on the tie his mother probably made him wear. As they pass, he sends me a look that screams 'Help!' as his dad offers a small apologetic nod.

My mom is parked directly across the aisle from us, standing by her car door while she finishes a cigarette. She's staring at the church. She seems to waiver on her feet, and I rush over, wrapping an arm around her shoulders.

"¿Estás bien? Qué puedo hacer por ti, Mami?" *What can I do for you?* I hate feeling helpless. The look on my mom's face is soul crushing. Tears rim her eyes, and she appears distant and unstable.

She glances at me, and then at Catherine, who had come up beside me. A sad sweet smile fights its way to her mouth without reaching her eyes.

"I'll be fine, *mi amor*. I just need another moment."

I nod, unsure of how to proceed. I wrap my arm tighter around my mom's shoulders and she sags into my side. My heart thumps heavily against my chest and my eyes sting. Catherine steps around me, taking my mom's hand carefully and squeezes.

"We can stand here as long as you need, Nelly." The affection in Catherine's voice is like a balm to my torn soul. I give her a grateful smile that I worry might actually come across as a grimace.

My mom tightens her grip on Catherine and stands straighter.

After another moment, she says, "Let's head in." My mom doesn't let go of Catherine's hand as we walk toward the front doors of the church.

Once inside, we are greeted by somber faces. The church is mostly filled with family this early, but a few of my dad's older friends, mostly retired policemen, are milling around. The casket is closed and pushed up against the wall right in between two sets of double doors that lead into the sanctuary. There are bouquets of flowers surrounding the pitch-black box that glistens as the sun hits it through huge cathedral windows on either side of the lobby.

My chest tightens and I freeze by the doors, looking around but having trouble processing what I'm seeing. In a blur, people come up and talk to me. At least two men from the police force shake my hand, but I can barely register what they're saying.

"I'm so sorry for your loss."

"Your dad was a great man."

Was he a great man, though? Memories of the last few years living with my dad flood my mind.

My dad drunkenly stumbled into the house, scaring my sisters late on a Saturday night…

***

"AMAYA! NADIA! LUCIA! NELLY!" Dad stumbles through the door. The smell of whiskey hits me square in the face. His coat hangs from one arm, and he looks scared and frantic.

"Papi! Shhhh, everyone is sleeping." I stand up from the couch where I was sleeping, waiting for my disorderly drunken father to come home.

He freezes.

"Who the fuck are you?" He puffs out his chest.

"Papi, it's me, Nathan." I slow down and put my hands up, showing him my belly in a way.

"Nathan lives with Carolina. You won't fool me, diablo." Dad stomps forward, ready to brawl.

"Carolina and I broke up. Remember? I moved back in a month ago."

He's past the point of return.

"Liar!" Dad charges me. He tackles me to the ground and starts yelling. "NELLY, GRAB MY GUN! LUCIA, CALL THE POLICE." He punches straight down. I barely move my head out of the way, and the boom of his fist hitting the floor reverberates through the house. The weight of my father crushes my chest. I can barely breathe, but I can't fight back.

I put my hands up, trying to press against his shoulders or get leverage with my knee to push him off, but even drunk, his police training stands and he doesn't let me gain an inch.

"PAPI, IT'S ME!"

CRACK! His fist connects with my nose. I can feel it break under his fist.

My dad winds up again. A blood curdling little girl's scream hits my ears, but the sound is muted. My head is spinning and my ears pop. I'm trying to regain my composure, bringing my hands to my face to protect myself.

He stops, though, at the sound of my sister. I'm thankful. Surely, another punch would knock me unconscious. The lights in the living room flicker on.

"Oh, mi dios! Oscar, what have you done?" Mami says.

"Oh God, Nathan, Oh God, I'm so sorry. What have I done?" he says sheepishly.

Amaya stands in the doorway, face ashen as she looks between me and Papi. I can feel blood rushing from my nose and down my face. I look back at my dad, who looks like he's turning green.

***

My stomach churns violently at the memory, as well as the sight of my dad's casket, and I have to fight through a wave of nausea. I half walk, half stumble toward the corner of the lobby, my vision clouds over slightly. Bile rises in the back of my throat and the coffee turns sour in my stomach. I think I hear someone say my name, but I can't pay attention. I focus on my breathing.

Inhale one, two, three, four. Exhale one, two, three, four.

"Nathan, are you okay?" Catherine's cool hand rests on my lower back. I can feel it through my blazer, and I focus on it. Not trusting myself to speak yet, I nod slowly.

Inhale, one, two, three, four. Exhale one, two, three, four.

"I'm fine," I say finally, turning to her.

She definitely doesn't believe me, but she nods and takes my hand. "They're calling for the family to go sit up in front of the sanctuary."

"I guess we should go then." I let her pull me away from my corner of the room and we make our way to the front of the sanctuary.

The sanctuary is a touch smaller than a basketball court. The floor is at an incline with carpet that was originally red but that has turned into more of a burnt umber with age. The cushions on the wood pews are a much richer burgundy. They are replaced more often, but the fabric still shows the imprints of where people sit. The walls are a dark walnut and there is one large stained-glass window behind where the choir stands. The stunning glass illustration depicts an image of St. Isidore passing food out to the homeless. I remember hearing stories of how he was so devoted to the church and helping others he often would be late to work. It reminds me a bit of my dad.

Bethton Grove St. Isidore Catholic Church was established in 1926. The local Quakers helped build the church after renting out their basement to the group for ten years. When my parents moved here from the Bronx after getting married, their parents followed them. Then their families followed them. When I come to Mass, it's more like a family reunion since fifty percent of the congregation is Alvarez or Perez.

I look around at faces that are mostly familiar as people trickle into their seats. A few minutes later, the priest enters, carrying a golden thurible with smoke spilling from the top. He swings it in a motion that is vaguely circular but represents the Father, Son, and Holy Spirit. I follow the pattern to avoid looking at the casket as it follows the priest. My nephew Oscar walks a step behind the priest carrying a little decorative bowl to dump the ashes of the Frankincense in once they reach the pulpit.

I can hear the priest in the back of my mind as Catherine leans closer, taking my hand and holding it in her lap. I am barely following along with the motions of those around me, standing a second after everyone else and always being the first to sit down. The church feels too hot, like the candles on stage are growing bigger and sucking all the oxygen from the room. I hear my mom sniffle and dab at her eyes, but I am frozen in time, suspended above my body, unable to do anything.

I can't focus on the priest. His face goes from blurry to clear and back to blurry again. I feel like I'm under water, holding my breath, straining to take in my surroundings. No matter how hard I try, there is still no oxygen, and I still can't see anything.

At one point I am tugged to my feet and dragged down the aisle. My throat feels as if it's full of rocks as I go through the motions of communion and head back to my seat. I have the fleeting thought that I pass Cici in the line and it strikes me as odd. I can barely form enough thought to pay it too much attention. I don't know how much time has passed before I am tugged to my feet and a songbook is placed in my hands.

The Eucharistic Doxology starts as the priest sings. My head throbs as I stand as still as possible, remembering as a kid how excited I would get hearing the last song. My dad would place his hand on my shoulder to calm my anxious feet as we listened for the song to end.

My shoulders are heavy with the weight of the day and anxiety wells up in my stomach even though now I am old enough to hold still. After the song ends, the priest heads back up the aisle. The casket follows before me. The priest invites my mom and my sisters to stand at the back doors as people leave. Everyone is encouraged to head to the basement where there will be refreshments along with the food made by the tias.

I stand stonily next to my mom at the back of the sanctuary, shaking hands with people as they express their condolences, and head for the stairwell to go downstairs. I thought I would feel more relief that maybe if I got to the end of the service, things would feel better. But they don't. There's no relief from the tension in my neck, and my face hurts from pretending to smile as people walk by, telling me how sorry they are. My body grows heavier with every handshake, and my shoulders ache. More pain throbs behind my eyes as the last of the people walk by.

And then there is Catherine.

She smiles at me timidly, then she steps up and wraps her arms around me. For what feels like the hundredth time today, I pull strength from her. She doesn't move, holding me tightly as I lay my cheek against her forehead and breathe. I know she won't let go until I do, and today I feel particularly selfish and hold on until my own body feels recharged. When I pull away, we are alone. The family has started to head downstairs, and the sanctuary is quiet.

"Are you ready?" she asks when I don't make a move to head toward the stairs.

I nod but stand staring at the empty pews. The chapel seems lifeless now, just a shadow of itself with the candlelight casting weird shapes on the walls.

"I'm just ready for it to be over."

"I know. Let's go downstairs for a bit, and then we can get out of here." She takes my hand and kisses the back of my palm, snapping my brain back into reality. She pulls me gently in the direction everyone else went.

Eighteen

Nathan

The room is loud. I haven't been to many funerals, and I'm surprised and the white noise of chatter is almost calming. Maybe because I grew up in a big family, or maybe because it seems that nothing just happened, as if we came in from a wedding, not a funeral. The basement has yellow linoleum covering the floor, stained with age. The basement doubles as a fellowship hall and kids' space. The walls are covered in gimmicky posters with cartoon Bible scenes on them. Where the actual wall pokes through is a bright, almost canary yellow. There are white, round foldout tables that people sit at after they make their way through the buffet line.

Catherine and I hop in the line, filling our plates with traditional Mexican food and classic Midwest casseroles. The lights dim a touch and a nun pulls down a projector screen. Images of Dad appear. I heard Amaya and Nadia talk about doing this photo gallery for Dad. I watch as an unfamiliar baby turns into the face of a child that could easily be mistaken for me. Catherine takes my plate, and I let her without thinking. I step out of the line to let others go before me. I can't help but freeze, watching my father's life play out before my eyes.

An image of my father and mother going to prom pops up. Then him in his police uniform. Next, I know a tear runs down my cheek. Seeing my dad hold a tiny me. How does a young family man turn into an alcoholic? How do you go from having everything together to die in your fifties from fucking whiskey? The photos continue to scroll through, each one like another match in the fire of my heart.

Then it hits me in the chest on the last slide. Dad in his uniform the last time I saw him healthy. My heart sinks as it scrolls his birthdate and then the day he died on the screen.

There were so many memories and yet not nearly enough. My throat burns thinking of how many birthdays are left for each of my sisters. How many more school graduations, and Christmas Eves.

And he's just…gone.

And I'm left here to clean up his mess.

Sofia wishes I was him, and somehow I feel as if it's my fault that I'm not. So many years of advice and preparation that he selfishly took away from me. Now I'm left drowning, trying desperately to keep my head above water and wildly in over my head. I needed more time. I needed more help.

The lights get turned back up, and the silence is chilling. People sniffle and wipe their eyes, but as the lights come back up, so does the volume. Everyone around me seems to move on just fine. I scan the tables for Catherine. I see very few dry eyes. My eyes connect with Catherine's dreamy hazel eyes. She's sitting with Yuri and Mariposa, chatting. I make my way over to the table. I notice Sofia's head in that direction as well. My mom stands talking to the priest, Father Francis McClure. I slide in beside Catherine.

"… and then Nathan got beat with a wooden spoon." Mariposa laughs.

"What are you telling lies about?" I tease my younger sister.

"Uh, not a lie, I'm telling her about when you tried to turn your underwear drawer into a frog rescue." Mariposa deviously grins from ear to ear.

"It was one frog! I was six! How was I supposed to know it was dead and not just sick?" My cheeks flush with embarrassment. On the bright side, though, Mariposa seems to be over whatever issue she has with Catherine. It's a good sign when she tells embarrassing stories.

"That's so cute. Oh, stop pouting, it's endearing." Catherine gives me a little shove.

I look down at the plate, and what looked and smelled delicious ten minutes before suddenly makes me nauseated. The image of my father in the casket scrolls through my mind. He looked emaciated and like he was sleeping. His color was off from all the makeup. Mami wanted the yellow gone from his skin and they didn't get him quite dark enough to match his original skin tone. It was eerie—it *is* eerie thinking about him just lying in the sanctuary until we drag him to be buried.

A small hand squeezes my shoulder, pulling me out of my daymares. Nadia and Andria come sit next to Catherine, launching into a full-blown conversation about Andria's music. It lifts my spirits the tiniest bit to see my sisters getting along with Catherine.

"Nathan, you okay?" Amaya looks at me, eyes wide with concern.

"Oh, yeah, just thinking about *Papi*. Come sit with us." I pat the chair next to me.

She smiles wide, excited to escape Sofia's table and the surrounding chaos.

Growing up with mostly adult siblings, I can only imagine how overwhelming the younger kids are to her.

"Thanks. Oscar keeps asking me to play hide-and-seek and I just don't feel like it today." She plops down next to me, leaning into my side. "Can I have some of your bread?"

I scoot my entire plate toward her, not really feeling like eating. She takes it and starts eating everything. "Sofia said I needed to eat all of my tortas before I have anything else, but *Tia Sofia* made it with mayo, and I don't like mayo."

"Have what you want." I kiss her head.

Catherine sighs, looking at her own plate of food but mostly pushing around what she's grabbed.

"So, Catherine, Amber said you haven't lived in Bethton Grove for more than a year. Where were you before?" Yuri pipes up, obviously trying to diffuse the somber atmosphere at the table. I see Catherine flinch. It's obviously still a sore subject. I'm sure it must trigger her memories of Marcus. I look around the room quickly, realizing I didn't even pay enough attention to see if Catherine's family was here. I remember she said her dad and mine were friends. I don't see anyone who resembles the woman I met in the coffee shop the other morning.

"I grew up here, but I lived in Georgia as an adult. I moved back here when I broke things off with my ex."

"I met Cici and your dad before the service. They seem nice." Yuri is not picking up on the tension at all.

Catherine looks at her blankly. "They can be."

It's like a light goes off above Yuri's head and she quiets back down, shooting a nervous look at Mariposa.

"Amaya, what are you doing over here? Oscar and Catarina are looking for you." Sofia walks over, already glaring.

Amaya looks at me with a pleading look.

"She's eating right now, Sof. She will play when she's done." I glance at my sister over my shoulder.

"She already has food at our table."

"And I told her she could sit here." I turn in my seat to face Sofia. I'm already annoyed with Sofia for even existing at this moment. I just want her to go back to her table and mind her own business.

"I already took care of everything for her today. Don't undermine what I've done."

"No one's undermining you, Sof," Mariposa speaks up.

"Nathan is! I already told Amaya she needed to finish what she had before she got more!" Sofia's voice has gotten incrementally louder with each word.

"Sofia," I start. "It's been a rough couple of days. Just lay off, would you?" I keep my voice level and low, trying really hard to avoid the scene that I can feel coming.

Sofia huffs.

"Mom is here, Sofia." Mariposa sits up a little straighter, draping her arm around Yuri's shoulders. "She can take care of Amaya. She is her kid, after all. Just because Dad died doesn't mean you suddenly have to be Amaya's mom. Just let her be today."

I feel like I can visibly see something snap inside of Sofia. Her face has been growing redder by the second.

"How dare you? Someone has to take care of her today. *Mami* cannot have another responsibility."

"Then leave her with me and you go take care of your own children," I answer coldly.

"*¿Perdóneme? ¡Cuido de mis propios hijos! ¡A diferencia de ti, yo puedo manejar la responsabilidad, no salir corriendo y vivir con una mujer blanca impía!*" I see Mariposa lean over mouthing the translation to Yuri and Catherine. *Excuse me? I am taking care of my own kids! Unlike you I can handle responsibility, not run off and shack up with some white godless woman!*

Catherine's hurt eyes drop down to the table.

"ENOUGH! Stop using Spanish to talk down to us. You know it's not day to day for us. You WILL NOT…"

"Sorry, I forgot you all decided to forget about your culture and your family! Running off to do what you damn well please without thinking of the consequences and leaving the rest of us to deal with it!" Sofia hisses at me.

"No one's forgetting that, Sofia," Catherine speaks up, standing slowly. "It's just been a hard few days. Let's just calm down."

"Sofia–" I say, but she interrupts me, turning fully to Catherine.

"I will not CALM DOWN!" Sofia takes a confrontational step toward Catherine and I spring to my feet. "My family is FALLING APART. My father is dead, and half of my siblings are doing everything they possibly can to say fuck you to our family. You have distracted Nathan from his duties, and now that *Papi* is gone, there will be nothing left! It will be me left to take care of *Mami* and Amaya because no one else cares enough to do it!"

My sister is shaking, staring at Catherine with raw, hot venom.

"*¿Que esta pasando aqui?*" Mariposa leans over, translating again. *What is going on here?* My mom is walking slowly toward the commotion, looking at me confused.

"No, no, *Mami!*" Sofia says sarcastically. "*English only please.* We don't want to offend anyone!"

"Sofia! Enough!" I say, stepping forward another step. "You're being completely ridiculous. You aren't even the one who cares for Amaya and Mom. I am–"

Sofia cuts me off again. "No, Nathan, it's not enough. Because the changes you are making are NOT what *Papi* would have wanted. You have gone so far from what he wanted from you, and now you're bringing some white girl around, parading her in front of our family like you have no respect for anyone. And you let Mariposa parade her homosexual relationship around here like it's nothing! This is ridiculous–"

"Enough!" I say. "It's not about what *Papi* would have wanted! You asked me to step up and make choices. I don't care if you like them, but I am making choices. And I am sticking by them."

"You will ruin our family with what you are doing! Think of Amaya! She won't get any of the childhood we did because *Papi* is already gone. You are not teaching her what is right and wrong. You are letting her see your mistakes and bad choices. She doesn't have consequences, she doesn't–"

"Sofia! This is uncalled for." My mom tries to butt in.

I glance around. Everyone in the room has gone silent. They all look to be in various states of shock, horror, and surprise. I catch Catherine's hard expression out of the corner of my eye.

"You are so out of line right now, Sof. This isn't like you." I say quietly, hoping to bring down the volume of the argument a little, but my sister isn't catching on.

"No, Nathan, this isn't like you! You have basically given up on our family. You weren't there like you needed to be! This is no different than when you were with Carolina. You're choosing a girl over your family again! You're letting her make choices for you. I mean, for heaven's sake, you missed your own dad's death because you were too busy fucking her!" She points accusingly at Catherine.

"Stop it!" Catherine is shaking slightly but her voice is level and assertive. "Sofia, I know you're stressed. I know it's been an exhausting few days, and I know you're upset. But you have no right to talk to me or Nathan like this. He has done everything he can for your family. I have watched him give you more and more attention over the last few days, trying to placate this *tantrum* that you have been throwing, and nothing is ever enough! Let go of this because you are the one tearing your family apa–"

Lightning fast, Sofia strikes out, and the slap that connects with Catherine's face breaks everything. My mother gasps in horror, placing her hand over her mouth in shock. Mariposa and Yuri are on their feet, moving toward us, and the twins are still sitting, frozen, with their mouths agape. Time seems to slow around us, and I can't breathe in stillness before the panic.

Carlos whips out of his seat, which I haven't seen him do since he was a quarterback in high school, grabs Sofia and speaks words into her ear that immediately stop her from fighting back. The fire in her eyes dies as she looks between me, Catherine, our mother, and the rest of the family. It's like she's waking up from sleepwalking. Her expression is dumb and confused. And then everything falls back into motion. People start talking and screaming around us, extended family and friends closing in around us on all sides.

I close the distance between Catherine and me. She's holding her cheek in her palm and looks a bit shaken, but still manages an adorable smile. My heart stutters in my chest, and my pulse drowns out all the surrounding sounds.

"Fuck, are you okay?" I take her hand from her cheek and want to throw up for the tenth time today as I see the welting finger marks spreading on her cheek and jaw.

I whirl on my sister, seeing red. "HOW FUCKING DARE YOU!"

Carlos steps in front of his wife and holds up a hand. "Nathan." His voice is supposed to be soothing, but it does nothing to quell the rage in my head.

"Fucking take her somewhere else, Carlos," I breathe. I turn my back to them, focusing my attention back on Catherine. She's handling all of this better than I think I would if our situations were reversed, even though my chest twists with guilt for bringing her into it. Next thing I know, Amaya climbs from her chair onto the top of the table. She stomps her feet, the sound ringing as the plastic folding table groans under her.

"NO MORE! ENOUGH!" A battle cry comes from the small girl. While she's standing on top of the table, it's more powerful than that. A nun on a podium admonishing her students is more accurate.

"Sofia, you are embarrassing right now. How can you not see everyone around you is fine? Just because you're not okay doesn't mean everyone else isn't okay. The only one *Papi* would be disappointed in right now is you! I'm fine! You keep using me as an excuse to throw a tantrum! I have a *Mami* who takes care of me! My dad may be dead, but he never took care of me, really. He was very sick too much! Nathan took care of me! He has an awesome girlfriend who YOU just HIT at our *Papi's* funeral. How disrespectful of his memory! Thats what the *tias* keep saying!" Amaya scolds Sofia.

Sofia turns from blank, to embarrassed, to tears, turning into Carlos to cry.

Amaya takes a deep breath and continues. "Half the kids I go to school with have gay parents. Nathan is making the same decision *Papi* would make because Papi included Yuri, even if he didn't understand."

It's true, our father didn't understand, but he loved Mariposa. If one of us loved someone, so did he. They clashed at first, but Dad would rather have his daughter be happy than worry about sinning.

"*Mami* lost her husband and YOU'RE yelling at her! Enough Sofia. Just stop." Amaya folds her arms for emphasis.

The room feels huge as silence follows my youngest sister's outburst. But she doesn't waiver as she stares everyone down.

"Please get off the table." My mother is ashen, her eyes brimming with tears.

"You have said your bit. Now I think it's about time for everyone to wrap things up. Catherine, come to the kitchen with me and I'll look at your face. Sofia," my mom turns to my sister. "Go have a cigarette and cool off. When you come back in, you had better have a new attitude. Honestly, you're lucky *Papi* wasn't here. He would tell Catherine to press charges."

With a last look, my mother leads Catherine away and my sister walks quickly toward the stairs. Once she is out of the room, everyone seems to collectively sigh.

Amaya has disappeared, probably to check on Catherine, and I need some air.

Nineteen

Nathan

The sanctuary lights are still on. I was going to go outside, but there is no way in hell that I can look at my sister and not lose my shit. Instead, I head into the deserted hall, heading toward a pew at the front of the aisle, hoping to sink in and become invisible to the world.

The sound of my sister's hand connecting with Catherine's cheek still bounces around in my head and my nausea returns. I lean forward, resting my elbows on my knees and cradling my head in my hands. How could I have let things go so far?

I hear one of the doors at the back of the sanctuary open, and I try to sink deeper into the pew. The door is off to the side of the main doors and leads to a staircase that takes you under the sanctuary. There are bathrooms down there, and a room for the priest to change in and out of his robes. It also has a massive storage room that holds communion stock.

"Here you go, Francis! That's the last box. This should be enough communion wine for four months, so if you call me before that, I *know* you've been dipping into the church's stash again!"

Cici's voice carries into the room from behind me.

Father McClure laughs deeply, and I hear Cici laugh, too.

"When are you going to come back to Sunday Mass, Cecile? We miss you!"

"I'll stop in when I can. It was good to see you today."

There's some more shuffling, but I still don't turn to look. A soft thudding of footsteps fills the hall, and then a figure stops at the end of the pew I'm sitting in. I look over and Cici stands there, one hand on her hip, her face placid and relatively void of emotion.

I nod, and she seems to take that as an invitation to sit. I shift uncomfortably, remembering Cici's feelings about me and Catherine. It makes me hesitant to acknowledge her and what she wants right now. I barely have the energy to func-tion. I'm not sure I can handle a Cici talk right now. But when the woman wants to talk, or sit, or do anything, it's kind of hard to tell her 'No.' I also don't want to give her the wrong impression. I desperately want Cici to like me and to support what Catherine and I are doing. I don't want them to be at odds over me. I want to prove that I am worthy of Catherine's love, even though I'm starting to think I never will be.

Cici's hair is wrapped in a low bun, but some of her wild silver curls peek out around her face. She has on a long, dark gray skirt and flowy black top.

"Long day?" she asks, folding her arms across her chest and staring forward at the pulpit.

"Something like that." I rub my hands over my face, trying to wipe the exhaus-tion away, but the moments I have my eyes closed just make the exhaustion seem more intense. It takes effort to pull them back open, and I barely feel like I can form sentences. My heart is still thudding in my chest, the only sign I am still alive and not a ghost sitting in a pew waiting for hell to swallow me up. Or maybe this is hell.

"I saw your sister standing outside when I was coming in. She was yelling at her poor husband about some stupid fight with my niece."

I cringe at Cici's tone. She doesn't sound angry, but I feel like a child caught in a lie. She knows the truth, but she's waiting for me to tell her myself. "Yeah, unfortunately Sofia slapped Catherine. So Mom sent her to time out," I say it in a way that sounds like a joke, but my tone falls flat. All the fight has left my body. I drag my hands across my face and sit up. I lean back and stare at the ceiling. There is no comfort here, no comfortable way to sit, no comfortable way to admit my mistake. No comfortable way to occupy a room with Cici without her seeing more than I ever want.

The roof of the church was redone a few years back and the beautiful architectural ceiling was replaced with popcorn texture. I hate it. Just like I'm coming to hate every corner of this church. The sound of my sister's hand connecting with Catherine's face reverberates around in my head and just feels amplified by the empty auditorium.

"Are you kidding! Shit, what happened?" Cici sounds furious. I know Catherine is her niece, but the questions irritate me.

"Tempers were high. Catherine tried to help, so it didn't end well." I try to keep it short, letting her get the hint that now's not the time.

"Catherine is very anti-conflict. I can't imagine Catherine doing anything to instigate it."

I haven't heard Cici angry. Usually, even in serious moments, she is lighthearted. Part of me wants to turn to her, to ask her how well she really knows Catherine, but now doesn't seem like the right time. Because after what I know Catherine has gone through over the last few days, she doesn't strike me as anti-conflict. Someone who's anti-conflict wouldn't tell her stepmom to back off in a coffee shop.

"She didn't exactly fight Sofia. I did," I state plainly. "Then she stood up for me and Sofia hit her."

"How the fuck does that mean my kid gets hit?" She turns angrily at me.

I fucked up. That's what it means.

"She shouldn't have been hit. Sofia doesn't think I'm acting like the 'Man of the Family' and lost her mind." I roll my eyes, thinking back to her tantrum, and my anger boils. "I'm not really sure what you want me to say here? Everything has been fucked up for the last few days, and even longer than that if I'm honest. And I am one person."

"What did you do then? How did you protect Catherine? She is only one person, so shouldn't she be your singular focus? All she has ever done is deal with men's shit, clean up their messes." Cici's voice hits me almost as hard as Sofia's hand hit Catherine. I don't know how to tell Cici that I can't completely devote everything to Catherine. I did that once before with a partner, and we see where that got me. Catherine knew what my family was like, and she understood I cannot pick between her and them. I know Cici wants me to, but that is more triggering to Sofia and my family than anything else. I can't afford to not be completely present.

Cici sighs, not backing down, but I can see her mind working. "Nathan, I'm really not trying to attack you today of all days, but I worry for Catherine, and I worry that one or both of you is going to end up hurt. You both deserve better than what you've been given."

"Is it your business? I understand your concern for Catherine. I worry about her, too, and I am constantly trying to protect her. But you have to understand that it's my family that we are talking about. It's not like you protected her from yours. Nothing I say is going to help my case with you, anyway." I sit up and can't hold back my anger. "You can't hold your own family together, and you are asking about mine?" I know that response is probably a low blow, but I'm not the only factor in this shitstorm of a week.

Cici bristles at my response, sitting up straighter and turning even more to face me. "Yes, because YOUR family is chaos. Catherine doesn't deserve that. She already ran away from that… She's been on the wrong end of enough abuse for a lifetime. You don't get to question my family and my choices. I have always thought of Catherine first." She accuses me, my choices.

How dare she compare me to him–

"YOU HELPED CREATE THE CHAOS!" I shout angrily, instantly regretting what I've said. "I would never put Catherine in danger. I care for her deeply. But I don't know what you want from me! If it wasn't this today, it would be something else another time! It's like you have this idea I'm a fucking mess like my dad!"

Cici is quiet for a moment, her jaw ticking. She sucks in a deep breath and exhales. A knot forms in my stomach. I've had enough fighting today, but I deserve this retaliation.

"I'm sorry, I really am. If I could've banned your father from my bar, I would've. I carry guilt from all my patrons who struggle with addiction, especially Oscar. If sick people don't want help, it's impossible to help them. Everyone in Oscar's life tried, including me. But at some point, once you get told to 'Fuck off' enough times, you take a step back." She pulls her glasses off her face and cleans them, pausing for a moment. The void of emotion on her face just twists my gut more. I know she cared for my dad deeply. Everyone around him cared for him.

"About seven years ago, when your father was a once-a-week-er, I had another person like him. Every day I was open, he was there, just as your dad eventually did. His wife reached out to me and asked me to ban him from the bar. I obliged. It didn't matter much to me. Two weeks later, another bar let him drive home drunk. He killed himself and a family of four. I've known both of your parents for a long time, Nathan, and one day your mother asked me to do what the other wife did. She was angry. Angry like you're angry right now. She kept calling and calling. Yelling, telling me I was taking advantage of your dad for a quick buck, eventually pleading.

"I told your mother what I will tell you now. Would you rather he was with me, where he is safe, or drinking at a Buffalo Wild Wings where no one gives a shit?" She turns and her eyes are deep like Catherine's. I could imagine in her youth they both look very similar. "This isn't really about that, though. Your family is toxic, violently so. It started with Oscar. I loved him, but he destroyed your family, not me. Not my bar. Not anyone but him. It sucks that you're cleaning up his mess. But don't put it on Catherine to help or fix it. One sister hits her, and another steals her home. You can't tell me that's not toxic. I can't let you poison her like that. It's not that I don't like you. You're a smart guy, with a stable job, and I believe you love her. But you're a package deal with your family. You can't tell me you're not. You all live within five minutes of each other. I am not okay with her having a family that's just as toxic as her parents were." Her voice carries anger… and heartbreak.

I'm stunned into silence for a long dragging moment. The infuriating part is that she isn't completely wrong. I know that my family's behavior this week has been an absolute mess. I know that we all have had only the wrong responses. But we are all flailing, we are all at a loss, and we all needed guidance that we never received. Does Cici not understand that now my entire family has to figure out how to live again? We've been in limbo for months, maybe even years. It feels like I don't know how to handle anything right now. I don't know the right response. I don't even know what to say to her at this point.

"I understand this is fucking rough, losing your dad. Both my parents are gone. My dad was about ten years my mom's senior. Dad got pneumonia when he was eighty. Mom died of cancer right after Catherine graduated from college. But you can't use Catherine to get over your grief. You can't allow your family to make her live on eggshells. You need to figure your shit out and don't drag Catherine into it." She pauses and looks at me, her eyes piercing.

I grit my teeth. "You're right in some ways."

"You seem pretty angry about it."

"I am honestly furious. Mister Macho is not me, I am not that guy. For Christ's sake, I'm a fucking librarian. I don't organize event things, I've never split up fights or had to keep the peace. I'm not intimidating enough for that. I've only been with one other person. I'm not using Catherine." Anger fills me. "But you're right. Dad destroyed our family. Dad died a slow, awful death. The man killed himself. He left without telling me how I am supposed to do this. He taught me how to fish, how to be independent. He taught me how to shoot a gun. He taught me right from wrong. He even taught me to change diapers for my siblings because he said if the women feed them, we change them. He never taught…" I choose to end it there. I find myself defending him, but what do I have to defend? My throat feels thick, and it hurts to swallow. With painfully startling clarity, I see what Cici is saying. I understand her worry. I understand that she doesn't think I will be a suitable partner for the reasons I just explained. But that means nothing. It doesn't mean that I won't learn, or that I can't try. "But you're right, he was toxic, and he's poisoned me. And yet, the fact that you've reduced me to the sum of the worst of my family is probably the most insulting thing anyone has ever done to me."

"Nathan, I am not trying to insult you. I just want desperately to save you both from your own choices, before things actually get out of hand. Before either of you get sucked into something you cannot escape. Please don't do this to Catherine. Don't throw her to your sisters. Catherine deserves a welcoming, loving family. Lord knows her family has not been that. She doesn't have siblings; she doesn't have the connection to her family the way you do. If your family expects you to be present, and present without her, don't you think you owe them that? Figure your shit out before you drag her into any more of this." She places a hand on my shoulder closest to her, pleading with her eyes.

"I never… I could never." I shake my head and put my face in my palms. My anger turns to sadness as I realize that the one thing I have been aching to have still can't happen.

"She needs to figure out her shit, too. It's not just you, she can't pull you into her messes either. She needs to find a place of healing with her dad. She can't have a healthy relationship with anyone till she heals, truly." She stands up and squeezes my shoulder. "Nathan, you're a good kid, but timing matters. And all this is going to end in more heartbreak. Catherine has had enough of that in her life."

"I know…" I mutter. Doubt and pain are blurring my vision. Maybe I am making a terrible mistake. I know I cannot watch Catherine being attacked again. I cannot listen to my family berate her and talk down to her. I cannot watch them talk about her behind her back or to her face. Maybe I am ruining her and this relationship before it ever starts. She deserves stability, love, and connection, and I have never been sure if I can offer her that. If I can't do it, then maybe it is best that I let her go. My throat tightens painfully and my eyes burn with tears I've been holding back for too long.

"Then you need to let her go, for now. It doesn't mean never, but you can't be with each other when you both are messes." Cici walks away from the pew and pauses. She turns back to me. "Nathan?"

"Yes?" I look up at her, my face tacky from the tears escaping my eyes.

"Get Catherine to talk to her dad. Show me you're not poisonous. Help her start healing." She turns back and goes to leave.

"I will…" I mutter as I stand to go find Catherine. For the millionth time in my life, I feel stuck. I feel incapable of having the things I want because I don't know how to get them, and no one will help me. I am alone again.

Twenty

Catherine

I texted Nathan a few minutes ago that I'd be waiting for him by the car. I haven't seen him since all hell broke loose downstairs, and I figured I'd give him some time to cool off after all of that. My face still stings a bit in the cool autumn breeze even though Nelly helped me ice it, acting as a painful reminder of the afternoon that couldn't have gone any worse if we'd tried.

My mouth is still sour with anger and humiliation, and I can't wait to go back to the apartment and scrub my tongue of the taste. I don't even know how to process what happened. My heart is heavy because I understand the sorrow that Sofia feels to some extent, but I still can't fathom ever speaking to my family like that at such a vulnerable time. And I hate that my desire for things to calm down resulted in even more heartache. I'm once again reminded of Cici's words:

I just want to know your choices aren't healthy for you or Nathan, and it's my job to point out when you're not making well thought-out decisions.

I wonder if I am really making the right choice trying to start a relationship with Nathan again at this point. But I also don't think I could walk away again. It almost broke me in half the first time, even though I knew it was necessary.

I don't know if I'm strong enough to do it again.

"Hey." My thoughts are cut short when Mariposa and Yuri walk up to where I am sitting. Yuri is smiling while Mariposa looks sheepish.

"We saw you out here and just wanted to check on you before we left." Yuri says, linking her arm through Mariposa's. "How is your face?"

"I'm fine," I say blandly.

Yuri gives Mariposa a look, and the girls seem to have a silent conversation. Then Mariposa turns to me. "I'm sorry for being a bitch."

I'm a bit surprised, but I don't think I let it show. "It's fine." I look over her shoulder, hoping Nathan is going to step out any second and save me from having another conversation right now. But luck doesn't seem to be on my side lately.

"I mean, it's really not. I think you're cool, and I know my family is crazy, but you're a badass for handling everything the way you did."

Yuri smiles, looking back and forth between the two of us.

"Hey." Nathan's deep voice causes all three of us to spin at the same time. I didn't even hear him walk up to us.

"Hey." I try to smile, but I can feel it doesn't really work. There's a tightness in my jaw and neck that I can feel when I move my mouth to talk.

"I think we should probably get going." Yuri nods to Nathan. "Thank you for what you did today," she says.

Mariposa takes her hand, nodding. "Yeah, Nathan, thank you. I know everything is shit right now, but I appreciate what you did for us." She pauses, and I think she's done, but then she seems to decide otherwise. "I don't know if it means anything at this point, but I think you have done a great job handling everything, and I'm glad you're my brother."

My throat feels a bit tight, but Nathan barely seems to register anything that's being said. I smile at the two girls as they start to head to their own car. My stomach starts to churn because something seems off. The energy flowing from Nathan is charged with emotions I don't understand and that weren't there before.

"How's your face?"

My hand goes self-consciously to my cheek. It's hot to the touch and aches. "It's fine. It really wasn't that bad," I lie. I can still trace a bit of raised skin. It seems to be in the shape of fingers, but I haven't seen it, so I don't know for sure.

He nods, and I can tell he doesn't believe me. He takes the keys from my hands and helps me to a standing position before walking around to open my door, and then he skirts the front of the car to get to the driver's side. Nathan grips the steering wheel angrily, and for some reason, I feel a bit like I did that night in the winter when Nathan picked me up from that club when I was drunk. Like the sum of my own actions has put us in this questionable position.

Once we are settled into the car, I finally ask, "Where were you?"

He's quiet for a moment, pulling out of the church parking lot and back onto the street before he answers me. "I was sitting in the sanctuary. Cici actually came to drop off wine, and we talked for a few minutes."

"Oh." I still haven't talked to my aunt since yesterday morning, and I am a little afraid of what she may have said to him.

"Yeah." He's quiet, and I can see the tightness in his jaw as he clenches his teeth. My heart sinks as I realize the conversation probably didn't go well. "I don't really know what to say at this point. She sure has a lot of opinions about life, doesn't she?" He rubs his neck, embarrassed. I think that was a failed attempt at humor, but I can't tell. *Too bad she didn't get slapped.*

My heart skips a beat, and my stomach rolls uncomfortably. He has this wild expression clouding his eyes, like he might start laughing or crying, or maybe he's just going to stop the car and get out. I can't tell, but it's making me sick. "What did she say?"

We are both silent for another moment before he speaks.

"You should talk to your dad."

"Is that what she said?"

He looks uncomfortable and I can tell that was a lot more to what she said than just her saying I need to talk to Dad. Cici always has an opinion. I know this.

"It doesn't matter what else she said." He grips the steering wheel tighter. "But I know she's right. You need to talk to your dad. I can't stand in your way."

"Did Cici say you're in my way?"

"Not exactly, but I caught the gist of it all. You don't deserve what happened to you today. My family is shattered right now. It's unfair for you to be trying to walk into my family and still have issues with your own. You don't deserve that." His voice is flat and emotionless.

"Where is this coming from?" My heart is racing. I think I want to cry, but I swallow hard, holding back the stinging in my eyes and throat. I have a sinking feeling in my chest, and I hate it.

He's quiet again for a long moment and a trickle of anger is building behind my ribcage.

"It's not coming from anywhere. I know this, but Cici brought some extra things to light today." He still hasn't looked at me.

"Is this about your dad?" I ask.

"It's about everything, Catherine." His words are clipped and slightly harsh. For the first time since I met Nathan, I hate the way he says my name. It sounds like it pains him, like I might be an annoying child who has asked 'why' too many times.

I'm catapulted back to the way Marcus would yell at me when I'd do stupid things, and it infuriates me. I thought Nathan and I were supposed to be in this together. We were doing these things and talking. And now I'm starting to feel like a stranger, like in the last hour someone else has taken Nathan's place. That dark cloud from a few nights ago is sucking all the air from the car, drowning out my thoughts with its ominous presence.

"It's about how ruined my family is acting, and how little I have a grasp on right now. It's about me trying to find myself again and be the person my family needs right now. I don't want these things to ruin your life. I'm already damned at this point, and it's ridiculous for me to be so selfish to drag you down with me."

"What are you even talking about right now? I thought we already had this conversation, that we decided to do this together?" My vision is blurring around the edges, and I feel like I can barely take a breath.

Silence again fills the car and I count the trees as we pass them on the road.

We are pulling up to the only stoplight in town when Nathan finally looks at me. He sighs deeply and reaches for my hand, but stops short and then reaches for the steering wheel again. That single moment, or lack thereof, shatters my soul. I want to cry out, to beg for an explanation, to reach for him myself and tell him I'm not letting go until we figure this out. But there's a wall between us that wasn't there this morning and I'm afraid it's never going to go away.

I huff out a breath and slump back in the seat.

"You really should try to fix things with your dad. You don't want to end up like me, sitting by a casket, wishing you had been slightly less spiteful and actually tried." He says quietly, turning the car onto the main stretch of road in town. "You deserve better than you're giving yourself right now."

We pass Soups and The Diner before I can find my voice again.

"Who cares about my dad right now? What's happening? What did Cici say to you? Why do I feel like you're trying to get rid of me?"

"People make mistakes–"

"Are you saying us getting back together was a mistake?" My heart slams into my throat. I feel like I've been slapped for a second time today and I see stars.

"No, I was talking about your dad."

"Fuck my dad. I need to know what's going on with you right now. You're scaring me."

He lets out a breath through his nose, and his nostrils flare slightly. He's angry, but I don't care. "Because right now I feel like I'm talking to my aunt and not the man that I am in love with. Definitely not the one who claims to be in love with me."

"Catherine, please. I really don't have the strength to fight about this right now. I'm exhausted, and it's been a long day."

"I know." I school my expression into nothingness, staring blankly out the front window. "Let's just go home for now."

Another long pause. "I think you should stay at your apartment tonight." Nathan says, each word slamming into me like a shard of glass, cutting my soul into pieces.

"What?"

"I just think I need some time by myself tonight. I need space to think things through, and I think it would be best for now if we didn't spend the night together. Right now, I can't handle distraction.

"Now I'm a distraction? Is this like some fucked up case of the *Body Snatchers*? Did Cici somehow replace you with an alien and you're just faking being Nathan? Because I feel like this is some sort of sick joke at the moment and I'm not loving it. What about last night? Or this morning? Was that a lie, too?"

Nathan blows a big breath of air out through his nose. "No, Catherine." He sounds like a parent correcting a child.

"Well then, I'm not sure I understand. Either you are lying right now, or you were lying then. I'm going to get whiplash."

"Catherine, it's not you. I just need some time, it's me. I'm just fucked up right now and I feel like I'm spiraling. I don't know what you want from me."

My head is doing its own sort of spiraling freefall, and anger boils through my veins, making my body feel hot. "What the fuck, Nathan? No one ever actually says that whole 'It's not you, it's me' bullshit. It's always the other person who's the problem."

He pulls in front of the coffee shop, not bothering to pull into the small parking lot, and throws the car into park so fast we lurch a little. "You know what? Maybe it is you right now." He turns in his seat to look at me. His gaze is cold and unwavering. "My dad just died and you're mad at me because I want a little space? My life is crumbling. Maybe Cici is right and we are just using each other–maybe I am using you–and all of this will wear off in a week or two when. our emotions calm down. Maybe I was just looking for you the other night because I was desperate to feel something. I don't know. But right now I can't deal with it, and I'm exhausted from having to explain myself and do every-damn-thing to keep people happy. I don't need another person breathing down my neck asking me repeatedly if I'm okay. I don't need you constantly telling me that my family doesn't matter or that their feelings don't matter and only mine do. Because it doesn't feel fucking true, and it's not helpful. I sure as hell don't need to feel guilty for not wanting to deal with anything else right now."

I don't think Nathan realizes how loud his voice has gotten, and I do my best not to shrink down in my seat as he lays out one blow after another. This is so much more painful than Sofia's hand hitting my face. I try closing my eyes against his words, but that only makes them echo around in my head, bouncing from one side to the other. Hurt and rage are bringing tears to my eyes, but I blink through the sting. Maybe he is right.

"Okay, I'm sorry," I say shakily.

He closes his eyes and takes a deep breath. "Catherine–"

"No." I hold up my hand to quiet him. "I'm sorry. I am out of line. You're right. I mean, what was I even thinking? Of course you need space. Thank you for your fucking honesty." I can't keep the biting tone from my words.

"Catherine–"

"Please stop. You're right. Now I know. You want space and I can give that to you. Don't worry about it."

I pull out my phone, sending a quick text to Amber that I'm going to be coming back soon. When I look back at Nathan, there's a mixture of hurt and distress painted all over his face. I'm pretty sure in that moment I see regret, too, like he would eat every single word he just threw at me if he could, but it's too late.

"I'll let you be." I go to open the car door and he grabs my arm.

"Please, try to understand," he mumbles.

"I do understand. I understand you don't want me around right now. And you're right. Maybe I forced this faster than I should have. I get it. I don't want to be in the way. So just let me know when you're ready to talk, and if you don't think you'll be ready to talk anytime soon, let me know when I can get my stuff." I can't help it as a single tear falls down my cheek.

I pull free of his grasp and open the car door. I don't wait for his reply as I slam the door and cross the street, quickly heading toward my apartment. It's a second thought that I should have kicked him out and gotten my car, but I just needed to get out of the situation. I will go back and get it later tonight or something.

I can't do anything right. I made a mess of his dad's funeral. I shouldn't have gone. If I had said nothing to Sofia, just sat there quietly. If I hadn't left his side, maybe he wouldn't have run into Cici. I just want to run back and tell him he's wrong and hold him tight. I turn back around and he's already walked back into the cafe.

I feel tears stream down my face as my heart sinks. How do I do this? How do I fight for us? Everyone I love leaves—Mom, Dad, my friends, and now Nathan. *Why me*? I feel myself shaking. I squat on the sidewalk, putting my face into my hands and scream. A rush of anger fills me. What have I done wrong? What about me makes everyone leave? Cici is the person I would like to call. I want her to tell me how to fix this. I know what she would say…

I pull my phone back out of my pocket and dial a number I haven't used in so long.

TWENTY-ONE
Catherine

The sun is low in the sky when I find the park bench off to the side of the library. It's the same park bench I sat on when Marcus texted me back in the winter. I'm not sure if it's the chill of the night air or the memory that makes me shiver. The same giant lions sit guarding the doors, the one with the nose rubbed raw still sits next to me. The same worn path still leads back through campus, statues of old dead white men littering the makeshift park in the middle of it all. So much has changed this year and I don't even feel like the same person anymore. That girl was a crumpled piece of discarded paper hiding from the wind, desperate to not get swept away. She doesn't exist anymore, and the person I am now can stand tall, bracing against the storm. Although right now I don't feel very secure.

I mentally shake that thought free and remind myself–I am not the same person who runs anymore, I can fight my own battles.

I remind myself of this repeatedly as I wait for my dad to show up. When I texted him, he answered almost immediately that he would walk over. As I wait, checking my phone every few seconds, I wonder if he's really going to show. I don't have much faith in him anymore. That hurts my heart just as much as the rejection I'm afraid is at the end of this conversation. I know Nathan is right. Even if I hate that Nathan fighting with me pushed me here, I need to talk to my dad. I deserve to at least have this conversation.

I've been sitting here for a few minutes now, going over what I want to say, because I've realized—I want to have this talk with him. I don't know what good it will do. I don't know if we'll leave here better off, or if we'll still be in the same place after. I don't want to be bitter; I don't want to feel spiteful. I don't want to feel dread take me by the neck every time I think he's going to be around.

Someone clears their throat and I look up. I was so lost in thought I didn't even hear my dad walk up. I shoot to my feet, brushing my hair away from my face.

"Hey," I say. It comes out squeaky like I'm out of breath.

"Thanks for texting me," my dad says.

I nod, and then we just stand there, staring at each other. When he looks at me, I wonder what he sees. I look nothing like I did a year ago. I hate wondering whether he's proud of the changes I've made.

My dad is a proud man. He always stands up straight with his shoulders back. When he was younger, I can imagine he was a force to be reckoned with. I remember as a little girl seeing him in his police uniform, thinking he looked like a superhero. His salt and pepper hair and dark eyes make him seem intimidating in the late afternoon light. The shadows on his face look harsh, and even though his eyes sparkle, his expression is unreadable.

"Do you want to walk around for a bit?" I ask finally when I can't take the tension of the standoff anymore.

He nods, and we head around the back of the library. We walk slowly, not bothering to pick a destination. The silence feels like thorns to my skin. Part of me still feels the rage and hurt I had the other day, but mostly I am tired. I've done too much fighting the last few days and I just want to be done.

My dad clears his throat again and shoves his hands into the pockets of his olive green jacket. "You know, I met your mom on this campus."

We've never really talked about Mom since she left, and my heart instantly feels heavy. "Oh?" I knew they met here when she and Cici and Dad all lived here as kids.

"We walked around campus kind of like this the first night we met. Your aunt had a noise complaint called in and I went to break it up. I was often sent to clean up her messes in those days. Your mom was at that party, and I ended up walking her back from the library late that night. We walked this path many times. That building over there," he points to a brick building next to a large tree. "That was Cici's and your mom's dorm. She was so easy to talk to then, and so beautiful. I was so caught up in the newness of the way she made me feel. Then you came along soon after." He sighs and wipes a hand over his eyes. "You remind me so much of her sometimes it almost hurts."

I cringe at his choice of words. There are very few times I'm compared to my mother at all. I have always resembled my dad and Cici more than her, so I don't know what to say or what to ask.

"Lisa told me about breakfast yesterday."

"Dad–"

He cuts me off. "She told me what you said, and I have to say something first."

I stay quiet, waiting for him to speak. It's almost like second nature to quiet myself when he speaks. He does it so rarely.

"I know I haven't been there like I should be. I'm not proud of it. If I'm being honest, I saw some of the warning signs in your relationship, and I overlooked them. With your mom sometimes we had… similar issues. But we had you, and I didn't know how to get up and walk away. Even if I wanted to, I don't think I could have. I didn't have the strength because I loved your mom. I still do, weirdly. I so desperately wanted that family for you, I couldn't leave.

"I think I just so desperately didn't want the same ending for you with Marcus. I didn't want you to experience the heartbreak that I felt so much. I just hoped it was a new relationship issue and they would go away. Every time you came home, I talked myself out of the pain I saw, talked myself out of keeping you to myself. By the time I had a feeling that things had gotten terrible, I didn't want to admit my mistake. I didn't want the shame of knowing I let you walk back into danger."

"It felt like you didn't believe me–didn't see me," I stutter.

"I see that now. I'm so ashamed that I didn't see how bad it really was. You were right the other day. I overlooked it and now I have to live with the consequences my choices have created. I just know what it's like to love someone who doesn't truly love you back."

"Dad…" I whisper. He has never talked to me about my mom.

"I loved her so much, but her depression tore her apart. She was never the same. Or maybe that was the real her. She got pregnant only a few months after we started seeing each other. Nothing I did was good enough. Every day, I took the low blows. She slung insults and sometimes even plates."

Like Marcus.

He continued. "We had good times, but they became fewer and fewer. I resented her. She didn't love me. She loved you. She was just so mentally ill. I know she was cold. I'm sure it's hard to believe she loved you, but she did. You were a perfect little girl. Oh, Lord, Kitty, if only Bailey Mae was half as behaved as you were. I never had to raise a hand to you. Timeouts were a rarity. You were the best snuggler, too. I miss coming home from work and passing out with my princess on the sofa." He smirks, reflecting on times past. A distant look tells me he travels back to that same sofa in his mind some days. There's sadness there that I recognize as the same sadness I feel when I think about my parents. "I wanted it all to work so bad, Kitty. I did everything I could to try to shield you. The worst thing I could imagine was you experiencing that. So I couldn't see what was going on. I was too busy covering my eyes. I am so very sorry."

"I just wanted you to see me so badly." Tears well up in my eyes.

"I know." He slows his pace and turns to me. He walks up to me and places both his hands on my arms. I accept the gesture and step into his embrace. "I see you now. I am so damn sorry. Kitty, I messed up hard. You have changed so much, and I saw none of it. I'm here now. My eyes are open and so are my ears. You came to us and we didn't hear you either. I am so damn sorry." I can hear the tears in his tone, and it shatters me all over.

I sob into his chest, clinging to him like I did as a little girl. I am so angry. I hate how much I just want to forgive and be done. But I also want to resent him. Resent him so deeply I forget he exists. I can't though. I just want my dad. At the end of all of this, I just want a chance at the thing I thought I couldn't have. A family. Even though resentment might feel easier than forgiveness, I don't want to waste my time. I don't want to waste another day where I don't have the opportunity to share my life with my family.

I wipe my eyes and step out of the safety of my childhood. Back to reality. We are now standing in the middle of a common area in between some buildings of Bethton Grove College. There are enormous maple trees all around us, their leaves vibrant with shades of yellow, orange, and red. Every few seconds, a leaf drifts from the trees as the wind tumbles through the branches. A few college students are intermingled in the trees, talking at picnic benches or playing frisbee around the open spaces. Some have blankets laid out with books scattered around the edges. It reminds me a bit of a modern version of one painting hanging in the library, *A Sunday Afternoon on the Island of La Grande Jatte by Georges Seurat*. The print hangs right next to Nathan's office.

My dad is the first to break the silence again. "I understand if you are still mad at me. I don't fault you for it. But don't take it out on Lisa or Bailey Mae. I wish I could explain it to you, but without you, I wouldn't have them. You taught me what genuine love was. When you were born, and I got to hold you, I thought, 'Wow.' It changed my entire perspective on what I thought loving someone could be. I want you all to be a family. They are dying for a relationship with you." He sounds pained, his eyebrows are creased in concern. "I'm not asking you to forgive me now, or maybe ever. I know I was part of the damage. But they are really trying. You can be mad at me as long as you need to, but don't make them suffer for it as well."

"That's never been my intention," I whisper. "I just don't know what to do anymore. I'm not the same person who I was in Georgia. Over the last year, I have changed a lot. I don't even know what to do anymore or how to talk to you guys. Because every time I think about trying, I just don't even know where to begin."

"Well, we are going to be in town for the next week. Maybe we could have dinner one night, talk for a bit?"

I want to jump at the chance, but I can't help being cautious. I feel like a stranger in my family, and I don't even know how to open back up to these people after the things I endured.

"I think we could make that work." It feels like a leap of faith, like a step in a direction where I can't see the end.

"You don't have to do it for me." My dad says, hurt and resignation lingering in every fine line of his face. "But at least consider trying again with Lisa. She wants you to come see the baby in a few weeks when he's born. She loves you more than you realize, and breakfast was very hurtful for her."

"I know. I feel bad she got a lot of the brunt of my anger towards you… Wait… It's a boy?" I feel like an asshole because even in all of this, I never asked. But I remind myself they also never told me.

A small smile touches my dad's lips. "Yeah. Thank God. There is so much estrogen in the house. She won't decide on a name, though. For the longest time, she was convinced it was another girl."

"That's really exciting. I'm happy for you guys." And I genuinely mean it. I am happy that they have this life together.

"We really want you to be a part of his and Bailey Mae's lives. I hope you will consider having dinner while we are here, and then coming down to visit after the baby is born."

I nod, still unsure but feeling better about the whole situation.

"I don't want to be mad at you anymore," I say finally. "And for now, I am willing to agree to dinner."

My dad nods but says nothing for a really long time. We keep walking, looping back up the far side of campus. I wonder if he was expecting me to never want to see him again and is surprised. I know that's how I feel.

"If it would be easier, why don't you bring Nathan with you?" He gives me a pointed look. "Lisa said you guys have been spending a lot of time together."

I freeze at the mention of Nathan. My dad must see the look on my face because he follows quickly with another statement. "Or not. It can just be us."

"It's not that. He's just dealing with a lot right now and I don't know how long it's going to be before we are actually ready to do anything together." There's a lump of emotion in my throat that I have to fight through to speak.

"I understand that. Whatever you think is best, or whatever you guys need." My dad clears his throat again. "I have been friends with Oscar and Nelly for many years. I have no doubt Nathan is a good man."

My heart hurts just thinking about Nathan. I feel like a person dying of thirst, and I can't keep water from slipping through my fingers. We were so close to getting things right, and something else stepped right in the way. Maybe we really aren't meant to be here together. Maybe it's one of those sad stories where we will forever pick the wrong moments to try. Everything hurts as I look at my dad again, who's just staring like he can't figure out the part of the story he's missing.

"Well, I think I'm going to head back to Cici's. She wants to play some board game or something tonight with us." He sighs. And I can't help but smile because

Dad hates sitting for long periods of time doing stuff like that.

"I need to get back, too."

"Think about what you want to do for dinner and let me know. I love you, Catherine. I know I do a shit job of showing that to you, but I really do."

I turn and, without thinking, throw my arms around my dad's neck. I don't remember the last time I hugged him. He seems shocked for a second and doesn't move, but then slowly hugs me back. My eyes sting as I hold on, tears threatening to spill out.

I don't say 'I love you' back. I try, but no sound comes out, so I just hold on a few minutes longer, hoping that he understands. When I finally let go, his eyes are misty too.

Twenty-Two

Catherine

The light is fading quickly as I walk back toward my apartment. My purse feels heavy on my shoulder and my feet are aching after the long day. Everything around me is glowing in the early evening light, bathed in shades of gold and pink. I love this time of evening in the fall. The rich orange and red of the leaves make the trees seem as if they are on fire.

My chest aches at the idea of going back to my little apartment with Amber after staying at Nathan's for the last few days. As I approach the modern white and blue building, it appears like a hollow shell to me, not as the home that I have loved so much over the last six months. How am I going to come back here and live after Nathan? I don't know if I have the strength to do it again. But I'm also done running. I have built a life that I can live with, and if that means no Nathan, then I can figure out how to be okay with it.

I walk up to the door of our apartment, feeling a bit lost and out of place as I fumble through my bag for my house key. It seems foreign to me now, sitting on the same keyring as Nathan's apartment key. My heart takes up the familiar drum of pain and disappointment as I insert the key into the lock and let myself into my already decently loud apartment.

Music blares through the hallway leading to the kitchen and living room. I doubt anyone heard me come in as I slide off my shoes and trudge toward the sound. Halsey's "Without Me" blares through the apartment. The girls are singing in the kitchen. I'm not really in the mood for what they're doing, and I feel guilty for walking in here and potentially destroying their fun time. I pause right before the doorway to the kitchen, realizing I could turn around and go somewhere else. I could go to Cici's, although I'm not sure board games with the person partially responsible for ruining my night is what I want. After today, I'd rather chance it with the girls.

The small space is fuller than it's been since I moved in. Amber and I cook together on the weekends sometimes. Usually, we have the tv in the living room turned to face the kitchen island so that we can watch murder documentaries or cooking shows. More often than not, Amber and I don't even cross paths in the evenings. I tend to be at work or on my way to work as she's coming home, so if we see each other, it's brief. Amber, however, does sometimes leave leftovers in the fridge for me with little sticky notes with encouraging phrases written on them. That is a shiny piece of her personality that I am forever grateful for. Amber has some sort of sixth sense when it comes to knowing if the bar is going to be busy and when I'll come home starving. I love her for it.

It takes a moment for any of them to notice me standing in the doorway. Mariposa sings dramatically while holding a wooden spoon. She's perched on the counter in something that is probably supposed to be pjs but looks way closer to expensive lingerie. It's a deep green sleep set, a tank top and a pair of shorts, but the back is completely see-through black lace, and she has no bra on. Her hair is down around her shoulders, brushing the middle of her back as she sings.

Yuri is in a pair of black comfortable looking pj-pants and an off-the-shoulder black shirt that has strategic rips down the side. They look like a couple from a fashion magazine modeling fancy sleepwear. Yuri's black hair is put up into a sort of ponytail, showing off the amazing curves of her cheekbones and jawline that girls like me would kill for.

Amber, however, is in a pair of leggings, her favorite old flower-print t-shirt, and a pair of rainbow unicorn slippers that always make me happy when I see them. She is dressed like a child, somehow making it seem effortless and kind of cool. Like she's wearing all the clothing ironically, when in fact she isn't.

Yuri sees me first since she's the only one facing in my direction.

"Catherine! You're just in time." She smiles widely at me, closing the space between us quickly and pulling me into a quick hug. "We were just about to pull the brownies out of the oven!"

"Catherine! You're here!" Amber squeals, dropping the oven mitts on the floor before dashing across the small space to throw her arms around me. Yuri steps back and out of the way quickly, having to duck to avoid Amber's flailing arms. "I'm so happy you're here! I love you soooo much!"

Yuri picks up the oven mitts as the timer goes off and pulls the brownies out.

"Are you high?" I take Amber's hug, wrapping my arms around her slender waist. My throat feels tight, and I hang onto her a little longer than usual, using her affection as a hard reset for my emotions.

"She's so high. Andria hooked us up. She is jamming with some of Nick's friends tonight," Mariposa chimes in, hopping off the counter.

"Remind me again who Nick is?" I ask. Amber is still hanging on my shoulder, smiling at nothing.

"One of my cousins, the one who thinks he's a badass for selling cheap vapes with his friends."

"Soooo high." Amber echoes with a hiccupping giggle.

Mariposa comes up to me and wraps an arm around my shoulders in a sort of side hug. The simple act has Amber bouncing on the balls of her feet, smiling like a maniac.

"I knew you guys would be the bestest of friends!"

Mariposa rolls her eyes at Amber, but I can see her affection even through the fake annoyance. "Go put your pjs on." Mariposa gives me a smile. "We are having a girls' night. Do you want an edible or a blunt?"

I smile uneasily. "I prefer to smoke my weed."

"I'll get another one out then. Hurry!" Mariposa makes a shoo-ing motion with her hand and sends me down the hall to my room.

Even though the girls have taken over my room, mostly, everything is still neatly organized. They each have their own sides and their own bag. Well, Yuri has one bag. Mariposa has three. They are lined up on the floor and pushed against the wall. My dresser is untouched, and all of my things have been left alone. It doesn't even look like they actually slept in my bed last night. The covers are pulled up over the pillow like I usually do in the morning and the comforter is spread flat. It surprises me after seeing the way Mariposa left our bathroom the other day.

I grab a change of clothes from the dresser next to my bedroom door, settling on a pair of yoga pants and a hoodie. The rest of them look cute, but I just can't muster it right now.

Stepping back into the little hallway connecting my bedroom and the bathroom to the rest of the house, I can see that the party has made its way into the living room. The girls are setting up the coffee table with bags of chips, fresh brownies still steaming from the glass dish, a few bottles of wine, a bottle of whiskey, and an ashtray. The music is considerably quieter now and I am thankful for that as I step back out into the open.

"For someone who seems so quiet and kind, you sure watch a lot of creepy shit, Amber." Yuri flips through stuff on one of our streaming services.

"Most of it is probably my fault," I say, peering to see what she's looking at on the TV.

I don't look nearly as fashionably comfortable as the rest of them, but at least I'm finally out of the stuffy outfit I've been wearing all day.

"Come sit!" Amber motions me down to the floor next to her. As I sit, she pours me a shot of whiskey.

"Thanks," I mumble, throwing it back before settling back against the couch. Mariposa hands me a smoldering roach and I smile at her, hitting it twice before handing it back. The familiar burn in the back of my throat is comforting as the effect runs through my body, relaxing all my tense muscles.

"What's wrong?" Amber peers at me, concern touching the corners of her eyes. She knows me so well at this point that even if I tried to hide it, she would know.

"I saw my dad tonight," I mumble. "Right before I came here."

"Oh, no." Then she pauses, looking at me, confused. "Since when is your dad in town?"

"He came for, uh, Oscar's funeral." I peer over at Mariposa, trying to gauge her reaction to me talking about her dad's funeral today. She seems relatively indifferent, still puffing on the last of the roach. Yuri is rubbing her back in slow circles, watching everything. My heart aches seeing their connection.

"Oh, is that why you and Nathan stopped by to get stuff the other night? Is he staying with Cici?"

I nod. "He is. Along with Lisa and Bailey Mae. Oh, and Lisa is pregnant."

"Oh, Catherine. Why didn't you tell me?" Amber wraps a slender arm around my shoulder.

"I just didn't know what to say. The other night I just felt ambushed. Cici didn't tell me they were showing up and things went to shit quickly."

I tell them all about my dad showing up, and everything that happened at her house. Then finding out Lisa was pregnant and trying to have breakfast with her the next morning and her commentary on my life.

All three of them listen carefully, but Amber is the only one who asks questions as I speak. I figure Mariposa and Yuri probably just don't know enough to ask, and I'm perfectly okay with that. I watch Mariposa, hoping that I don't make her uncomfortable talking about my dad, but her face barely changes from cool indifference as she listens. I briefly wonder about her and Amber's friendship. They seem even more opposite than I thought Amber and I were at first.

"Shit, man, that sounds rough," Yuri finally speaks when I stop to pour another shot of whiskey, but this time I sip it instead of drinking it all down at once. The heat from the alcohol grounds me again, seeping from my stomach into every part of my body.

I shrug. "Then tonight my dad actually apologized. I really want things to be okay. I'm not the same person who I was, and I just don't want to feel stuck again."

Yuri nods at me, and we all settle into some sort of semi-comfortable silence together.

"How come you aren't staying with my brother?" Mariposa peers over her wineglass at me, arching a perfect eyebrow in a way that doesn't seem judgmental, but it could turn that way at any moment. Her face is free of makeup, and she still looks completely flawless. I wonder what her skincare routine is like.

I let out a sigh, grabbing a bag of Cheetos and popping them open before answering. "He felt awful about Sofia and when Cici found out, she said some… things… He just thought we needed some space, I guess. So I volunteered to come back here for the night."

Mariposa's eyebrow arches even higher.

It's uncomfortably quiet in the room now, and Amber clears her throat. "You need to tell him to get his shit together. He's letting Sofia get into his head just like he would when we were kids."

"I understand where he is coming from though–"

"Listen," Mariposa cuts me off, sitting forward in her seat. "I'm sorry I was a bitch to you the other day. I'm going to be shady and play the dead dad card, but in all honesty, I see the way he is with you. You know, he called me about you early this year. Told me all about the girl he worked with, how you were with our family and even Dad. I heard it in his voice then, and I saw it in his face this weekend." She sets down her wine. "He has no idea what he's talking about. I don't care what anyone said to him. He's being a dick, and he knows it. He's never been good at asking for what he wants. And he's even worse at asking for help. I don't know if that will ever get better. My brother is undoubtedly in love with you. And you need to get your head out of your own ass long enough to realize that this is a rare time where he needs you to fight for him.

"Our family doesn't know how to mind their own business. They will ask him to give and give and give until he has nothing left. He needs someone to help him stay grounded and help him hold on to himself. Because he doesn't want the things that they do. He's struggling to be the person who they want and still finds himself in this chaos that our family creates. And for some reason, he has picked you."

"I don't think it's a random reason," Yuri pipes up. "I saw the way you tried to diffuse the family today. Even I don't have the balls for that."

Mariposa nods. "You have something going on for sure, Catherine. Nathan sees that. He gravitates to that. You're strong. In this situation, you need to be strong enough to tell him to get over himself or whatever construct of life that he thinks he needs to follow and pull him back into the light."

"I just don't want to put him in a situation where I ask him to choose me over his family. How can I do that?"

Mariposa sighs deeply, leaning into Yuri. "Maybe it's not the worst thing for him to choose you over them. Sofia doesn't like you because she thinks if he chooses you first, things will end up like they did with Carolina. She dragged him down and had him wrapped so tightly around her finger he couldn't get away. She made him choose her over them all the time. But you're not like that. She didn't want to share him or his attention. You see him, and you care about him and what's best for him. There is a difference."

It's interesting to me that she says 'them' like they're not her family. I guess after the fight that I witnessed about her relationship with Yuri, maybe Mariposa really doesn't feel like it's her family anymore.

"Our dad never would have wanted him to feel the way Sofia is making him feel. He never would have expected Nathan to take his place if he knew something like this would happen. Most of us are grown. We have our own lives and Dad always knew that. He never expected us to do anything but be ourselves. I believe Dad raised us that way. He made it so that we could stand on our own two feet. Sofia doesn't know what she's talking about. She's always felt like she needed someone to lead her. She needed Dad, she needed religion, she needs her husband, and now she thinks she needs to cling to Nathan."

Yuri speaks up when Mariposa pauses for a breath. "I don't know much about the family. I haven't been around enough to know what's going on, aside from what Mariposa has told me. But I have seen the way Nathan looks at you… And I don't care what he may have said to you, he didn't mean it." She's quiet for a moment, taking a sip from her shot glass. "I remember once in the beginning of our relation- ship–" she motions vaguely between herself and Mariposa, "–I had some anxiety about our relationship, and I was scared shitless after I brought her to meet my friends. We had some mixed reactions."

Mariposa leans closer into Yuri with a slightly hazy expression in her eyes. I don't know if she's reliving the memory, or if it's the weed taking its hold.

"I was so afraid of the ridicule I might face, I tried to break up with her that night. It was the biggest fight we ever had. I felt lost and trapped at the same time. Like I was waking up inside of my life, but I had no control and did not know what was going on. I had this perfectly constructed identity, but I felt like I was made of glass, and if anyone looked too closely, I might shatter into a million pieces. I thought I knew who I was until *someone–*" she throws a loving look at Mariposa, "–challenged every piece of me I thought I knew. It was scary, and at the time it seemed easier to step back away from the edge, to preserve all of my glass edges from potentially shattering and hurting people I cared about. I am thankful every-day that Mariposa didn't let me. When I took a step back, she took two steps closer. And she proved to me I was worth the effort of finding myself, even if it meant pushing myself over the edge and challenging who I thought I was. Sometimes we think we are made of glass, but really we are diamonds."

"Either I'm really high, or that was some of the most profound shit I've ever heard." Amber is staring at Yuri in awe, and I place my hand on her knee and giggle.

Mariposa smiles at our friend and continues where Yuri left off. "Nathan is too afraid to ask you to be that for him. I can't tell you what to do," she pauses and then shrugs, "but I'm going to, anyway. You need to go find him. Because he is free-fall-ing right now. He is lost, and he's trapped between his own carefully constructed personality and what he really wants. And he needs you to care enough to help him. Nathan takes care of everyone, and no one takes care of him. He needs to know that you're going to still be there if everything truly falls apart–if he shatters. His identity has been so rooted in Dad and Mom and the family that he has no idea who he is outside of that. And if you ask me, it's unfair he's even in this position. But he stepped into it willingly, and no one stopped him. Our family is full of heartbreak, and he deserves his own little piece of happiness."

"So what should I do now?" Everything the girls have said seems to seep into my bones, charging my body with anxious but determined energy.

"You can't stay here tonight," Amber says firmly, breaking her silence.

"You're kicking me out of my own apartment? Again?" I add jokingly.

"You're damn right. You cannot stay here. We do not have enough room. So you better go find Nathan and talk this shit out with him." She takes my hand, squeezing it. "Catherine, I love you, but you also deserve your own little piece of happiness. You and Nathan have both suffered enough for a lifetime, and you deserve the safety he provides for you, and he deserves to be fought for."

I nod slowly, looking at all three girls. "I guess I better get going then…"

"My brother is an old man." Mariposa giggles. "He goes to bed soon, so you better hurry."

I can't help but laugh as I stand. "I'm going, I'm going. Thank you, guys."

Mariposa leans farther into Yuri and lifts her glass to me.

Remembering what Amber said about wanting to have dinner or drinks before they leave. I say, "Once everything is settled, before you go back to New York, we all should have dinner."

Amber beams at me, and I know she sees it for the olive branch that it is.

It's a little past nine as I grab my purse where I left it, checking my phone to see if Nathan called or texted. I try not to get discouraged when I see nothing.

The cool night air pricks my whiskey-warmed cheeks as I close the front door behind me.

Twenty-Three

Nathan

As I watch her walk away into the evening air, I know I just completely fucked up. I get out once she has safely crossed the street, half running across campus away from me and the stupid things I said.

I step into The Grove. I half expected Larry to be here, but then I remember Cici is holding a little gathering for people who knew Oscar at the bar tonight. The sun is just passing golden hour, warm light dancing in the cozy coffee shop. But the silence is deafening.

Thanks for your fucking honesty.

Catherine's anger had rolled off her in waves. It was an assault like I have never seen from her before. I deserve every word. Now that I am alone, though, I realize what I said in the car was the biggest lie I have ever told. Every word, every emotion, was a misdirected attack. I lashed out like a child, so afraid that I wouldn't be heard. I just kept talking. Unlike a child, though, I knew the weight of my words and spewed them out anyway. I couldn't be mad at the people I wanted to be mad at, so I found the closest living person.

Turning on my heel, I head back out the front door and back to the car. I don't know where I am going yet, but I can't sit in silence all night. I can't be alone with my thoughts right now. I consider leaving the car here. Maybe Catherine will come back. I doubt it, though. I rationalize taking it, telling myself I will drop it off at her apartment or something a little later. I'll text Amber to come out and take the keys. I put the car in drive and pull out of the sprinkling of students heading back to wherever they go on Sunday evening.

When I was in college, it was always off to Mom and Dad's for the obligatory family dinner. All of us filled our roles. Each of us has sat in the same spots at the table for over thirty years, only adding or removing chairs for boyfriends or girl-friends. Well, the ones who were brave enough to meet Mom and Dad. My fresh-man year, I missed Sunday dinner once and Dad called me to inform me that unless I was in the ER, I was not to miss dinner or he'd stop paying the parents' portion of my tuition. Every Sunday was like clockwork.

Now it won't be...

Now the chair, Dad's chair, will be empty. There won't be dinner tonight. Mom will reheat leftovers from the funeral lunch on sad paper plates. Then Mom and Amaya will sit on the couch with Nadia and watch Jeopardy. Nadia will get all the answers since Dad won't be there to compete with her. She might not even attempt to guess out loud without him. It will be silent as Alex Trebek awkwardly interviews contestants instead of Dad interjecting, "OF ALL THE THINGS YOU COULD PUT DOWN FOR HOW INTERESTING YOU ARE AND YOU PICK THAT? WHO CARES THAT YOU HAVE FORTY-SEVEN CATS!"

I turn onto Baymore Street, where the Chinese place is. China Oasis, the best worst Chinese food I've ever had. You can smell the grease and fried rice smell through the AC unit in the car. I pull in front of the tiny building. It was originally an old 1930s house until the Zhao family bought it and converted it to a Chinese restaurant back in the eighties. They've run it ever since. The open sign flashes but the 'N' is out so it just says 'OPE.' How midwestern for a Chinese place.

I think about parking, heading inside to place my order and then waiting at the loft for Catherine. I can't though. She's not there, so I just keep driving. I just imploded things with her, and I can't sit and wait, hoping that she's going to see through my bullshit and come back. She's smarter than that.

She knows I don't deserve her.

I pick up my phone at the next stop sign and hit the contact app.

"*Mami*…" I can feel the tears well up in my eyes.

"Yes, *Mijo*? What's wrong?" Her voice sounds weak and tired.

"I just… I just really need my mom right now." A tear falls down my cheek. I feel like a broken cup. There are so many cracks–so many pieces of mine that are missing; I don't know where the leak is coming from anymore, or maybe it's coming from everywhere. But at this point, I'm becoming so empty it doesn't matter anymore.

"Oh, *Mijo*." Her voice breaks. "Please come over. I am always here for you. You know that, Nathan." She rarely uses my real name.

"I'll be there in five." I hang up, punch the dash to feel something else, to hold back the tears.

I pull into my parents' driveway. Well, I guess it's now my mom's driveway. The lights are all on. No one would know by looking at the house, but it's the emptiest it has ever been. The cars that had been packing the street are gone. The people who tried to fill that emptiness went with them.

My mom is sitting on the porch, and from the car I can see the dim red light at the end of her cigarette. Since I left The Grove, the sun has begun its slow descent. The sky that was brilliantly bright a few moments ago, now is turning orange and pink. The sun is not quite to the point of setting, but the light has dimmed considerably in the last half hour. Everything is bathed in light shades of pink. Mom is wrapped in a colorful blanket that stands out in stark contrast against her black funeral attire. When I get out of the car, she waves her free hand slightly and gives me a sad smile. My heart aches with the pain of the last few days, and my limbs feel heavy as I walk to the front porch.

I take the other rocking chair next to my mom, leaning back, surveying the street I grew up on and the front yard I played in. So much and yet so little has changed. The big old walnut tree in the yard still stands tall. It's shed most of its leaves already. The ones that remain have turned an off-shade of yellow-brown, and the yard is scattered with dark brown ones. The neighbors' houses are all still various shades of brick, white and gray, lined up in perfect rows to either side of the old, paved street. As the shadows from the houses grow longer, the streetlights are coming on slowly.

But my dad is gone, and according to my sister, the family is falling apart.

"What an exciting day," my mom says quietly, tapping her cigarette ashes into an old flowerpot.

I snort but don't reply immediately, "I guess you could say that. What happened after I left?"

"Well, I helped Catherine get some ice. Then went back out and helped the family pack up. They were all equally impressed and horrified by your girlfriend and your sisters. But I'm pretty sure your tias think Catherine's amazing."

I run my hands through my too-long hair and lean back into the rocking chair. I exhale deeply. There is just enough chill in the air to blow smoke rings with my breath as one of my niece or nephews would. The childish thought ceases and there is silence.

"*Mami*?" I whisper.

"Yes, *Mijo*?" She taps the ash from her cigarette once again.

"What am I going to do? *Papi's* gone." The words singe coming out of my throat.

She takes a long drag of her cigarette. The silence allows time for tears to well in my eyes. I don't try to push them down this time, leaning into the sting in the back of my throat and the way my nose burns. Waiting for an answer seems like hours, even if it is a few seconds. My mom is like a dragon hoarding her treasure trove of wisdom. All the answers sparkling underneath that cigarette. She blows it out and a cloud forms in front of her, unlocking the treasure trove of advice.

"*Yo no sey*." She sucks on the cigarette.

"You don't know?" My jaw drops. Not once in my life has she ever not known.

"*Si*," she says, blowing both her smoke and my hopes for an answer away.

"What do you mean? I don't think I've ever heard you say you don't know." I sound angry, but I don't mean to.

"Well, you obviously haven't been with me when I've been pulled over for speeding." She smirks at her own cleverness. I know it's at my expense, but I'm happy to see a glint of a genuine smile from her. Not the fake one she has been showing people for the last few months. "Let me finish this cigarette. Where's your girlfriend?"

I sigh loudly to let her know I'm displeased with the lack of response.

"She's meeting with her dad," I groan.

"Michael Martin? I didn't make the connection until the funeral. He's a good man. He has always been kind to *Papi* and me. I remember once when *Papi* got shot." She gets sullen.

"Yeah, after Mariposa was born." I push her to say more.

"You all were so little. Michael actually came up to Philly and helped while we stayed in that dinky apartment." She laughs, probably recalling how all five of us were shoved into a two-bedroom apartment. Dad hadn't wanted to sell the house behind my *Abuelos*. With mortgage and rent, they couldn't afford anything bigger. "His wife was home, only a few months pregnant. But Michael came to help clean and help with you all."

"I didn't know that," I stumbled on my words.

"*Si*. He did. It was only for a few days, and you were young, so I'm not surprised you don't remember. His wife didn't enjoy our company much, so when we moved back here, we never reconnected. She was not a fan of how loud you all were. So, Catherine, being an only child makes sense." She tosses her filter to the ground, reaching with her pink house slippers to stomp out the spark.

"Your cigarette is finished?"

"*Si, Gordito,*" she says plainly.

"Well, I really would appreciate an answer." I need you to guide me.

"I don't have an answer for you. I don't know what you're going to do, Nathan," she says firmly.

"But…" I start to interrupt, but she puts up a hand.

"You asked me. Do not interrupt, Nathan Francly Perez Alvarez." Mami uses a tone that only a mother can.

"*Lo sientos, Mami.*" I can't help but respond as if I'm a child again.

"*Gracias.* Now, back to what I was saying. I don't know what to tell you, Nathan. You need to figure out your life. You are thirty. We have always relied on you for support. Rescuing *Papi* when he needed, caring for your siblings, and giving up a personal life for us. But if I'm being honest, we never should have asked that of you. I never should have asked that of you. *Mijo,* I can only imagine how lost you feel. I am not in the same position as you. To me, your *Papi* died when he got that bed.

"Grief is a funny thing, *Mijo.* I remember telling *Papi's* hospice nurse my feelings. I was horribly embarrassed. I had let go of *Papi,* and yet he lay in that bed sleeping, withered like a raisin and yellowed like a banana. When he was lucid, I often told him he had turned into one of those little guys from Willy Wonka." She seems to fall into her own memories, clearly sad, but a smile is spread across her face.

"An oompa loompa?" I don't get how that's funny.

"*Si!* Now *no mas* interrupting, Nathan." She waggles a finger at me like I am still six. "She told me it was normal to have already grieved him, that the man I knew was long gone. She handed me a little card and told me to call it. It was a grief counseling group for caregivers of the terminally ill. They met on Tuesdays."

"Which is when Amaya would come to spend the night. Why didn't you say anything?" I interrupt again, and she thwacks me on the back of the head from her rocking chair.

"I SAID *NO MAS!* I said nothing because you would've told your sisters! Sofia would say I was sticking *Papi* in the grave while he was still breathing. I met other caregivers in the same position as me, *Mijo*. It was hard and emotional, which is why I had you take Amaya. I'd come home and not have an ounce of energy to parent or even be a person. I'd grab a bowl of ice cream, check in with the nurse, kiss *Papi* and go watch telenovelas. You and your siblings didn't watch him die like I did. Not that you didn't visit, it's just different.

"One woman there, Laura, her husband had ALS. She took me to dinner one night after a group session. I asked her many things. Just as you are asking me. She answered all of them until I asked her what I would do when he was gone. She told me she didn't know. There were so many options. I could curl up in a ball and give up on life. Which I can't do; I have Amaya and my grandchildren. Or I could keep ongoing and doing what I had been doing. *Papi* no longer was a partner or father, he was a shell of his former self. She told me I would cry when the shell was no longer there, and I have cried a lot. I screamed and yelled even before he passed. Then even more once he did. My tears have dried, though, and I must keep trudging on. I have a new normal that I had a taste of while he was sick."

I reach over and hold her hand.

She turns and smiles. "You will get a new normal. You've been waiting around not living life, *Mijo*. Your *Papi* would be angry if he knew what you had been doing, going to the gym and work, not living your life, waiting for a call that he was gone. It's time to find a new normal." She squeezes my hand.

"As the new man of the *familia*." I say solemnly.

"No," she says firmly.

"But Sofia…" I try to explain.

She cuts me off. "Excuse my language, but screw that."

I love the fact that Mami thinks screw is a curse word.

"Your sister is only saying that because it's easier to replace *Papi* then let him go. Once he became sick, she avoided him. It was easier for her to think nothing was wrong. That's what I learned in the group. Sofia is being selfish. I told her she needs to apologize to both you and Catherine. She cannot decide what you should do. You could never replace *Papi*…no one can. I don't want you to replace him. He was here, and he gave us what he could. The years that were good were so good." Her voice breaks and she clears her throat. "But I don't need a man here running things. Sofia lives the illusion that your father handled everything like when you all were younger. He has handled nothing in years. Before he even began drinking, he worked long hours as a detective. Even in this tiny town. I can care for myself and Amaya. I don't want you to fill *Papi's* shoes."

"But what do I do?" I can feel tears fall from my eyes.

"Whatever you want. Live your life, *Mijo*. Find yourself. You already found Catherine. Most would've left after that slap, but she stayed. I kept apologizing and she looked at me with the kindest eyes. She told me it wasn't the first time, she just hoped she hadn't angered the rest of us. You will have much more free time to spend with her. Travel. See all the things that Papi didn't get to if you so desire to fill his shoes. Get married, he will be there in spirit. You give him grandchildren. He will see them and watch over them. Give up and become a hermit if you want. I cannot tell you what to do."

My cheeks are cold with tears as more run down my face.

"I don't need another man of the house, or another Oscar Francly Rodrigo Alvarez. I need you to live your life," she finishes.

"*Mami*, I…" I choke out the words, but I can't finish the sentence without breaking into a loud sob. "Cici said…that I was using Catherine…that I'm poisonous…"

"Ah yes, the wise shaman of the town. Maybe you are using her, but that's not a bad thing. It can be, but isn't always. I used your *Papi* for comfort, friendship, and love. So you found someone who helps you get your mind off things. That's a good thing, and she will help you carry many of the awful weights of life. You will do the same for her. That is when it becomes a partnership. You are no longer using each other, you are sharing the burden. Because Nathan, life is heavy. I do not believe that God created us to go through life alone. You cannot carry it all by yourself, and I'm so sorry again that I have misled you to believe otherwise. You are not poisonous, you are kind, and knowing Cici, she meant that towards us, not you. She was angry. Nathan, it's time for us all to move on. To find a new normal. I will go inside and you will stay here, feel what you need to, have your grief, and return to that wonderful girl."

I can only nod.

"*Papi* loved her. I'm sure he couldn't be happier to see you both together again." She shuts the door, the newly fixed screen door clattering behind her.

I start to sob. Taking deep, agonizing breaths of cold air between each whimper; weeping for Dad. I am weeping because I don't know who I am anymore. Weeping because so much uncertainty is ahead.

TWENTY-FOUR

Catherine

It's gotten dark and my heart beats wildly against my chest. My stomach fills with nerves as I walk up the street toward The Grove and Nathan's apartment. I'm going over what Mariposa and Yuri said, trying to talk myself through what I'm going to say. But doubt clouds my thoughts the closer I get to his apartment. What if he isn't willing to listen? What if he really meant what he said? I hate that he really thinks I was just a distraction, especially after the night we spent together. I try to reassure myself that Nathan isn't like that. He isn't that kind of person.

But after what he said in the car… my faith is shaky. The image of his pained expression flares in my mind's eye, seared into my brain.

The windows above the shop are dark. Not even light from a tv seems to be visible. My car is still out front, so maybe he's already in bed. I look up, staring at the windows, trying to decide what to do–should I walk straight in? I still have a key. I could just let myself in, but then I risk startling him in his sleep, assuming he is sleeping.

Someone clears their throat to my left and I jump out of my skin, stumbling back a step as I whirl on the person intruding into my thoughts.

Nathan's head is tilted to the side, looking at me. His eyes are red rimmed, dark and puffy. It looks like he may have been crying and my heart teeters on the edge of shattering into thousands of pieces. Deep sorrow etches harsh lines between his brows and around his eyes. The whispers of wrinkles starting from his normally gentle smile seem more pronounced as he frowns.

"What are you looking at?" he almost whispers, but I can see a hint of genuine confusion. He looks up to the window of his apartment, to my car, and then back at me. It's like he's hoping to trace my train of thought by looking around.

"I was trying to see if you were home."

"Here I am." He lifts his arms up in a sort of shrug. One hand holds a brown paper carryout bag, so it lifts awkwardly like an imbalanced scale.

"What's that?" I point to the bag.

"Pasta. I needed some comfort food after today."

"Nathan, listen." I push my hair out of my face, turning fully to face him.

He interrupts me. "Can we talk upstairs? It's getting late."

I nod and he walks past me, acting more indifferent than anything, and my heart hurts. I hold back the anger that is welling up inside of me. I feel blindsided by his calloused change of personality. And I just want to scream.

I follow behind him in silence, locking the front of the store behind us as we head through the dark sitting area into the kitchen. The old stairs creak loudly all the way up to his apartment door as if protesting being used by us.

I don't try talking again until the door is firmly closed behind us and we are locked back in his apartment.

"Nathan–"

"Wait," he says, setting his things down on the counter in the kitchen.

"No, I'm done waiting. I have something to say, and you need to listen."

The muscles in his jaw tick as he closes his mouth stiffly, something like irritation flaring in his eyes. But at this point I don't care.

I stand up straighter, squaring my shoulders. "I understand what you were saying earlier in the car," I begin. "But I'm not willing to believe this is really how things are going to go between us. You don't get to shit on me. I *wasn't* out of line earlier. You'd think after the horrible things your family has done to you recently, you'd actually *want* someone who will put up with their bullshit long enough to care for you! Maybe if you pulled your head out of your ass long enough to see that, we wouldn't be having this conversation."

"Catherine, please. I know what I said earlier was shitty." That same pleading look is seeping back into his eyes, but I won't let myself pretend everything is okay.

"You're damn right it was shitty. And I get that you're tired. We are all tired at this point. But I refuse to believe you are being selfish for bringing me into this when I walked willingly. I refuse to believe that you so easily let someone else influence your own feelings. WE had an understanding. We were on the same page, and everyone else could go to hell. I knew what was coming, and I went anyway because I love you. I was more than happy to do it because I know you love me. You want me to face my problems, but when someone holds a mirror up to you and tells you to face your own problems, you don't like that. And the worst part is that I'm not asking you to face your problems the way Cici and Sofia want you to. I don't believe any of the things they want to change are problems you need to fix. You aren't the sum of your past, your problems, or your mistakes! At the end of the day, those things don't matter as long as you keep moving forward and keep learning. The people who actually love you and care about you will see and understand that. I see and understand that. You are not being asked to face your past mistakes. I'm asking you what you want going forward."

I take a deep breath, letting my words sink in. I look into Nathan's deep black eyes and see a storm of emotions threatening to break the flood wall. He already looks like he's been crying for hours. I want to hold him, but he needs to be held accountable.

"You don't get to shove me away when things get bad. I don't want you to just give me your nice, pretty, or perfect parts. That's not an actual relationship. You don't get to kick me out because you're spiraling."

I drop my purse on the table in the corner and try to get a handle on myself for what I'm about to say next. I don't want it to come off as anything but how I mean it. I school my expression and when I speak again, my voice is quieter. "Do you remember when you picked me up drunk that night? After I had gone to the club with Meghan, Sarah, and Ashleigh? I was drunk off my ass, and you told me then that for this to work, you wanted all of me. The same goes now, Nathan. I can't force these things from you, you have to give it to me. If you're in a shitty place right now, then fine. I am big enough to take it. If we are doing these things together, then we are doing ALL of it together. That means I'll hold your hand while you feel out of control. I'm willing to fight with you if we need to fight. When I know you aren't thinking straight, I'll take your shitty insults. I will not tolerate you telling me to leave.

"I don't want to wait for things to settle down. Because they will never truly settle down. There will always be something. Haven't we learned that by now? There will never be a perfect time for us. If we keep waiting for one, then we will be doomed to have nothing together. If you feel you need to fulfill some family role, I'll help you. We can run away together if you want to. If you want to find something else entirely, I'll help you come up with a plan. I care about you way too fucking much to be left in the dust because you're afraid of some stupid family backlash or something else. If that's all you're worried about, I'm always game. I will take family backlash if that means being next to you forever. The only way you will get me to leave is if you tell me you don't love me."

He stares at me. The annoyance has melted from his face, and a blank expression has taken its place. The indifference fills me with even more fire.

"Can you do that? Tell me you don't love me, and I will give you your key back right now. I will pack my shit, and we won't talk again."

His eyes glitter as he studies my face, taking in every infuriated feature. I don't flinch or move. He's still quiet and I can see the pulse fluttering in his neck unsteadily.

"You can't say it." The words come out softly. Not an accusation, just an observation.

He shakes his head, his Adam's apple bobbing as he swallows hard. "I think I like you even more than I did before."

I jolted back to his office the day I quit working at the library. When I was spinning out, I planned this elaborate explanation for why I needed the time. I was terrified of his response, terrified of the pain I might cause him. But he listened, and when I was finished, he said those exact words.

"I think I like you more than I did before."

"It was never about that," he says stiffly. "It was never a matter of love. I could never ask for anything from anyone, or maybe I've never been given the opportunity. I just feel like I don't know what to do anymore. I don't feel like myself. I don't even feel like I know myself enough to know what I'm supposed to feel like now."

"I understand that. But Nathan, I'm not asking you to have any answers. It doesn't scare me that things are unsettled right now. I don't need anything from you."

He flinches a little and sighs, running his hands through his hair. "I just don't want to feel like a burden. And I don't want to be the thing that puts a rift in your family, or holds you back."

I take two steps closer to him, taking his hands in mine. "You aren't a burden to me. You're grieving. There are valid reasons to be upset, stressed and lost. But don't push me away. You don't deserve what's been put on you. You don't deserve the burden you're trying to carry, and you don't have to do it alone. Our relationship is supposed to be an equal share of the burden. But I am not weak anymore. If you are struggling, let me help you carry it all."

He trembles slightly, shoulders dropping as he exhales a shaky breath. "I just don't know where to go from here."

I pull him closer to me, guiding his arms around me as I wrap myself around him, squeezing his torso tight against my body.

He doesn't respond right away, but slowly his body relaxes, his chin dropping to rest on the top of my head as his arms tighten around me.

"You don't have to have all the answers right now. Let's just get through the day. Tomorrow we can figure out the rest." I whisper. "I can love you through whatever it takes, and for however long it takes."

I bury my face in his chest. He smells faintly of cigarettes and the small bit of deodorant and cologne he put on this morning. I remember hearing once that if you hug someone, you should never be the one to pull away first, because you never know how long someone needs. So we stand there in heavy but comfortable silence, wrapped around each other, hanging on for dear life.

"I'm so sorry," he whispers. His breath runs across the top of my head.

He doesn't have to specify what he's apologizing for. I already know.

Finally, his arms loosen their hold on me, and he looks down. I rest my chin on his chest, looking up at him. His eyes are soft and tender, and I feel like I can see the pieces of his stress and pain falling away like pieces of ice as he thaws out his emotions. The food is forgotten behind him as he pulls me after him into the bathroom, turning on the water.

"Your water bill is going to be outrageous this month." I try for a little humor.

He makes a sort of breathy sound in his throat that may be a laugh, but it doesn't quite reach his eyes.

"Today sucked and I feel disgusting," he says.

As the bathroom fills with steam, we look at each other for a long time, as if assessing the damage even though it isn't visible. Finally, he steps forward and drags my hoodie over my head. I lift my arms, only breaking eye contact when the material covers my face. Then I'm standing in only my bra and leggings. Nathan's fingertips brush slowly down my arms, and fire sparks to life under my skin, following the trail of sensation his hands leave. He's still looking at me, and I reach for the buttons of his shirt, taking my time to unbutton each one before pulling the material from his pants and sliding it down his shoulders. Then I pull his undershirt over his head. He leans down slightly, helping me get it off.

I examine his skin, running my hands down his shoulders and chest, feeling the contours of lean, hard muscle under my fingers. Nathan is reaching for the clasp of my bra and expertly removes the thin fabric. And then he's dropping to his knees in front of me, and I can't breathe.

Nathan's lips brush each of my hips, and my breath hitches in my throat. My lungs no longer know how to work when he touches me, when he kisses me. He takes my leg in his hands, carefully removing my shoes and socks. His fingers graze my thighs as he runs his hands up my legs and then pulls my leggings off. He inches them down so slowly, over my butt, down my thighs, before he again lifts my legs to pull my leggings free of my body. Butterflies take flight in my stomach, battering my ribcage from the inside as he kisses me once, softly, right under my belly button.

I put my hands on his cheeks, watching his face as he rises, and I pull his mouth to mine, brushing lips and tongue as he runs his hands down my back. Then I'm reaching for his belt and pants, and it's his turn to draw in a ragged breath. His eyes never leave mine as I push them free of his hips. Then he's stepping out of them, pulling me close again, bare skin to bare skin. His mouth touches mine, then my jaw, my neck, and my shoulder.

"That doesn't replace talking," I say finally. My heart is racing again as he looks up and down my body.

"I know," he says quietly before opening the shower door and ushering me inside.

TWENTY-FIVE

Nathan

I wrap myself around her in the shower. I feel too raw to put words to my emotions yet, but the sensations of all her softness against all of my hard edges eases the pain that seems to seep from my soul. She wraps her arms around my shoulders as I lift and pin her against the wall. The hot water cascades down my shoulders and back, soothing away the discomfort of fatigued muscles as I take my time kissing her.

The confusion hasn't subsided from earlier. I still feel as lost as before, but as soon as I saw Catherine tonight, I knew for the first time that I truly needed her. When I got close enough to know it was her, I could have dropped to my knees. I don't care if my family accuses me of being selfish. I refuse to live the rest of my life without her by my side. Shame threatens to pull me into its grasp. I know I can never take back what I've said. She has offered me kindness, but I don't deserve it. I would be an idiot to lose her or take it for granted.

Her lips are pressed firmly against my neck when I slide into her against the shower wall, her legs wrapped around my hips as she exhales against my skin. Goosebumps trail up my spine at the sensation. When she pulls away, looking into my eyes, I know this time is different from any time I've had sex in the past. Her eyes blaze with love and lust, the hazel color beckoning me forward like the light that filters through a dense forest. Blazing golden sunlight and cool green moss, dragging me deeper, calling me closer than I've ever been to someone before. Her lips are kiss-swollen and slightly parted, her fingers digging into my shoulders as I slowly, painstakingly, move inside of her.

This is what old books mean when they say, 'making love.'

It isn't long before we are both breathing hard. Her quiet sighs and moans rip through my skin and pleasure coils at the base of my spine. I can't look away from her face as she tilts her head back and closes her eyes. The sounds that come from her as she orgasms have me shaking beneath her, ecstasy like I don't think I've experienced before coursing through me. But I still don't close my eyes, I don't lean in to kiss her, and I don't stop my rhythm, unable to pull myself out of this moment even if I tried.

She curls reflexively into me as I set her feet back down on the ground, turning the water off. But we don't move right away, clinging on as we catch our breath. I only move when she shivers almost imperceptibly, and I reach for a towel to wrap her in.

Safely in bed, we stare at the ceiling together, both aware that we need to talk but neither of us is willing to break the silence. Her cool hand is folded perfectly into mine and I count her breaths. There is so much I want to say and yet nothing comes out.

Catherine is the one to finally pierce the silence between us, shattering the surrounding barrier, the way ice splinters across a sidewalk.

"You forgot to eat your pasta."

I smile a little to myself. "I'll eat later."

"I talked to my dad."

"That's good. How did it go?"

She sighs and turns to face me, so I do the same, mirroring her posture, except I drape my arm across her hip.

"It was fine. Actually, it was good. We came to some sort of understanding. I know it came about in a really shitty way, but I am glad I did. I just wanted you to know that I did it, so next time you run into Cici, you can tell her."

There's no accusation in her voice, but I flinch anyway. "It wasn't like that."

"I know…are you going to tell me what she said to you now?"

I close my eyes. "She made it seem like I was dragging you into the depths of Hell and using you to escape my problems. Well, not exactly, but that's how it felt. She's really protective of you."

Her fingers brush my cheek. "I don't think it's always a bad thing to want to escape your problems. You're not using me if I'm doing it willingly. I think the whole point of being in a relationship is having someone who can distract you and help you take your mind off things if that's what you need. We also can work through things together. You don't have to get it all together first. Nathan, you deserve to feel safe, secure, and loved. Regardless of your past, the choices that your family has made, and the place you're stuck in now."

"I'm just afraid that she's right. I don't want my family to hurt you…I don't want to hurt you." My heart aches again.

"Are you going to throw a plate at my head and call me a whore?" She jokes, but I remember Marcus. My heart breaks knowing she's been through something much worse than I can ever understand. I tuck a piece of her soft, dark brown hair behind her ear.

"I would never, it's just…it's so fast. What if it's just the honeymoon phase of a relationship?" My heart sinks deep in my chest. The idea of me loving her and this is just a phase for her sneaks into my mind.

She grins, her full lips spread across perfect white teeth. "We already tried moving slowly. You saw how those relationships ended."

"But what if I hurt you?"

"You won't."

"What if you hurt me?"

"I won't."

"What if…"

She put her gentle finger on my lips, quieting me.

"There are so many 'what if's'. One thing I am sure of is that *you* aren't Marcus. I'm not *your* family or Carolina. *We* aren't the people we are with them. We're something *new* and new is scary."

"Sometimes, like today, I get so afraid that I will drag others down with me. So many people around me have blamed me for the shitty things that have happened. With my family and Carolina… I never felt like enough. I wasn't enough for her. I didn't do or say the right things, and that only made me want to try harder. And even at the end, when she was at her worst, it was always me or my family to blame. Sometimes it just feels like we are the problem. Like I am the problem." The words rush out of me in one exhale of breath. "And when Cici talked to me today, it felt like confirmation of the things I always feared for myself. I lashed out because I was afraid." I choke on the last few. The vulnerability leaves a weird taste in my mouth.

Catherine sighs, cupping my face in her hands. She looks at me and everything else melts away. Somehow, Catherine seems to have absorbed every painful confession, leaving me feeling lighter.

"I love you so deeply." She scoots closer. "Life is full of bad things, but you definitely are not and will never be one of them. I feel so safe with you. I finally have found a home. You feel the same. We'll be okay. We're not alone anymore. That I'm certain of." Gold seems to flicker in the forest of green in her soft eyes. She pulls her finger away and kisses me once again. I pull her closer to feel her soft curves and my heart pounds inside of my chest as I touch her.

"I will never doubt you again, my love." I don't think I've ever felt so safe either.

"Oh, I promise you will. We'll work through it again and again. I will always let you know I love you." Catherine's smile is contagious.

"Why are you so amazing?" A grin sprawls across my face.

"It's probably all the trauma I have." She laughs a deep belly laugh.

I can't help but roll my eyes. I kiss her again, savoring the feeling of the moment.

"What books do you have here?" she asks, looking over my shoulder.

"I don't know. A bunch of different ones. Why?"

Catherine rolls out of bed, walking over to the makeshift bookshelf I have in front of the window, and I gasp.

"You're naked! The window!"

She grabs a book quickly and crosses the small space back to bed, grinning the whole time. "There was no one out there. It's almost eleven on a Monday."

"That doesn't mean I want you to chance it!" I laugh a little despite myself.

She settles back into bed next to me, propping herself on a pillow and throwing her legs across my hips. Her hair is still damp as she lays it out behind her on the pillow.

"What book did you find?"

"*Princess Bride.*"

"A classic. I like it. That's always been one of my favorite comfort reads."

She smiles and opens to the first page. It's quiet for a moment and I consider turning on the tv. But then she reads out loud. Her voice is quiet, but as the words tumble from her, I close my eyes. Everything melts away as I focus on what she's saying. I don't speak again; I don't move. Peace settles into my bones as I allow myself to be swept away in the story. With every turn of the pages, the pain of the day seems far away.

I don't know when I fall asleep.

***

"I can't believe you kept me up so late." I yawn as I stretch, nudging Catherine awake. She is still not awake as I sit up. "Come on, it's a new day. It looks so bright out. Let's get dressed and go out."

"I changed my mind. I don't love you. I can't love a morning person." She peels one eye open and glares at me as I climb over her.

"Get used to it. I am only a morning person because I live in a cafe. Larry has everything bagels, and they sell out fast. I can smell them calling my name."

Catherine perks up a little.

"He has fancy coffee." I wiggle my eyebrows at her, feeling better than I have in weeks. Things are going to be okay, and the sunshine today seems to be there to prove it.

Catherine groans, sitting straight up. The blanket falls from her chest to her lap. Her breasts are exposed. Reminding me of the gentle embrace we had last night. I can't help but just stare at her beauty. The tiny window behind my tv shines on her, making her skin glow. Fuck, she isn't just an angel; she has to be a saint. Her hair is wild but in a sexy, tousled way.

She looks at me and tilts her head. "What?"

"You are just gorgeous, and I can't believe you let an *estupido* like me in your life." I am so fucking lucky.

"I love it when you speak Spanish to me." She gives me a sleepy smile. "You're pretty cute yourself." She winks at me sleepily, a morning gravel in her voice.

"Te gusta cuando hablo así?" I turn, crawling back into bed to kiss her gently. *"Eres tan hermosa en la mañana. Tal vez en lugar de café deberíamos quedarnos en la cama todo el día."* I kiss her jaw, and then her throat, eliciting the sweetest sounding gasp from her.

"I don't know what you said, but I could listen to you all day." She wraps her arms around my neck and I'm more than tempted to say 'fuck it' and never leave this room again. Coffee be damned.

"I said, 'You look beautiful in the morning.'"

She kisses me and my mind threatens to go blank.

"And I said, 'Maybe instead of coffee we should stay in bed today.'" My lips brush hers with every word.

"I like the sound of that." Her words are breathy and my dick twitches uncomfortably.

"Buuuut, I am pretty hungry," she says a moment later, and I laugh.

"Come on, coffee and bagels, it is then."

She drags her legs over and wobbly-walks to pick up jeans from the bag that she threw on the floor.

I walk to my closet next to the bed and open the door. "There will be plenty of room for you to put your stuff in here. We could probably get a second dresser right here." I motion to the spot right next to my dresser. "And your dresses can hang next to my suit jackets."

I walk to the front of the bed and pull open my dresser drawer and grab my red boxer briefs and a pair of black socks and slide them on.

"Ew, you put your socks on first?" Catherine laughs fully clothed but barefoot.

"Yeah, I'm not a heathen," I tease back.

"Socks are restricting. My toes need freedom." She smiles deviously.

"You are the weirdest person," I state sternly, but only to tease her.

"Says the weirdo who puts his socks on first," she jokes, but she seems to hesitate. I can see the subtle shift in her mannerisms, like she's fighting against herself and whatever thought popped into her mind.

"Hey, I'm not Marcus. I love when you tease me. Carolina never thought teasing was funny. You're right, we're not them." I pull out a pair of slacks and squeeze into them.

"Jesus, you really are a morning person." Catherine's belly laugh makes me smile in a way I don't think I ever have. I pull on a white shirt and slide on a black sweater. "That's it. I can't watch you get dressed, ever!" She giggles and walks away.

"What did I do?" I laugh a hard laugh I didn't think I would ever have without her.

I follow her as she slides on her black no-show socks and then black Vans. Catherine opens the door and starts down the stairs.

A small wave of sadness hits me from nowhere. My heart momentarily feels heavy and uncomfortable in my chest. I breathe through it, listening to Catherine hum as she seems to skip down the stairs. The sound shakes me free of the weight, and after a moment I can breathe normally again.

"Hey, wait up!" I feel a smile spread across my face. I'll be fine. Everything is already getting better.

"Coffee doesn't wait for slowpokes!" she shouts behind her.

I shake my head and put on my shoes and chase after her.

I run down the stairs and Catherine stands with her arms crossed across from Larry.

"Just talk to her. She is just so heartbroken over this," Larry pleads.

"She needs to apologize. Her meddling is ruining things for me," Catherine says sternly.

"Kitty, I know. You two are so stubborn. You both deserve better. I'm just saying if you start it, she will listen to you when you don't always listen to her." Larry sounds like my dad.

Catherine sighs loudly.

"I don't mean to interrupt, but I'm hungry. You have a customer as well." I hope Larry gets the hint. I don't want Catherine's morning ruined. We both need these happy moments.

Larry looks down and shakes his head. He turns and walks to the door.

"Thanks." She turns and squeezes my arm. "He's right, in a way."

"I didn't want to say it. I agree with him. My mom talked to me. You talk to yours." I tease.

"Defend in public, correct in private. I'll talk to her, but I'm gonna whine about it." She pours herself some cold brew out of the fridge. "Oh, a little whipped cream on top sounds fun." Catherine says gleefully.

"You're adorable. Will you make me one too?" I ask.

"Sure. Will you find me a donut?" She leans away from the counter and smiles.

"You know, I pay him an extra bit every month just so I can eat down here whenever I want." I wink at her.

"I'm going to gain so much weight," she groans.

"I love your curves." I love her big ass, too.

"Thank you." She hands me a coffee and I hand her a jelly donut.

"Nathan, take me to my aunt's, please." She looks at me and her eyes look like a storm of feelings.

"Of course." I kiss her on the forehead.

Twenty-Six

Catherine

"Text me when you're ready. I'm still on bereavement leave so I'll be just hanging out at the apartment," Nathan says before I climb out of the little Camry.

"Oh, you're coming with me." I smile.

"Wait, what? I don't know if that's a good idea. I'm kind of the problem." His voice shakes with concern.

"I know, but I need you here if I need to bolt." I smirk deviously.

"Well, I'll stay in the car then." Nathan crosses his arm and huffs. I can only imagine that he didn't get away with much as a child with that sour look.

"No. You'll definitely look like the problem then." I can't help but chuckle a little.

He exhales and groans. "Fine." Nathan puts the car in park. He gives me a teasing glare. We both get out of the car. I grab his hand and squeeze as we make our way up the old concrete steps.

Cici can be difficult when things aren't going well between us. She is a fixer. She has to help everyone. But when people don't fix it her way, she takes it as a personal insult. Cici once blew up at Larry for not standing up for himself in the way she advised him to.

I don't want that.

We walk up the steps into the large white farmhouse that looks misplaced in the subdivision that grew around it. No sign of Dad and Lisa's car; they must be out. I pull the screen door and reach for the handle of the front door. Before I have the chance to open the door, the doorknob turns and swings open.

"Well, 'ello love! Oh, and Nathan?" Charles stands before me in a fuzzy blue bathrobe, white boxers with black polka dots all over them, and a very charming wife beater.

"Hey, Charlie. Love the outfit. Is Cici home?" I say with a small grin across my face. It's hard not to burst into laughter staring at the normally posh Englishman in his pajamas.

Nathan waves awkwardly.

"Thanks. Old man chic is all the rage right now. Cici is in her room getting dressed. You can head up." Then he turns to Nathan. "I'm making breakfast. Give me a hand?" He smiles, but I can see hesitation in his wrinkles.

"She's still mad?" I walk past him to head up the stairs.

"Well, mad isn't how I would put it." He shuts the front door, and it creaks ominously.

"So, yes," I state clearly.

"Cici just wants the best for you." Charles says sheepishly.

"I know. If she didn't, I wouldn't be here." I make it to the bottom of the steps, then I turn to Charles. "We'll be okay. We always work it out."

"You have grown up so much. I remember many times you'd walk in this door ready to fight." His eyes look almost a little teary, but his smile shows that it's only from pride that he might shed a tear. He wraps one arm around my shoulders and kisses my forehead affectionately. It leaves gravel in my throat, and I smile at him.

"I know. She needs to see that as well." I pull away from him and start up the steps.

Each step creaks, warning Cici someone is coming. When I was little, we'd play hide n' seek. I'd hide under the bed from her and my dad because the steps were so loud.

I knock, and there is no reply, so I just swing the door open. There she sits on the edge of the bed in a pink mumu, scrolling on her phone with her gaudy turquoise reading glasses sliding down her nose.

"Well, well, look what the Kitty dragged in." She turns up and smirks at me.

"That joke wasn't funny when I was six, and it still isn't funny." I roll my eyes.

"Well, it's funny to me and that's all that matters." Cici turns her face back to the phone. "So, why are you here and not with Romeo?"

"Because I love my aunt and I know she's pouting in her room like a nine-year-old because of our fight." I cross my arms just like she would when I was younger.

She sets down her phone and stands up.

"I just want the best for you." She looks at me sadly, like a puppy. "Kitty, his sister hit you. You barely know him or his family. He's going through a rough time, and he might use you to distract himself. You're diving into a pool, and you don't know how deep it is."

"You know his family. Cici. Do you really think Nathan was raised to use people? You know his mom, his dad, and all of his sisters. You know Sofia is hot-headed. Do you think she would ever have hit me if her dad didn't just die?"

She stands and shakes her head 'no' while making eye contact with her new pink pedicure.

"Cici, I know you want the best for me, and for a long time, I didn't want that for myself. Now I do. Now I want to be happy. I need you to trust me that even if Nathan turns into a monster, you know who I will run to."

She looks up slowly, and her deep brown eyes connect with mine.

I step towards her. "You're my mom, even if you didn't make me. I'll come to you when I need you. The meddling needs to stop. It's hurting me, not helping me. You don't want Nathan to hurt me, but you're the one trying to unravel my life."

"I just… I don't want you to go through something horrible like Marcus again." She looks pleadingly into my eyes.

"Do you think Nathan is even remotely anything like Marcus? I don't wanna go through that again either, but I might. That doesn't mean I should hole up and be an old spinster." I wink at her.

"Hey!" She smirks.

"Am I wrong though? You're fiercely independent, so much so that instead of getting hurt, you don't let anyone in. How long have you and Charlie been together but not *together*?"

She shakes her head.

"I love you, but I'm not you. I'm not my dad. I want to move on. I want to heal, and I can't do that if you're angry with me."

"You're right. Never make me say that again." She steps up to me and puts her hands on my arms. "You aren't the little girl I used to know. Who the fuck is this wise old lady?" She giggles and wipes her eyes. "You may have not grown under my heart, but you grew in it. I am so proud of you. You are an amazing woman." She smiles. "Now enough sappy shit. Let's get super stoned. Charlie is making shit-on-a-shingle, and that's only good if you're high."

"You are so annoying. That's the only reason you keep him around is sex and food." I can't help but laugh.

"Of course, Kitty." She squeezes me tight. She's a few inches taller than me and I end up smothered in her shoulder. "I'm sorry. I love you."

We sit on the bed while Cici pulls out a joint, and we share it back and forth. The silence is comfortable, and when I hear the front door open and my dad's and Lisa's voices trail up the stairs, I don't feel the dread and panic I'm expecting.

Cici sighs loudly. "I can't wait for the day that I have my house to myself again."

"Bullshit. You love having a full house."

She rolls her eyes at me but stands and holds her hands out to help me off the bed. "Let's go see everyone."

Downstairs, Dad is pouring himself a cup of coffee, laughing with Charles as he assembles breakfast. Nathan sits cornered by my little sister while she lists every fairy from her favorite cartoons. When Cici and I walk into the kitchen, my dad freezes, a coffee cup halfway to his lips, and Lisa turns to stare at me as well.

"Good morning." Cici pushes past her brother, punching him in the arm, then reaching for coffee as well.

"Hey, Dad." The words taste foreign in my mouth, but I am determined to make this work. I swear I hear Lisa gasp dramatically and have to fight the urge to roll my eyes. I catch Nathan watching me out of the corner of my eye, and when I turn, he gives me the slightest smile and I breathe a little easier.

"Hey, I didn't know you'd be here," he says almost casually, rubbing his punched arm. But I can see the tension in his face.

"I was just begging for Cici to take me back."

My aunt snorts as she pours her coffee.

"Are you staying or heading out?" he asks cautiously.

"She's staying, and so is her boyfriend." Cici nudges her brother and gives him a look.

"I wasn't planning to, but it sounds like I don't have much of a choice." I smile at my dad, and his face lightens as a grin spreads across his face.

I turn to Nathan, and he mouths *Save me*.

I mouth back a big *No* and smile at him in a way that I hope conveys that I will pay him back generously later. Before I turn back around, I swear I catch him swallow hard and blush a little.

The kitchen moves again. Something about the atmosphere is different. The best I can do is compare it to when you fall and scrape your knee. Once you've scabbed, it no longer hurts, but the scrape is still healing. The reminder is still there, but I know I'm healing.

"I'm glad you're staying for a little!" Lisa comes to stand next to me, watching her daughter.

I try to think of a response, but nothing comes to mind. Guilt clouds my thoughts from our last encounter. Lisa turns to face me, expression blank, like she's preparing for whatever blow I might throw her way.

"I'm really sorry, Lisa." We stare at each other. She doesn't seem to know what to say, so I keep talking. "I lashed out the other morning, and I am sorry. I didn't mean for you to get in the crossfire of my old resentment for my mom, as well as my anger at Dad. I have never treated you the way you deserved." I pause, trying to read her expression, but nothing has changed. It's like she's completely frozen. "I never tried to have an actual relationship with you and then blamed you for the distance between us. That was unfair of me. So, I'm sorry, and I'd like to get to know you better."

"Oh." Lisa presses a hand to her mouth, fanning her teary eyes with the other hand. And then she's throwing her arms around me, almost toppling us both. "I have held none of that against you, Catherine." She squeezes me for another minute before pulling back and stepping away. She glances around the kitchen, taking in all of our family who are doing a great job of 'listening-not-listening'. Cici is staring extremely hard at her brother, who is staring very hard out the window.

Charles has turned himself away and is washing a cup with all of his attention.

Nathan has turned his attention back to my little sister, and I love him for it. He listens to her with the same animated emotion he gives to Amaya. I watch Lisa slowly wander over to them and offer a small smile as she approaches the table. Nathan stands quickly, pulling out the chair next to him and then helping her scoot her pregnant self in.

This man who owes me and my family nothing is more than I could have ever asked for. He talks quietly to Lisa and even smiles once before Bailey Mae is dragging him back into a sea of princesses.

I turn back and my dad is watching me quietly, switching between where I stand and my 'boyfriend' as Cici said. I study him for a second, enjoying the neutrality of my feelings in his presence. He looks better today than yesterday, well-rested and more peaceful. To my surprise, I find that I'm slightly sad that he and Lisa are going to be leaving in a few days. The emotions feel strange in my chest, and it feels like my ribs constrict around them.

My dad walks over and stands next to me, leaning in the doorway between the kitchen and the dining room. "So," he says, then clears his throat. "How'd you two meet?"

I choke on a laugh. "Uh, well, when I moved…" I pause, the awkwardness hitting me as his expression goes off for a second before returning to neutral. I start again. "When I moved here, I started working at the library on campus. Nathan was technically my boss."

"That's… nice…" Dad clears his throat again.

"He's been a really good friend to me."

My dad pauses for a moment, looking to where Nathan has said something that made Lisa laugh. "Oscar was a really good friend to me, too. So, if he's anything like his dad… I would say you're in excellent hands."

I smile at my dad, and he nudges me gently with his elbow before joining his wife at the table. Nathan smiles at me from across the room, and in that moment, I am absolutely sure that things are going to be okay.

The last lines of the poem that brought Nathan and me together run through my head:

And whether or not it is clear to you,

no doubt the universe is unfolding as it should.

Therefore, be at peace with God,

whatever you conceive him to be.

And whatever your labors and aspirations in the noisy confusion of life,

keep peace in your soul.

With all its sham, drudgery, and broken dreams,

It is still a beautiful world.

Be cheerful, strive to be happy.

Epilogue

Nathan

"*Mijo,* can you grab the stuff in the oven when you come in here?" my mother calls from the dining room.

"*Si, Mami!*" The tray is warm even through the potholder as I walk it to the dining room table. The house is full tonight. Bailey Mae and Amaya are talking excitedly about the new Disney movie they both love. Mike is sitting at the end of the table, and Mom is standing next to him chatting, holding a plate of arepas. I set the steaming food on the table and look around quietly.

Almost every chair is occupied except Dad's at the head of the table, the one next to it, and two in between Mike and Amaya. My heart hits my ribs uncomfortably as I look at it.

"Hey, are you okay?" Catherine's arms slide beneath mine and she squeezes me gently.

"Yeah, I'm good. It looks like Lisa and Sofia are getting along well."

She turns to where my sister and her stepmom are chatting. "Thank God."

Sofia looks over at us and gives a small approving smile, which Catherine returns. Sofia and I had a long talk a few days after the funeral. She didn't specifically apologize, and I don't think she ever will. However, we have come to an understanding, and I am hopeful for the future.

I nod. "Where are Cici and Charles?"

"She texted me a few minutes ago and said they were walking over, so they should be here any second."

As Catherine says it, there's a knock on the front door. Amaya and Bailey Mae shoot out of their seats, running to open the door.

And just like that, the house gets a little fuller, and surprisingly, my heart actually settles a little.

Cici walks right up to me, and I lean in to hug her. "Hi, Nathan." She plants a soft kiss on my cheek and then sweeps Catherine away from me, talking about work schedules for the following week amidst a bunch of other things.

With everyone here, it's time to sit. I walk slowly to my dad's old seat, and maybe I imagine it, but it feels like the room goes quiet around me. But then Catherine is beside me, pulling out the chair right next to my normal seat. I look at her and she gives me a reassuring nod.

With a deep breath, I pull the chair back and sit. My mom walks from Mike and stands behind Dad's chair and pulls it out to sit. She gives me a gentle pat on my arm. I don't need to take Dad's spot. Mom is here, a truly beautiful matriarch filling the role she was meant to.

I don't know who I am yet, but I know who I'm not, and it's not my job to be my dad anymore.

Food is passed around, there is laughter and conversation, and it feels as if the world is plunged back into daylight.

Catherine takes my hand under the table, content just as I am to watch our families get along. Cici, my mom, and Mike are talking and laughing about something my dad did when he was younger. Sofia is still engaged in what looks like an important conversation with Lisa, and Mariposa is talking to Charles.

Catherine nudges me, pulling me out of my thoughts. "It's great, isn't it? Everyone seems to be really happy."

"They do, don't they?"

"Are you happy?" She leans a little closer to me, squeezing my hand under the table.

"I'm happier than I've been in a long time." I close the distance between us and kiss her softly.

And it's the truth. My heart is full, and for the first time, I feel like I can clearly see my future. It may still be a little broken, but it's coming together slowly. Catherine and I have plenty of time to figure things out, and our families will be there and supportive on the way. I know I am where I'm supposed to be, and I'm excited about the future.

www.ingramcontent.com/pod-product-compliance
Lightning Source LLC
Chambersburg PA
CBHW011148190726
48288CB00010B/3232